The Rock and Roll Brontë Series

by Tracy Neis

♪ ♪ ♪

*Mr. R - A Rock and Roll Romance*

A modern reimagining of *Jane Eyre*

♪ ♪ ♪

*Restless Spirits*

An Alternate Take on

*Wuthering Heights* and *Agnes Grey*

♪ ♪ ♪

*Wildfell Summer*

A magical mystery trip through the pages of

*The Tenant of Wildfell Hall*

# Restless Spirits

Tracy Neis

An Alternate Take
on
"Wuthering Heights" and "Agnes Grey"

Restless Spirits
by Tracy Neis

Published by the author
All rights reserved.
Copyright © 2020 Tracy Neis

The characters in this book are fictitious. Any similarity to actual persons, living or dead, is purely coincidental and not intended by the author.

This book is protected under the copyright laws of the United States of America. Any reproduction or other unauthorized use of the material or artwork herein is prohibited without the express written permission of the publisher and author.

Cover and author illustrations by:
Karen Neis

Summary: A rock-and-roll reimagining of Wuthering Heights and Agnes Grey that unites the plots and characters from Emily and Anne Brontë's classic novels in a 1990's-era ghost story.

Library of Congress Cataloging-in-Publishing Data
Neis, Tracy
Restless Spirits / Tracy Neis

Neis Family Publications
Paperback Book ISBN: 978-1-7343600-1-1

For *my parents:*

Robert Reimer,
*Who wanted me to be a girl engineer,*
*But paid for me to be an English major anyway.*

*and*
Joan Dempsey Reimer,
*Who could hear the Banshees cry.*

R.I.P.

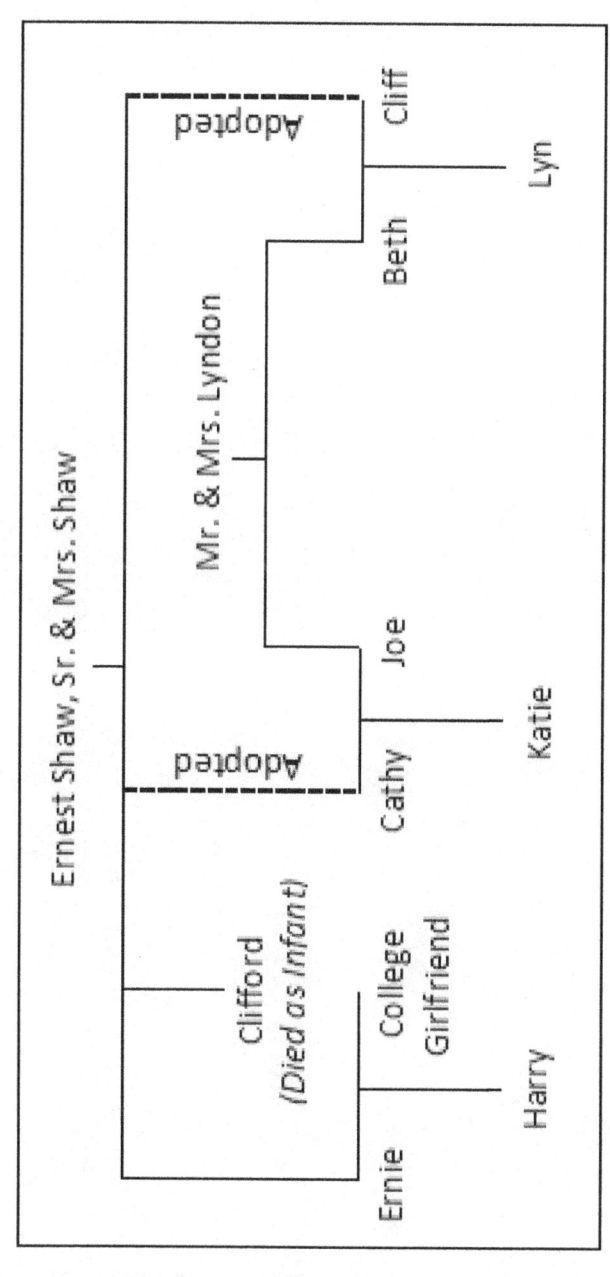

*I am not I; thou are not he or she; they are not they.*
— Evelyn Waugh, author's note to "Brideshead Revisited"

*I am he as you are he as you are me and we are all together.*
— John Lennon and Paul McCartney, "I am the Walrus"

# Chapter One
## A Dark and Stormy Night

The blast of the car horn jarred Jim awake. He tightened his grip on the steering wheel and straightened his Jaguar in the middle lane of the Interstate.

*Goddammit!* he cursed in his head. *I could have killed someone!*

He scanned the names of the towns listed on the overhanging green signs, searching for a place where he might pull over to grab some coffee. Pulaskiville. Steam Corners. Blooming Grove.

"Where the hell am I?" he grumbled under his breath.

A small knot of fear started forming in his gut. He cut his eyes to the side of the road and looked for the neon lights of a fast food restaurant.

When none came into view, he focused his gaze back on the red tail lights of the truck in front of him, hoping they might lead him on a straight and narrow path. But soon his mind was wandering again, recounting the myriad delays he had suffered this evening on his trip to Cleveland.

He had stayed much later than he'd planned at his friend Eddie's house in southern Ohio. Then he'd gotten stuck in the afternoon rush hour traffic just outside of Dayton. Driving into Columbus, he'd started singing along to Bryan Adams' new hit "Have You Ever Loved a Woman?" on the radio, and somehow missed the exit that would have taken him to Cuyahoga County. He was halfway to Zanesville before he'd had the sense to turn around and retrace his steps. When he finally made it back to the proper freeway, he'd found himself trapped in another traffic jam, this one caused by an overturned truck that had spilled its load of coffins across two lanes of the highway.

An image of the policeman who had directed traffic around the caskets sprang to Jim's mind. Illuminated by glowing red flares at his feet and pulses of yellow headlights across his face, the cop had looked like an actor from a carnival's haunted house. The irritated scowl he'd flashed at the drivers accentuated his ghoul-like appearance.

Jim pushed aside the memory and focused his eyes back on the truck's tail lights.

Four fat raindrops plopped onto his windshield in rapid succession. He turned on his wipers. Within minutes, their rhythmic motion had mesmerized him. Back and forth the wipers swished. Back and forth. His eyelids started to droop. His car started drifting into the next lane.

A second car horn jarred him awake.

*Fuck it all! I'm taking the next exit, whatever the hell it is!* he promptly decided. *There has to be <u>someone</u> out there who can sell me a cup of coffee!*

He eased into the right lane and looked for a turn-off. An unlit sign appeared a short distance in front of him, marked with dimly reflective letters. He tried to decipher the ghostly script in the glow of his headlights, but couldn't make it out. He briefly considered remaining on the Interstate—he didn't want to wander too far from his route.

*But what the hell,* he thought with a wave of resignation. *That road must lead somewhere. I'll just drive down it until I find a diner or bar.*

He pulled off the highway, turned onto an unlit road, and switched on his high-beams. The rain picked up. He adjusted his wipers to a higher speed.

In the distance, he spied the dark, boxy silhouette of a building, with a warm yellow light shining through a small window along its side. He drove closer and saw a hand-painted sign announcing the establishment's name: "Zilla's Country Kitchen." Smiling in relief, he turned into the restaurant's driveway. But his hopes immediately faded when he noticed only one other car in the parking lot.

The light from the building's lone window blinked off just as Jim killed his engine. A man stepped out of the restaurant, lifted his coat over his head, and ran towards the parked car.

Jim rolled down his window and called to the stranger. "Excuse me? Excuse me!"

The man ignored him. But after climbing into his car and switching on his headlights, he drove towards Jim and rolled down his window. "Sorry, Bud, we're closed for the night."

"Is there any place nearby where I can get an expresso?" Jim called back to him, trying not to sound too desperate.

The stranger laughed. "Shit, man, look around you! Does this look like the kind of neighborhood with a fancy coffee shop?"

Jim sighed. "I just need some caffeine. I have a lot more driving to do tonight."

"Where you headin'?"

"Cleveland."

"You're goin' the wrong way. Cleveland's north. Get back on I-71."

"I'm planning to. I just need some coffee first," Jim replied testily.

The stranger turned his head and stared blankly at the rain cascading down his windshield for a few seconds, then looked back at Jim. "Maybe you can get yourself a cup at the Black Bull," he suggested. "Katie usually keeps a pot going for her customers before they hit the road."

"Sounds perfect," Jim said. "Where's the Black Bull?"

" 'Bout a mile down this street. Maybe a little further. Don't know, I've never checked the distance. Just keep headin' east towards the Heights."

"Thanks!" Jim replied. "I owe you one."

The man laughed. "No you don't. The place is a dive. I usually try to avoid it." He rolled up his window and turned left onto the country lane, towards the highway.

Jim started his engine and considered following the stranger back to the Interstate, but then remembered how he'd fallen asleep at the wheel not once but twice.

*I need some caffeine!* he reminded himself. He mulled over the name Black Bull. It sounded like a pub he might find back home in Northern England. Taking that as a good sign, he turned right onto the county lane and headed east.

About a mile down the road, the street forked abruptly in two. No signs indicated where either branch led. Jim rolled his car to a stop and stared helplessly at the two paths. The left road appeared slightly wider than the right, though neither looked very promising.

"Christ, here goes nothing," he muttered irritably, and he veered to the left.

He checked his odometer periodically as he worked his way down the narrow country lane. Five-tenths of a mile. Six-tenths of a mile. He saw inky black fields to his left and rain-soaked patches of trees to his right. But the Black Bull failed to materialize.

*What the hell am I doing here?* he thought with a growing surge of frustration. He pulled a quick U-Turn and skidded on the slick pavement.

The rain started falling furiously. Jim's wipers barely cleared the windshield before a blinding torrent of fresh water blocked his view again. He downshifted and slowed his car to a crawl, then inched his way forward, searching for the fork.

An unmarked street appeared on his right. He turned onto it, but after bumping along its pock-marked pavement for a few dozen yards, he realized he was no longer traveling on the main road. He started turning his car around again. The beams of his headlights sliced through the diagonal slats of rain and flashed across a murky shape. A pair of shining eyes reflected the yellow light back at him.

"Fuck!" he shouted, slamming on his brakes. His car spun wildly, then skidded to a stop and stalled. Jim panted and looked frantically out the windows, searching for the animal that had spooked him. But all he could see was a dark torrent of rain.

He took a long, deep breath to settle his rattled nerves, then started his engine once more. He touched his foot to the accelerator and crept along the road at a dogged pace, hoping to avoid another encounter with the bright-eyed creature.

*It must have been a deer*, he told himself. *At least I didn't hit it.*

The car's radio signal deteriorated into static. He fiddled with the knob for a few seconds, then gave up in disgust and switched off the dial.

He crested a steep hill. Dense outcrops of trees blocked his view on either side of the road. His headlights flashed against a house in the valley below. He stopped his car and tried to make out the distance between the building and the road. The house looked small and dark, but its presence encouraged him. At least he hadn't wandered completely away from civilization.

He drove down the hill slowly and spied a mailbox along the side of the street. He pulled a little closer to it, hoping to catch the name of the road he was driving on.

Then he saw the glowing eyes once more. He slammed on his brakes, setting the car into another spin. It rolled off the pavement and crashed into a large rock protruding from a sunken gulley. The loud crunch of metal meeting granite made Jim's stomach lurch. The car's engine released a pathetic whining sound, then stalled once more.

Jim started frantically turning his key in the ignition. The motor responded with a hollow clicking noise that seemed to mock him. A bright orange "check engine" light appeared on his dashboard.

"Goddammit!" Jim yelled. He hit his fists against the steering wheel, then took another long, deep breath.

*Now would be a good time to have a cell phone*, he thought with remorse. His friend Eddie had just been showing him his new mobile a few hours earlier, but Jim had laughed off the device. "Why would I want one of those new phones?" he had argued. "They take away the best parts of driving and walking—being by myself and knowing that no one can bother me!"

He turned his face to the side and searched out his window for the house he had just seen. He couldn't make out its shape in the pouring rain, but he knew it wasn't far. Bracing himself for a cold, wet march across a soggy field, he opened his car door and stepped out of the Jaguar. A torrent of bone-chilling rain immediately doused him, plastering his clothes against his body.

His shoes sank into the wet earth with an ominous squishing sound and offered him little traction on the slippery grass. Hardly a few yards into his walk, he tripped over a fallen branch and fell face-first into the mud. A searing jolt of pain ripped through his right ankle and pulsed up his leg. He tried to stand back up, but his right shoe was stuck beneath the heavy branch. He scrunched up his toes and winced as he eased his foot out of his loafer.

"Fuck it all!" he shouted into the rain. He stood back up, slipped his mud-covered shoe over his sodden sock, and started hobbling towards the house. Each time he placed his weight on his right foot, another shot of pain coursed up his leg.

The ground beneath him was a mass of slippery ooze. Soon both of his shoes were sucked into the mire. He slipped them both off and threw them to the ground in disgust, then started limping towards the building in his stocking feet. He immediately stepped on a sharp object with his bad foot, and the pain in his leg magnified exponentially. He stopped to catch his breath and tried to draw comfort from the fact that his situation couldn't possibly get any worse.

Thunder rumbled in the distance.

"Jesus fucking Christ!" he screamed. He threw himself onto the grass and started crawling towards the house. A streak of lightning flashed above him. He looked up briefly and made out the building's silhouette across the sodden field. He repositioned himself and crept towards it.

When he finally reached the small house, he stood back up, leaned his weight on his uninjured left foot, and knocked on the door. There was no response. He twiddled the door knob nervously. The door opened.

"Hello?" he called inside. "Is anybody here? I'm lost! I need help! Please, is anybody here?" He ran the palm of his dripping hand against the inside wall by the door, searching for a light switch. He found a protruding, plastic knob, but when he toggled it, nothing happened.

"Hello!" he repeated. "Is anybody there?"

A cold gust of wind snuck up behind him and pushed him into the building. He staggered forward, then looked over his shoulder at the storm outside. Sheets of rain pelted the cottage's small doorstep. The wind began to howl. He sighed.

*Well, I'm breaking and entering then,* he chided himself, his insides churning with guilt, *but at least I'm not disturbing anyone.* He shut the door behind him and limped into the front room.

Lightning flashed again in the distance, illuminating the interior of the house through a gap in the window curtains and offering him a momentary glimpse of the furniture. He hobbled towards a table and ran his cold, clammy fingers over its surface. He bumped his hand against an old rotary telephone with a coiled cord. With a flurry of hope, he lifted the receiver and brought it to his ear, but there was no dial tone on the other end.

*It figures,* he thought with a fresh wave of disgust. He rested the phone back in its cradle and continued rubbing his hands over the table.

He found a small, smooth, cylindrical object and rolled it over in the palm of his hand. A scratchy, metallic wheel protruded from one side. Smiling at long last, he flicked the wheel with his thumb. A flame emerged.

"Thank you, Jesus!" he cried out in relief. Holding the lighter aloft like a fan at a rock concert, he examined the table more closely and discovered a cone-shaped candle, covered in an ornamental pattern of long, twisting tendrils of wax. He hadn't seen a candle like that since the Seventies. He lit its wick and returned the lighter to the table.

Using the candle as a torch, he limped through the small cottage, leaving a trail of puddles behind him as he examined each room.

The house appeared deserted—the rooms smelled musty, and there was no sign of food in the kitchen. Yet the furniture was neatly arranged. An antique upright piano stood in the back corner of the living room. Knick-knacks and doilies adorned the table-tops. Framed posters and paintings hung from the walls.

Jim hobbled down the building's small hallway and stepped into the last room at the back of the house. By the dim light of his candle, he caught a tantalizing glimpse of a carefully made bed, covered with a crocheted afghan. He stared at it longingly for several seconds, his breath catching in his throat. Then he stepped closer to the mattress and ran his fingers over the bumpy, zig-zagged pattern of the blanket.

A warm rush of calm immediately started swelling within him, like a pleasant buzz building after taking the first hit on an especially good joint. The bed seemed to be calling to him, inviting him to lie down and leave his troubles behind for a while.

*I'll bet this is how Goldilocks felt after she finished eating that goddamned porridge!* he thought, curling his lips in a wry smile.

He rested the candle on the nightstand and started unbuttoning his shirt.

*I'll just crash here for the night and figure out what to do in the morning,* he promptly decided. He stripped down to his damp underwear and noticed that his right sock was drenched in blood. He left his wet and filthy clothes in a pile beside the bed and slid underneath the musty-smelling sheets.

He closed his eyes and tried to ignore the wrenching pain in his right foot. The rest of his body ached with cold and fatigue. Raindrops pummeled the rooftop in a steady rhythm that soon started lulling him to sleep. But then the urgent cry of a woman's voice called him back to his senses.

"Let me in! It's Cathy! I've come home!"

He sprang up with a jolt. The voice was at his bedroom window. His heart started racing as he tried to think of the best way to explain his presence to the stranger.

"Let me in!" she repeated, her desperate cry rising over the sound of distant, rumbling thunder.

Jim slipped out of bed, wrapped the afghan around his shoulders, and limped over to the window.

"Come in! The front door's unlocked," he called to the woman. "I'm a stranger. My car broke down and I'm hurt, and I need a place to stay for the night. I'm sorry. I hope that's okay."

"It's Cathy!" the woman replied. "I've come home! Let me in!"

"The front door's unlocked," he repeated.

The woman continued her clamoring, so Jim opened the window to speak to her directly. There was no screen behind the glass pane, and rain immediately started streaming into the bedroom. Jim pulled back the curtain and looked outside. There was nobody there.

*She must have finally gone round to the front,* he decided. He grabbed the bottom latch so he could close the window.

A hand reached in from outside and clamped around his wrist. A cold spasm pulsed through him, as if he had broken the surface of an icy pond and was being sucked into the frozen depths beneath. He tried to shake himself loose. The hand tightened its grip.

A wave of numbness started creeping up his arm, then swept into his torso. It moved down his right leg and settled into his throbbing, injured foot.

The stranger released him at last. He fell to the floor beside the open window. He tried to scream, but his voice was frozen in his throat.

The rain started to drench him afresh through his sodden afghan, and his consciousness began to slowly drift away. He closed his eyes and surrendered himself to a powerful, dream-like vision of a yellow-eyed creature, laughing at him in the dark.

# Chapter Two

## An Ungentlemanly Host

"Who the hell are you, and what the devil are you doing in my house?"

Jim flinched. The stranger's bellowing voice shook him out of a feverish nightmare. He tugged instinctively at his wet afghan to cover his ears. He tried to curl himself into a tighter ball on the hardwood floor, but his injured right foot throbbed in protest when he attempted to move his leg. A moan escaped from his lips.

"I said, who the hell are you?" the angry voice repeated.

Jim opened his eyes but couldn't make out his interrogator's face. He could only see the black silhouette of a large man standing in front of the open window, with blinding sunlight streaming in behind him. Jim tried to sit up, but as soon as he raised his head a few inches off the ground, his stomach lurched. He felt like he might black out again any second.

"Answer me!" the man demanded.

Jim swallowed back a sob. "I'm hurt," he somehow managed to whisper. "I hurt my foot."

"Those your clothes?" the man shouted, pointing to the pile of wet garments on the floor beside the bed.

Jim nodded.

"That your car down by the gulley? The Jaguar?"

Jim nodded again.

"You left your keys in the ignition," the man informed him.

Jim closed his eyes and sucked in a deep breath. "It won't start," he replied hoarsely. He started saying, "The check engine light—" but didn't have enough breath to finish his sentence.

The stranger crouched down beside Jim and laughed menacingly. "You're in a real fix then, aren't you?" he taunted.

Jim opened one eye and sized up his companion. He had strong features—a large hooked nose, deep-set black eyes, high cheekbones, and a heavy jawline. His skin was tanned and weather-beaten. He didn't look young—his face had a fair share of wrinkles—yet he had a full head of thick, jet-black hair. He was big, muscular and broad-shouldered, and looked like he could pick Jim up and throw him bodily out of the house without even breaking a sweat.

Jim struggled to sit up once more. He felt groggy and lightheaded. The throbbing in his foot was growing worse by the second. He sucked in another deep breath and started to squeak out a pathetic apology for showing up uninvited at the house. But the stranger interrupted him.

"You've got a British accent."

"Yes," Jim agreed with a roll of his eyes. "I know. I'm from England."

"What are you doing in Ohio?"

"I was driving to Cleveland, to meet a woman at the new—" Jim had to suck in a deep breath before he could finish his sentence, "—Rock and Roll Hall of Fame."

"Looks like you didn't make it," the stranger scoffed. He shifted his gaze away from Jim's face and examined the bruised foot peeking out from the sodden afghan.

"Damn, your foot looks hideous," he noted casually. "Turning green. Want me to amputate it now and get it over with?"

Jim winced and tried to draw his leg back under the afghan, but he could hardly move it. The stranger grabbed Jim's foot in his large hands and started examining it. The rough touch of his calloused fingers against Jim's torn skin felt excruciating. Jim cried out.

"It's not broken," the man stated bluntly. He rested Jim's foot back on the ground with surprising tenderness. "But it's swollen something awful right by the cut. Looks like a nasty infection has set in."

"Ah, Christ," Jim whispered under his breath.

The man ignored Jim's remark. "How'd it happen?"

Jim fell silent for a long moment while he tried to remember the events of the previous evening. "I caught my foot under something," he said at length. "A branch, I think. I must have twisted my ankle."

"Must have sliced a ligament too," the man added. "That cut looks bad. You're gonna need something to drain out the puss."

Jim drew in another deep breath and attempted a polite smile. "I'd very much appreciate it if you could call me an ambulance." The long sentence took the wind out of him, and he started to feel faint again.

"Don't believe in doctors," the stranger replied succinctly. He stood up, walked away from Jim, and sat down on the edge of the bed. "Do more harm than good. They'd probably shoot you up with a whole mother-load of antibiotics. Do you know how much damage antibiotics have inflicted upon this earth over the past fifty years? They're altering the whole nature of the ecosystem. Destroying the planet's immunities. Weakening the human race to the point where we won't be able to fight off even simple colds without drugs before long. And for every germ the antibiotics kill off, there's another one right on its heel, stronger than the last, just waiting to come up and get'cha."

He crossed his arms in front of his broad chest and sneered. "Nope. Don't believe in doctors *or* antibiotics."

*Great,* Jim thought, the sense of hopelessness he had experienced last night returning with a vengeance. *This bloke is completely mental.* He tried once more to sit up straight while he considered ways to change the man's mind.

"What's your name?" the stranger asked after the awkward silence had stretched to a breaking point.

"Jim. Jim McCudden."

"Like the piano player from the Pilots."

"Yeah, that's me," Jim replied with a slight nod. "I was one of the Pilots."

The man started to laugh. "No shit! I've got me a sick, naked celebrity on my floor!"

Jim blushed and closed his eyes once more. His mind started conjuring up images of a speeding ambulance carrying him away from this wretched cottage, its flashing lights and blaring horn heralding his return to a familiar world of safety. But then the pain in his foot became so unbearable that he had to cast aside his fantasy and focus all of his mental efforts on not crying.

"You should be in bed," the stranger declared, calling Jim back to reality with a sharp thud. "You'd probably be a lot more comfortable on this mattress than you are there on the floor."

Jim flashed his companion a dirty look.

The man barked out a laugh and returned to Jim's side. He lifted Jim off the floor as easily as he might scoop a small child in his arms, and carried him to the bed. Then he bent down and examined Jim's foot once more. After running his hands gently over Jim's swollen ankle, he turned his attention to Jim's face and touched his forehead with the back of his hand. He felt the pulse points in Jim's neck and pulled back Jim's eyelids to inspect his pupils.

"I'll go back to the Heights and make you up a pot of tea," he said once he had finished his assessment. "It'll help with the pain. And I'm gonna think about the best thing to do for your foot. But I want to look at some of my books first before I try anything. I'll send Nessie down with the tea once it's ready. I'll be back soon."

"P-please," Jim stammered. "You're very kind. But really, if you could just call for a doctor—"

"Told ya, I don't believe in doctors," the man replied curtly.

"But I do," Jim countered.

"But you're not in a position to do anything about that now, are you?" the stranger reminded him. "From how I see it, you're trespassing on my land, you've broken into my house, you can't walk, and you're as sick as a dying dog. I don't think you've got any choice but to trust me, now, do ya?"

Jim glared at his host but offered no argument.

The stranger pulled the musty sheet, blanket and quilt over Jim's chest. "You rest now. Nessie'll be here in just a few. The tea will help. Trust me. I know what I'm doing."

Jim sighed. He felt frightened, cross, and slightly nauseous. But at least he was a little more comfortable now that he was lying on a soft bed, under a dry cover.

*Might as well just do what this bastard says until I get my strength back,* he urged himself. *What choice do I have, anyway?*

The large man stepped away from the bed. But then he noticed the flickering candle on the nightstand. The flame had burned a deep, uneven crater in the top of the pillar. Long, messy drips of hardened wax spilled over the intricately curled tendrils on the candle's side.

"You burnt Cathy's candle!" he shouted. The veins in his neck popped, and his swarthy face flushed beet red. "You asshole! You had no right to touch her things!"

Jim rolled his face over the pillowcase and glanced at the misshapen candle he had left burning overnight. Then he looked up into the damning eyes of his furious host. His own eyes grew wide with fear.

"I'm sorry," Jim said meekly. "I didn't know it was meant for show." He sighed in remorse, then added as an afterthought, "Is she okay?"

"Whad'ya mean, 'Is she okay?'!" the man barked back.

"She was here last night," Jim answered slowly, calling to mind the strange, incessant cry of the woman at the window. "Cathy. In the rain. She was trying to get in."

"You saw her?" the man asked, the anger in his voice instantly replaced by a tone of incredulity.

"No," Jim replied. "But I heard her. And—" He fell silent while he struggled to remember the details of his encounter with the woman at the window. "I touched her."

"Damn you to hell!" the stranger bellowed. He smacked Jim hard across the face with the back of his hand and sent him reeling back into unconsciousness.

# Chapter Three

## The Piano Teacher

Maggie Grayson smiled at her young student as he fingered the final chords of *The Wild Horseman*. "That was very good, Robbie. I think you're just about ready for the recital."

Robbie McCudden lowered his head and stared into his lap. "Thank you, Miss Grayson," he said quietly.

Maggie picked up Robbie's sheet music and made a few notations in pencil in the margins. She wanted to write, "Don't be so nervous! You'll do just fine!" But she knew that would be pointless. Robbie played piano very well for a child of nine, but he *always* grew nervous in front of crowds and tended to make a lot of mistakes at his recitals.

Robbie's older sister Clara coughed.

Maggie turned her head towards the dark-haired girl. "Is your mother here yet?"

Clara stared out the front window of the small townhouse and stroked Maggie's cat, Percy. "Of course not," she replied. "Mum's always late."

Maggie threw a glance at the clock on her mantelpiece. It was four-thirty-five. The McCudden children's lessons were supposed to have ended five minutes ago, and Maggie had hoped to deposit a few tuition checks in the bank before it closed at five. But she knew Clara was right. Philippa McCudden always collected her children late.

Maggie had dealt with many thoughtless parents throughout her teaching career, but Philippa was by far the most insensitive. She seemed to take a perverse pleasure in reminding Maggie that driving her children to and from piano lessons was an extremely onerous task—a tiresome burden which she only performed because she had been ordered to do so by the judge who awarded her custody of Robbie and Clara. The piano lessons were *entirely* her ex-husband's idea, Maggie had been informed on multiple occasions, and if Philippa had had any say in the matter, she would have pulled her kids out long ago and enrolled them in more useful social activities, such as sports or dance classes.

Maggie looked back at Robbie. "Well, let's practice your scales one more time while we wait, why don't we? It'll help keep your fingers feeling loose."

Maggie watched Robbie place his fingers on the keys, then turned her attention back to Clara. The gangly young girl was an extremely gifted piano player. Though not quite twelve, Clara was already tackling pieces that Maggie hadn't mastered until her first year of college. Yet the child relied too heavily on her inborn skills and uncanny sight-reading ability. Clara could play songs almost note-perfect the first time she tried them. Yet she seldom rehearsed her pieces with true dedication. After a few lessons, she inevitably grew bored with her assigned songs and wanted to move on to new selections.

Robbie, however, was an entirely different type of student. He was often intimidated by the songs she presented him and quick to insist they were too hard for him. And yet, with appropriate—and at times, excessive—encouragement, he was usually able to play them beautifully. He also brought an emotional expression to his playing that belied his youth and hinted at a truly artistic temperament. Sometimes his playing became almost too personal. Even now, as he worked his way through his scales, Maggie could tell he was feeling anxious.

"Here she comes!" Clara called out from the window seat as a silver BMW pulled up in front of Maggie's townhouse. "And she's got Jean-Claude with her."

Robbie's fingers jammed up, and he stumbled over his last scale.

Maggie gave Robbie an encouraging pat on the back, then closed the cover over the keys. "Who's Jean-Claude?" she asked politely.

Clara snorted. "He's this bloke Mum hired to teach us French. Mum's rented a house in Saint-Tropez for the month of August, and she expects us to be fluent by then so we can fit in with the natives."

Maggie's eyes widened in surprise. "Well, that should be marvelous fun for you both," she said hesitantly, trying not to sound too envious. "I can hardly imagine spending a whole month in the South of France! I'm lucky if I can squeeze a weekend in Blackpool into my summer holiday. Have you learned much French yet?"

"I can say *ooh-la-la*," Clara answered with a roll of her eyes.

Philippa McCudden knocked on the front door. Maggie asked Clara to let her in. Percy jumped to the ground as soon as Clara stopped petting him and sauntered towards the hallway.

Philippa burst into the house and very nearly stepped on the cat. Percy hissed at her, then made a quick break up the stairs to the next floor. Philippa scowled at him, then turned to the piano and noticed her son still sitting at the bench.

"Oh, you're running late with your lesson, Miss Grayson," she chided. "I thought you would be finished with my children by now."

"We were just practicing scales while we wait—" Maggie began, but Philippa cut her off.

"Come now, you two, gather your books. We haven't got all day!" She reached into her Louis Vuitton purse and pulled out a leather-bound checkbook. "I'm going to have to post-date this check, Miss Grayson," she said as she began scribbling with her Cross pen. "My ex is returning to Manchester this weekend after his latest American gallivant, and he's going to have to cough up his next support check straight away if he knows what's good for him."

Robbie cringed in embarrassment while he slipped his sheet music into his tote-bag, but Clara came to her father's defense.

"What are you talking about, Mum? Dad always pays you on time! Early, even."

"The French lessons, darling," her mother replied in a sing-song voice. "Tutors don't come cheap, you know. And your father is responsible for paying *all* of your educational expenses. We're running a little over what we had budgeted for the month."

"Does Dad know he's paying for us to have a French tutor?" Clara challenged.

"He will when he comes to pick you up this weekend, and I tell him," Philippa replied.

"We're going to Dad's house this weekend?" Robbie exclaimed. "I thought we weren't going to see him until the recital!"

"I've left a message on his answerphone," Philippa said. She handed the post-dated check to Maggie and slipped her pen and checkbook back in her purse. "Something has come up, and I have to go away for the weekend. You two will be staying with your father."

"Is anything wrong, Mrs. McCudden?" Maggie asked, noticing the edgy tone in Philippa's voice when she mentioned her sudden need to go away.

"Oh, don't be silly," Philippa replied with a wave of her perfectly manicured hand. "I'm going to a party at an old friend's house, that's all. But I only just found out about it, and I simply cannot miss it. I do so hate not hearing about things until the last minute. It wreaks havoc with my schedule. Come now, children, Jean-Claude's in the car. We mustn't leave him waiting!"

She stormed out of Maggie's house, pulling Robbie along by his left hand and leaving a cloud of expensive-smelling perfume in her wake.

Maggie examined Philippa's check and realized she wouldn't be able to cash it for two more weeks. Her cheeks burned in irritation. Then she glanced at her clock. It was four-fifty-two. She would never get to the bank on time.

She walked to her desk—an antique roll-top that used to belong to her father—and placed Philippa's check at the bottom of her pile of tuition payments. She started reaching for her stack of bills to pay but stopped herself just as her fingertips brushed against them.

*I'll worry about those later,* she decided. *Right now, I'm going to have a nice glass of wine.*

She stepped into her kitchen and pulled a small goblet out of her cupboard. Then she grabbed a bottle of white Zinfandel from her refrigerator and filled her glass half-way. She took a small sip.

The wine tasted sweet on her tongue and warmed the inside of her mouth. She closed her eyes and swallowed back a small tug of guilt. She knew her mother would disapprove of her secret indulgence.

Then she tried to push aside the fear that pricked at her gut—her fear of a strange woman's voice that might start haranguing her at any moment. This past month, it seemed, every time Maggie poured herself a small glass of wine, she heard the voice urging her to stop.

The first time she'd experienced the hallucination, she'd brushed it aside as her guilty conscience nagging at her. But lately, the voice had been growing more articulate and insistent. Last week, the invisible speaker even introduced herself and claimed her name was Agnes.

*Keep away from me this evening!* Maggie implored the voice. *I need this drink!*

She knew she could never survive her weekly meetings with Philippa McCudden without a glass of wine to look forward to afterwards.

Maggie thought about Philippa—gorgeous, gregarious and aggravating Philippa—and sighed. Then she stared into her wineglass. The rose-colored Zinfandel had formed small, delicate rivulets along the inside of the goblet from being tipped up and down.

"I need this drink," she acknowledged aloud as she brought the glass back to her lips. The wine would take the edge off the pain she always felt when she thought about Philippa. Because it hurt to hear Philippa rebuke and berate the man she had once been married to and thrown away.

Maggie took a large sip of wine and closed her eyes.

*Yes,* she admitted to herself. *It hurts to hear Philippa rebuke and berate the man I love.*

# Chapter Four

## The Story Teller

"Yoo-hoo! It's me, Nessie! I brung you your tea!" a cheerful voice called into Jim's bedroom.

Jim opened his eyes and lifted his face towards his visitor. His bruised cheek stung afresh, and his right foot started throbbing unmercifully once more.

A large Black woman in a floral-patterned caftan stepped into his room, carrying a battered plastic tray that held a teapot, a sugar bowl, and a chipped blue ceramic mug covered in yellow smiley-faces.

"You awake?" she asked Jim.

"I am now," he grumbled.

"Then sit up. You can't drink tea while you're lying down," she replied.

Jim tugged his blanket over his bare chest and struggled to prop himself into a sitting position. But as soon as he shifted his weight, a wrenching pain shot up his injured leg. He fell back against the mattress with a loud groan.

Nessie laid her tray on the bedside table. "Here, let me help," she offered. She slipped her hands under Jim's armpits and hefted him up in one quick movement. Before stepping away from the bed, she deftly pulled his pillow up with her left hand and placed it against the headboard so that Jim could rest his back more comfortably.

Jim stared at her in dumbstruck awe. The woman had a commanding presence and was obviously strong, yet she also radiated warmth. He hadn't expected to wake from his morning assault and find such a person by his side. But then again, he thought begrudgingly, after the bizarre occurrences of the last twelve hours, he hardly knew what to expect anymore.

Nessie smiled down at him, revealing a gleaming gold incisor, and pushed her slipping, horn-rimmed glasses back up the bridge of her nose.

"Thank you," Jim mumbled. "You're quite—strong."

"I used t' help my daddy sit up," she explained. "He couldn't use his legs much either. Now let me pour you your drink. Cliff says it's kinda bitter an' you'd prob'ly be wantin' some sugar in it."

"What's in it?" Jim asked as he watched Nessie pour tea into the brightly colored mug.

"Haven't the faintest idea," she replied. "Just another one of his magic potions, I s'pose."

Jim scowled. "I won't drink this unless I know what's in it."

Nessie's eyes twinkled and she started to laugh. "Now don't you go worryin' yourself," she said after making a deliberate effort to wipe the grin off her face. "If Cliff says this'll make you feel better, then it'll make you feel better. That man knows his tea. Whenever I'm feelin' under the weather, he always brews me up just the right thing to cure whatever ails me. Don't matter if it's a headache or a cold or just my monthly curse. That man's got a gift."

Jim accepted the mug from Nessie with obvious reluctance and took a small sip. He coughed and cleared his throat. "This tastes awful."

She took the mug back and stirred in a few sugar cubes. "Does this help, or do you need more?" she asked.

He took another sip. "It'll do," he sighed.

She let loose a deep, hearty laugh. "Here. Let me have a smell," she said, taking the mug away from him and placing it under her nose. "Phew-eee! This reeks worse'n that potion he used to brew up for my poor ol' daddy." She handed the cup back to Jim and sat down on the edge of his mattress.

"So where am I, anyway?" he asked after taking a larger sip.

"You're at the Grange. My old home. Though I live with Cliff now, in the house over the hill, a few hundred yards west as the crow flies. Can't see the building from here 'cause of all them maple trees in the way. Everyone in these parts calls it the Heights, since it stands on top of the tallest hill in the county. But it ain't really that high. Northern Ohio's kind of flat, you know."

"Mmm hmm," Jim agreed. He sipped his tea and mulled over her reply as a calming sensation started spreading from his throat to his chest.

*So this large, friendly Black woman lives with that violent, raving lunatic,* he noted. *They certainly seem like an odd couple.* He cleared his throat.

"Is Cliff your—I mean, are you two, um, well, together?"

Nessie eyed him incredulously, then broke out in another full-bellied laugh. "Is Cliff my sweetheart? Oh, Lordy! What a thought! Hell no! He owns this place, and I just sort of—well, make do. You know. I help him do whatever needs to be done."

Jim nodded. "I see. So you're his maid."

"No, I am *not* his maid," Nessie said. Her smile vanished and her voice and face both grew instantly serious. "I grew up here, 'long with Cliff. In both houses, I s'pose you could say. We both did. This here place is my real home, but Cliff offered me a room at the Heights a few years back, so I moved there. Saves me walkin' up that hill every day to go to work."

Jim nodded and took another large sip from his mug as he tried to make sense of her explanation. He wondered if the tea was affecting his ability to think clearly. As far as he could tell, he was as clear-headed as ever. But the pain in his foot seemed to be subsiding. In fact, his whole lower body seemed to be growing numb.

He tried to piece together the information he had gleaned so far. *The bastard's name is Cliff. And this nice woman is called Nessie. But how does that strange bird from the window fit into the picture?*

"What about Cathy?" he asked. "She's from here too, right?"

Nessie hung her head and lowered her voice to a whisper. "Uh-huh, that's right. Cathy grew up at the Heights too, 'long with Cliff and Ernie."

*Well, that certainly clarifies things,* Jim thought irritably. He swallowed another sip of tea and managed to mask his exasperation with an awkward smile. "And do you all live there still?"

"Oh, hell no," she answered, lifting her head back up and focusing a gentle gaze at Jim's bloodshot, grey eyes. "Ernie lives over at the Black Bull now, on the top floor. You know, Katie's place. But Cliff and me, we still live here, 'long with Harry. He's a big help with the greenhouse and the mail-order business. When he's not dinkin' with his trucks, that is."

Jim dimly recognized the names "Katie" and "Black Bull" from his conversation outside the restaurant last night, and made a mental note of the new character "Harry." But then he realized Nessie had omitted a name in her long-winded response. "And Cathy?" he asked.

Nessie turned her face away from Jim again and stared at the floor. "Cathy don't live here no more," she said sadly.

"Oh," Jim replied. He was about to say that Cathy had stopped by the previous night during the rainstorm, but then Nessie looked back up at him. He noticed a strange, wistful expression in her soft brown eyes and abruptly decided to refrain from any further discussion of the peculiar woman at the window. Instead, he redirected the conversation back to the man who was holding him captive. "What can you tell me about Cliff?"

Nessie smiled broadly again. "Lordy! I could go on and on! What d'you wanna know?"

"Can I trust him?" Jim asked, rubbing his hand against his sore jaw. "He says he's going to treat my foot, but I would much rather see a doctor."

"Well, as long as you're shackin' up on Cliff's property, you gotta do what he says now, don't you?" she answered, her voice stiff with resignation. But then she reached across the bed and patted Jim's free hand reassuringly. "But don't you worry. Cliff's a good man—never you mind what everyone else says about him. I've known him since he was a little boy. He's like a younger brother to me. And if he says he's gonna help you, then he's gonna help you. He ain't thrown you out of this house yet, now, has he?"

Her words did not inspire much confidence, but Jim tried to remain optimistic. He took another sip of tea.

"Now drink up," she insisted. "Cliff wants you to finish the whole pot."

Jim sighed. "So what is he, anyway? Some kind of homeopath?"

Nessie glared at Jim as if he were crazy. "Who? Cliff? He likes girls! What are you suggestin'?"

"A homeopathic *doctor*," Jim clarified. "You know. A doctor of alternative medicine. As opposed to a regular doctor who went to a traditional medical school."

"Oh," she replied coolly. "I misunderstood you. Thought you was implyin' somethin' funny." She stood up from the mattress, grabbed the wooden captain's chair that was propped against the wall, and dragged it to the side of the bed. After refilling Jim's mug and adding a few more sugar cubes, she took a seat. "Well, I don't know what no homeopathic doctor is, but Cliff's had lots of learnin'. He's studied with some of the wisest men in all of Asia. Or so he's tol' me. Knows all about getting your yin back in touch with your yang."

*Great*, Jim thought, closing his eyes and leaning back against his propped-up pillow. He said a short silent prayer that his strange host would not be inflicting acupuncture upon him next, then looked back at his talkative companion. "When was Cliff in Asia?"

"Long time ago," Nessie replied.

"Why did he study medicine there, instead of at an American university?"

"It's a long story," she answered.

Jim sat in silence for several seconds, waiting for her to elaborate, but when she said nothing more, he tilted his head and offered her a calculated smile to prompt her.

"Well, it would seem that I've got some time on my hands just now. Why don't you tell me some more about Cliff while I drink my tea?" he proposed, then added courteously, "if you don't mind."

"Oh, I don't mind," Nessie said. She settled herself more comfortably in her chair and stretched out her feet. "Finish up your mug now. It's prob'ly best to drink it hot."

"Cliff is—" she began, but then she stopped abruptly. "Maybe I oughta start with how he came here," she said after a moment's reflection.

Jim nodded. "Please do," he agreed.

Nessie smiled and crossed her arms in front of her ample chest. The fabric of her caftan bunched up around her bosom, and she took a moment to straighten it out before she continued speaking.

"First let me tell you a bit about Mr. Shaw—God rest his soul. Mr. Ernest Shaw, *Senior,* that is. He owned the Heights since way back when. After the war, when my daddy was lookin' for work, Mr. Shaw was the only man in the whole damned county who'd hire him."

A sour look crossed Nessie's face. "Daddy had a bit of a record," she admitted before adding defensively, "but he was poor, and he ain't never done nothin' but steal a little money to buy food for his mama and pa. But back in those days, wouldn't nobody hire a Black man with a police record. 'Cept for Mr. Shaw, that is. He was a good Christian. The Holy Spirit moved in him, my mama always said. Mr. Shaw believed my daddy was contrite and wanted to serve the Lord. So he took my folks in and paid Daddy to work as his field hand. And he let them live in this very house where you're lyin' just now.

"Daddy was so grateful to Mr. Shaw. Couldn't say enough good things about him. He even named me after him. I'm Ernestina Dean, but you can call me Nessie. Everybody does." Nessie flashed Jim another warm smile before continuing her tale.

"Now Mr. and Mrs. Shaw had themselves two little boys," she elaborated. "Ernest Junior, and a little baby named Clifford. But then one day, 'fore anyone even knew what was happenin', that baby took the polio and died. And right after that, Mrs. Shaw and my daddy, they were both stricken too and ended up cripples. Mrs. Shaw had to use a wheelchair after that, and my daddy, well, he could shuffle 'round this house on his crutches alright, but he couldn't work the fields no more. But Mr. Shaw let us stay on his property still. He was a good man."

Nessie looked up at the ceiling momentarily, as if she were directing her speech to Heaven. Jim waited patiently for her to collect her thoughts and took a few more sips of tea.

"So my mama went to work at the Heights after that," Nessie eventually said. "She took care of Mrs. Shaw *and* kept an eye out for me and little Ernie too. A coupla' years passed like that, and then Mrs. Shaw, well, she had some second or third cousin named Patty who got herself in a fix. And you know how it was back then. Wouldn't do for no respectable girl to have a baby with no husband around. So the Shaws took her in too. Like I said, they were good Christians, and they didn't judge people. And after Patty had her baby, the Shaws adopted that child and raised her like their own daughter. That was Cathy—the lady you was askin' 'bout earlier.

"Patty went away after that. She stopped by the Heights every now and then to look in on her chil'. But then she got married and had a whole new passel of brats, so she stopped comin'.

"And then one day—I'm not exactly sure when, I think it was maybe in 1960?—a preacher man came to town. He was gonna stage a revival just outside of Cleveland. The Shaws heard about him from their pastor and invited him to stay at the Heights while he was settin' things up. He brung along this little heathen chil' that he used in his show. Said he was a Red Injun boy he'd rescued from some tribe, though I ain't so sure that's true. This boy couldn't speak no English and didn't have no manners. And he was so covered in dirt he looked almos' as dark as me. Now the Shaws, being good Christian folk, they took pity on that poor chil'. I'm not sure what they told that damn fool preacher—if they said they'd watch the boy for a coupla' weeks, or if they asked to adopt him. But after that preacher went to Cleveland to put on his show, he never came back for his boy. And so he stayed here with us."

Nessie winked at Jim. "Mr. Shaw baptized him in the local church just to be on the safe side, 'cause he started thinkin' that preacher wasn't a genuine man of God after all. And he re-named that boy Clifford, after his sweet little baby that the angels took."

Nessie leaned towards Jim and whispered in a conspiratorial tone, "Just between you and me, my mama always said that Cliff had a bit of the devil in his soul." She smiled slyly and leaned back in her chair again. "But don't you mind that. Cliff ain't so bad as folks make him out to be. He never was. But he sure as hell never fit in anywhere outside of the Heights.

"The local school wouldn't take him at first, since he couldn't talk right. And even after my mama scrubbed him up real good, he was still kinda dark lookin'. But he was too white to go to Asa Mahan Elementary with me. So Mrs. Shaw kept him home with her while Cathy, Ernie and me went off to school ev'ry mornin'. She taught him how to speak and read and write and do his numbers. And Cliff was always gentle as a kitten 'round Mrs. Shaw. And 'round my daddy too, whenever he saw him. Seemed to know the crippled folk couldn't hurt him. But he was skittish with just about everyone else, even with Mr. Shaw at first. He was like a wild animal."

Nessie took off her glasses for a moment to wipe the lenses with the fabric of her caftan, and rolled her eyes. "Cathy took a shine to him, though. Once he started speakin' proper, that is. Wasn't long 'fore they became insep'rable, like two peas in a pod. That first summer, after Cathy got out of school, the two of them started runnin' off to the edges of the farm and playin' in the meadows every day. Come September, Mrs. Shaw tried puttin' Cliff into regular school, since he could talk now. But the other kids bullied him somethin' awful, 'cause of the way he looked. So Cliff started playin' hooky. And Cathy—well, she got to playin' hooky so much too, that Mrs. Shaw decided to keep 'em *both* at home and teach 'em herself.

" 'Course, that didn't sit well with Ernie, Junior. He never much liked the idea of havin' this wild chil' in his house to begin with. Used to call Cliff 'Heathen' or 'Prairie Nigger' whenever he thought no one was listenin'. And he sure as hell didn't like the fact that his mama and daddy made *him* go to school and work in the fields, while they let Cliff stay at home and run around all day doin' nothin'. Nossir. Ernie never took to Cliff. And he'd punch the livin' daylights out of any kid who'd call the two of them brothers."

Nessie sighed, then refilled Jim's mug and added a few more sugar cubes to his drink. "After Mrs. Shaw died, things got worse," she continued. "Mr. Shaw made Cliff and Cathy go to regular school then. Though they cut their classes so much, they both kept gettin' suspended. They played outside on the nice days and hid in this house with my daddy whenever the weather turned bad. But Ernie would catch Cliff sometimes, when he was walkin' home to the Heights. He and his buddies would gang up on him. It got pretty ugly."

She stopped speaking for a moment when she noticed Jim had stopped sipping his tea. "Drink up. Cliff'll be mad if he gets here and sees you ain't drunk it all yet. And you sure don't wanna make Cliff mad."

Jim rubbed his bruised cheek self-consciously and took a large sip of tea. His entire lower body was quite numb now, and he was beginning to feel light-headed as well.

"Well, now, where was I?" Nessie mumbled. "Oh, yeah—Ernie and his buddies used to jump Cliff whenever they got the chance. Beat him up pretty bad sometimes too. But Cliff wouldn't rat on 'em. He had too much dumb pride. He lied to Mr. Shaw whenever he asked about the black eyes. Said he'd fallen out of a tree or slipped on a rock while he was out explorin'. And since Cliff was always off and about who-knows-where, Mr. Shaw didn't doubt but that he was tellin' the truth.

"Things got better for Cliff when Ernie went away to college. But then he'd come home for Christmas or the summer, and he'd make Cliff's life a livin' hell all over again. He tormented that boy somethin' awful."

Nessie clucked her tongue and shook her head. "Some folks just don't have no feelings for anyone who looks dif'rent from themselves. Some folks—well, some folks just don't deserve no one's pity, I s'pose."

Jim nodded and sipped his tea. "So, Ernie hated Cliff, but Cathy still loved him," he surmised.

"Mind you, that's where things get complicated," Nessie replied. "Cathy and Cliff—well 'bout this time, when they were fifteen or sixteen years old, they went off together one mornin'. But that evenin', Cliff came back to the Heights alone. Turns out, the two of them'd snuck onto some neighbors' property a few miles down the road. Cathy twisted her ankle real bad, and the family—they were called the

Lyndons—they insisted she stay at their place for the night. Mr. Shaw drove over to check on her straight away. But once he made sure she was okay and saw how happy she was to be stayin' at the Lyndons' fine house, he went ahead and let her sleep there.

"I never could get the whole story out of anyone, but I guess what happened was somethin' like this: Cliff and Cathy went off that mornin' to spy on Joe and Beth Lyndon—these two rich kids who were about the same age as them. Well, lemme take that back. The Lyndon family *used* to be real rich, but they'd been fallin' on hard times for a while by then—sellin' off their best acres and lettin' their field hands go. But they still kept up their fancy ways. Sent their kids to private schools and didn't go to the local church. Nossir. Wasn't good enough for 'em. Drove thirty miles round trip each Sunday to one of them Episcopalian churches. That whole family never paid much mind to common farmers like the Shaws.

"But anyhow, after Cathy spent that night with those Lyndons, things were never quite the same 'tween her and Cliff. They started gettin' into fights, and Cliff started actin' like some jealous hothead, and—well, like I said, I don' know the whole story.

"Not long after that, Ernie came back from college without graduatin'. Got some girl in the family way and had to marry her. Mr. Shaw said they could live at the Heights, but tol' Ernie he had to work for a livin' now."

Nessie rolled her eyes once more. "No one liked Ernie's wife very much. 'Specially not me. She was real uppity. 'Spected me to wait on her hand and foot, like I was her personal maid or somethin'. But anyhow, she had her baby—little Harry. And a sweet little boy he was. I started takin' care of him, almost like a nanny, 'cause my mama had passed on by then, and Ernie's wife sure as hell couldn't be bothered with changin' diapers or boilin' bottles.

"Then, not long after that, Mr. Shaw died. He wrote in his will that all his property was supposed to be split three ways equal 'tween his three kids—Ernie, Cathy and Cliff. But since Cathy and Cliff were both still underage, he named Ernie their legal guardian. Mr. Shaw set aside some money for my daddy and me too, an' wrote in his will that we could go on livin' at the Grange for the rest of our lives without havin' to pay no rent. So God bless Mr. Shaw. Like I said, he was a good man. My daddy always said he must've gone straight to Heaven, and got a good seat up there right next to Jesus."

Nessie looked up to the ceiling once more and smiled again. Then she took Jim's mug and checked to make certain he had finished every last drop of tea.

Jim watched her carefully. She seemed to be moving in slow motion. He lifted his hand to reposition his blanket. He seemed to be moving in slow motion too. He turned his head towards the bedside table and felt a rush of dizziness. As Nessie rested the smiley-face mug on the plastic tray, he realized something was missing from the tabletop.

*What used to be there?* he wondered in a stupor.

"Now, as you can imagine, things got pretty bad for Cliff after Mr. Shaw passed on," Nessie continued, calling Jim out of his reverie. "Wasn't long 'fore he moved out of his bedroom at the Heights and started livin' with Daddy and me here at the Grange. And things got worse 'tween him and Cathy too. So it didn't surprise no one when Cliff took all his money out of the bank the day after he graduated high school, and just up and left."

Jim stared at Nessie with bleary eyes. Her body seemed to be shifting in and out of focus. He glanced back at the table and, with a flash of insight, realized that the half-burnt candle was no longer there. He closed his eyes and heard the front door to the house opening.

"I'm back, and I've got my knives!" Cliff called out, slamming the door shut behind him.

"Speak of the devil," Nessie laughed. "I guess he done come back!"

# Chapter Five

## A Celebrated Herbologist

Cliff stepped into the bedroom, carrying a beat-up Coleman camping lantern in his hand. Over his shoulder, he had slung a patched, burlap tote bag that bore the threadbare remains of some garishly-colored crewel-work embroidery. Cliff lifted the lantern over his head and proclaimed in a booming baritone, "I'm searching for an honest man!" Then he laughed at his own joke, placed the lantern on the nightstand, and focused a steely gaze at Jim.

"You drink the whole pot?" Cliff asked.

Nessie answered for him. "Yep. I made sure he done that."

"Thanks," Cliff said. He slipped the bag off his shoulder and rested it on the floor. "Lemme see your foot again," he added, yanking the covers to the side of the bed.

Embarrassed to be wearing nothing but underwear in front of Nessie, Jim reached for the sheet and tried to cover himself back up.

Cliff laughed at him. "Still got some of your daddy's pajamas around here, Nessie? Or did you throw them all away?" he asked indifferently.

"I think I might," she replied. "Couldn't bring myself to look at his clothes right after he passed, and I ain't never bothered to sort through 'em since."

"Could you please fetch a pair for our modest guest?" Cliff asked in a condescending tone.

"Will do," she answered. She stood up from her chair and left the room.

"I have clothes of my own," Jim said, struggling to maintain his dignity. "In my suitcase. In the boot of my car."

"Harry towed your Jaguar to the barn so he could work on its engine," Cliff said distractedly as he examined Jim's foot. "I can't be bothered going there just to fetch you some P.J.'s."

"Please," Jim interjected. "It's a hire car. You don't need to fix it. The company will take care of all that. If you could just call a motor service, I'm sure they could tow it to the nearest Hertz office."

"Already had it towed," Cliff repeated. "Up to the barn. Harry'll fix it for ya. He's good at that sort of thing. Likes cars. Always has, ever since he was a boy."

Cliff lifted Jim's foot. Jim braced himself for a fresh stab of pain, but he felt nothing. Cliff glanced at Jim's face and laughed once more. "See? Tea worked! Foot's numb."

Nessie returned to the room, carrying a pair of purple polyester pajamas spotted with orange paisleys. "Oh Lordy, just seein' an' touchin' his things again gets me feelin' all funny inside," she said. "I can just picture him wearin' these, sittin' in his rockin' chair, smokin' a doobie and listenin' to records on the stereo."

"Those were the days," Cliff replied with a wry smile. He lowered Jim's foot and grabbed his bag, then started pulling out items and resting them on the mattress. Without looking at Jim, he announced, "I'm gonna clean your wound, lance the blister, and rub some ointment on the cut. I'll stitch it back up if I need to."

He pulled some bandages out of his bag and asked Nessie to boil up a pot of water on the stove. "I just turned the water main back on, so let the tap run a little before you collect anything in the pot, please. Wouldn't want to use rusty water on our guest's foot now, would we?" He threw a snarky leer at Jim, then turned back to Nessie. "I'm pretty sure there's still some gas connected to the stove. Need a match for the burner?"

"I'll see if there's one in the cupboard," she replied. She draped her father's clothes over the back of the captain's chair and walked out of the room.

Cliff continued explaining his plans to Jim. "After the water boils, I'll add something to it. Then I'll soak the bandages in the solution and wrap them around your foot. They'll draw out the infection."

"What are you going to put in the water?" Jim asked nervously.

"I just told you, something that will draw out the infection," Cliff replied disinterestedly. He lifted Jim's foot again, placed a small ceramic bowl underneath it, and began pouring clear liquid over it from a large glass bottle. Then he pulled a white cloth from his stack of items and doused its surface with a brown liquid from a smaller glass bottle. He started rubbing Jim's foot with the damp cloth.

Jim clenched his hands into fists. "What are you doing to my foot?" he asked, hardly daring to breathe.

"Weren't ya listening to me earlier?" Cliff replied. "Told ya. I'm washing it."

"What's in those bottles you're using?" Jim cried. Tears of frustration started welling in the corners of his eyes.

"Distilled water and hydrogen peroxide," Cliff answered without looking at Jim. "Is that too weird for you? Most people I know approve of using such items in first aid situations. But if you'd prefer, I can wash your foot with prune juice and Draino."

"Sorry," Jim mumbled. He wiped his eyes with the back of his hand and turned his head to the wall. The dizzy feeling that had started enveloping him before Cliff's arrival had been replaced by a stomach-clenching wave of fear.

Cliff continued washing and wiping Jim's foot. Then he took the bowl off the bed and replaced it with a towel. "I'm gonna go see if Nessie's water has come to a boil," he announced as he picked up two scalpels, a long needle, and a small bag of dried herbs from his pile. "I'll be right back. Don't go anywhere."

Jim braced himself for the encroaching procedure. He wracked his brain, trying to think of any way he could possibly extract himself from this situation before Cliff returned with his knives. But his mind drew nothing but blanks.

When Cliff and Nessie returned, they each crouched by the foot of the bed.

"You might feel a small prickly sensation," Cliff warned Jim. "Kind of like a tugging. But it shouldn't hurt. If it does, you let me know."

"How should I let you know?" Jim asked, not daring to meet Cliff's eyes.

Cliff laughed. "Don't worry. I'm sure something'll come to ya. If you can actually feel what I'm about to do, you'll probably just scream."

Jim closed his eyes and tried to think of something pleasant to distract his racing thoughts while Cliff and Nessie worked on his foot. Images of his children's faces immediately sprang to his mind. He wondered when—or if—he would see them again. Their piano recital was coming up, he remembered.

*Surely, Cliff will release me from this house by then,* he hoped. *Or maybe I'll feel strong enough in a day or two to just walk out of here by myself.* He wondered if he should say a prayer.

Then he called to mind the heart-shaped face of Robbie and Clara's piano teacher back in England, and daydreamed about her for a few wistful moments. She was so calm and lovely, and genuinely kind.

*Why did I ever marry a bitch like Philippa?* he chided himself. *Why didn't I choose a woman more like Maggie Grayson?*

Jim steeled his nerves and snuck a glance at the bottom of the bed. Cliff was already wrapping his ankle in thin strips of white cloth.

The mildly pleasant, lightheaded sensation he had been experiencing earlier started to return. He watched Nessie walk out of the room, carrying the water pot. He saw Cliff rest his foot on top of a towel, but he couldn't feel anything from his waist down.

"There, now, that wasn't so bad, was it?" Cliff asked Jim in a patronizing voice. He pulled the wooden captain's chair closer to the bed and sat down. "Good news is, you didn't slice your ligament. It's just a small tear. Should heal pretty cleanly. Bad news is, the cut was deep, and a wicked infection has set in. You're gonna have to stay off your feet completely for the next few days."

Nessie returned to the room. Cliff asked her to dress Jim in the purple pajamas. Jim started to protest, but Cliff cut him off. "She knows how to take care of a crippled man. You're in good hands. Stop complaining."

Cliff scooted the chair out of the way while Nessie dressed Jim. Then he asked her to find her father's old bedpan. Jim started complaining once more, but Cliff reminded him that he had just drunk a large pot of tea and had to stay off his feet. "Don't think your bladder's gonna hold out till you're well enough to use crutches," he noted in a mocking voice.

Nessie returned to the room with a bedpan and handed it to Jim. Then Cliff asked her to go back home and make up a plate of food for their guest. She nodded and leaned closer to Cliff.

Jim closed his eyes while they exchanged a few short whispers. A fresh wave of exhaustion started tugging at his consciousness. He listened to Nessie's footsteps as she stepped out of the room, then heard the front door close. He felt sluggish and irritable.

*If I pretend I'm asleep, maybe that asshole will go away too,* he thought with a faint glimmer of hope. But he heard no more footsteps on the bedroom floor.

He opened his eyes and stole a quick glance at his host. Cliff was reaching into his embroidered bag and pulling out some rolling paper and a small packet of herbs. Jim watched in dismay as Cliff assembled a fat cigarette and slipped it inside a roach clip.

"Now comes the fun part," Cliff announced. He offered the joint to Jim with one hand while he pulled a lighter out of his shirt pocket with the other. "Smoke this down to the clip."

Jim summoned his last ounces of courage. "I don't smoke pot anymore," he protested.

"This ain't pot," Cliff replied.

"Then what the hell is it?" Jim demanded, struggling to maintain his composure.

Cliff leaned back in the wooden chair and folded his arms in front of his chest. "Is that any way to talk to the man who just saved you? The way your infection was spreading, you'd have lost your foot before long, and maybe even your life. I don't know how your parents raised you, but mine always taught me to say thank-you when someone offered me help."

Jim took a deep breath and counted to five in his head before he ventured a reply. "I do appreciate your help," he said when the silence between them had stretched to a breaking point. "It's just that—I really would much prefer to go to a hospital."

Cliff frowned. "Well, you stalled your car in the wrong place then." He took the cigarette away from Jim and held it out in front of him. "This cigarette contains a unique blend of herbs which will heal your infection, keep your fever at bay, and help your ligament mend itself. It will also numb your pain and make you sleep very deeply while all that healing is going on. I grew the herbs myself. I have customers from all over the world who are willing to pay considerable sums of money for blends such as this one. If you went to any herbalist in Hong Kong, any Siddhar in South India, or any homeopath in Heidelberg, and told him that Clifford Shaw of Cautley, Ohio, not only gave you some of his medicine for free, but administered it to you himself—why, that person would be green with envy! I am a world-renowned expert in both Zhōngyào xué and the Ayurvedic arts. And I am telling you, once more, to smoke this cigarette down to the roach clip."

He handed the cigarette back to Jim and offered him the lighter. Jim closed his eyes and sighed. Reluctantly, he lit the tip and took a puff.

"Inhale," Cliff barked.

Jim brought the cigarette to his mouth again and inhaled deeply.

"You don't have to hold your breath like that," Cliff admonished him. "This isn't marijuana. You can smoke this like tobacco."

Jim smoked in silence while Cliff watched him. When the glowing tip of the cigarette started deteriorating into ash, Jim threw a nervous glance at his host. Cliff pulled a cut-glass ashtray out of the top drawer of the nightstand and offered it to Jim. Jim tapped down the ashes, then looked away from Cliff and continued smoking.

After a few minutes, he started feeling very tired. He tried to stub the cigarette out in the ashtray, but Cliff ordered him to stay awake and finish smoking. "I'll keep you company. I'm going to take the wet bandages off your foot in an hour and replace them with dry ones. I imagine you'll probably be fast asleep by then."

Then Cliff directed Jim's attention to the camping lantern and showed him how to turn it on. "Wouldn't want you to wake up tonight and be all afraid of the dark," he sneered.

Jim sensed his mind drifting off to a vague sort of place, somewhere between a drunken stupor and a blissed-out high. He was still aware of his surroundings, but felt powerless to respond to them. He heard a voice that he recognized as Cliff's.

"I'll have Nessie leave your food on the nightstand. If you wake up hungry, go ahead and eat anything she's left for you. It should all be easy to digest."

The volume of Cliff's voice seemed to fade in and out.

Jim's eyelids started drooping. He felt a small tug on his hand and realized Cliff was removing the cigarette from his fingers. He rolled his head over the pillow and started giving in to a powerful urge to sleep. He felt Cliff's warm fingers press down gently on the pulse in his neck. Then he sensed Cliff's face leaning over his head. Cliff's breath felt hot and moist on his skin as he whispered in his ear.

"If Cathy comes back tonight, ask her if she has a message for me."

# Chapter Six

## The Irritant

Maggie stood on her front doorstep and waved goodbye to her last student of the day. She watched the child's mother drive down the long, narrow street, through the columns of identical, grey terrace houses. Then she collected her mail, brought it to her kitchen table, and put a kettle on for tea. While the water came to a boil, she sat down and sorted through the letters.

*Bill, bill, advert, bill,* Maggie noted irritably. But then she found two personal letters tucked inside a flyer from her local grocer—a note from her sister Maureen and a card from her friend Ellen Nussey. She tore open the second envelope and found an invitation to a surprise fortieth birthday party that Ellen was throwing for their old school chum Mary Taylor.

Maggie sighed. Her own fortieth birthday was approaching in a few months, and she knew no one would be throwing a surprise party for her. Yet after a moment's consideration, she felt a stab of gratitude for that presumed omission. She really didn't feel like celebrating a day that would officially announce to the world that she was a middle-aged spinster.

The kettle started whistling. Maggie got up to fill her teapot and fetch a clean mug, then returned to the table and read her sister's letter while the tea steeped.

"Bad news and good news," the letter began. Maureen's two children had both been home from school for more than a week with sore throats, but her husband Benedict was having an article published in the next edition of "Church Quarterly."

Maggie smiled to herself as she tried to imagine the look on her brother-in-law's face when he'd received the news. No doubt, he had been equal parts chuffed and embarrassed by the honor.

Maggie put down the letter for a moment and sighed. Maureen seemed so happy. She had followed in their mother's footsteps and married a soft-spoken curate from a small Northern parish when she was in her early twenties, just as Mum had done all those years ago. Ben even looked a bit like their dad, and his preaching style was remarkably similar.

*Maureen didn't crave romance and adventure like I did,* Maggie thought. *She just wanted a simple life in a small town with a kind-hearted husband by her side.*

Maggie threw a cursory glance at the birthday party invitation sitting beside her teapot.

*I'm almost forty,* she reflected. *Romance and adventure have passed me by. And as for finding a husband, well—*

She brushed a lock of hair off her face, then picked her sister's letter back up and read the rest of her note. She turned the page and discovered her mother had scribbled a postscript on the back:

*Hello, love! I've been doing some spring cleaning and found a few treasures in my closet. Watch for a package coming your way! I'm sending you that old daguerreotype your dad used to keep on top of his desk in the rectory. I remember how you used to like it.*

Maggie closed her eyes and tried to recall the face of the woman in the sepia-tinged portrait. But all she could remember was a conversation she'd once had with her father about the photograph. He had caught Maggie staring at it and started teasing her, claiming she'd put on a costume and posed for the picture herself since the woman looked so much like her. Maggie had pretended to be offended, and claimed she looked nothing like the Victorian matron. Then her father had ruffled her hair and told her the woman in the photo was the wife of a curate who had served at the parish a hundred years ago. He'd found the daguerreotype in a box of old books, and offered to show Maggie the woman's headstone. But Maggie had demurred, insisting that she'd rather think of her "look-alike" as a guardian angel than as a corpse lying in a church cemetery.

*She couldn't have looked that much like me,* Maggie thought as she slipped Maureen's letter back in its envelope. *Otherwise, I'd remember her face better.*

She poured herself a cup of tea, then heard a knock on her front door. She walked down her hallway and flinched when recognized her visitor through the peephole. Standing on her doorstep was an impeccably dressed but obviously frazzled Philippa McCudden.

Philippa rushed inside the house as soon as Maggie opened the door. "I do so hope I'm not barging in," she began. "But I find myself in quite desperate straits. My ex is apparently taking a secret holiday that he failed to tell anyone about, and absolutely cannot be reached. I had to sack my regular babysitter last month, and haven't had the chance to interview any new applicants yet. And my mother insists she has plans for the weekend that she cannot reschedule, not even for the sake of her own grandchildren! So what am I to do? I need someone to watch Robbie and Clara. I know you're fond of them, Miss Grayson. And they do seem to behave well for you. So I was wondering—I was hoping—I really *hate* to say this, Miss Grayson, but if I have to *beg* you, I will. Could you *please* watch my children this weekend? I know it's very last-minute, but I figured you'd be free, and I'll pay you, of course, as I'm sure you could use the money.

Would it be okay if I dropped them off after school on Friday, say at about four o'clock?"

Maggie stared into Philippa's heavily-kohled eyes, struggling to remain composed as she tried to imagine what could have possibly prompted her to propose such an audacious request.

*I'm a college-educated music instructor!* she wanted to yell back. *Not a nanny-for-hire! And how dare you imply that I have no plans for the weekend? You know nothing about my personal life!*

Maggie narrowed her eyes and pursed her lips, hoping she could somehow magically project her thoughts at her rude visitor.

*Money? You think I could use some money? I could have used the money you were supposed to have paid me for last month's tuition! How are you planning to pay me for this weekend of babysitting? Will you post-date another check?*

She ran her fingers through her shoulder-length, mouse-brown hair, and drew in a deep breath to calm her nerves. "Mrs. McCudden, I'm not sure what to say," she began.

"They won't be any trouble," Philippa insisted, her voice beginning to crack. She lifted her right hand to smooth back a rogue strand of her perfectly highlighted, ash-blonde hair. The light from the overhead hall lamp bounced off the large diamond on her ring finger and sent a rainbow of sparkles cascading across the wall.

Maggie swallowed hard. She had long since noticed that Philippa, though divorced, continued to wear her impressive engagement ring, even though she had switched it to her right hand and discarded its matching wedding band.

*Why do I let that bother me?* Maggie asked herself, struggling to direct her anger at the more pressing matter at hand.

"They'll just read or watch telly," Philippa pleaded, breaking Maggie's reverie. "And they can play with that—" She took a deep breath and somehow found the grace to refrain from adding an adjective before finishing her thought,

"—cat of yours. Honestly, I promise they'll stay out of your way. I would *so* appreciate it."

Her voice rose in pitch as it grew increasingly frantic. "I realize I'm catching you by surprise, but I'm sure my ex would be so happy to know his children were in the capable hands of their piano teacher the weekend before their recital."

*Oh lord, help me!* Maggie thought. She clenched her hands into fists to force herself from lifting them to Philippa's throat. *You mentioned your ex-husband on purpose, didn't you? I don't need to project my thoughts at you, you horrid woman. You can read them already. And there's no way that I can say 'no' now, is there?*

"Mrs. McCudden, I—" Maggie mumbled sheepishly.

"Oh, do say yes! Please do!" Philippa implored her.

"I—" Maggie faltered. "I suppose I could probably watch them for the weekend."

"Oh, you are a saint!" Philippa squealed. "I *knew* you would do this for me!"

Maggie squared her shoulders and tried to appear stern. "Though I'm not quite sure where I'll put them up. I just have one bedroom. I use my other upstairs room for storage."

"I'll bring along their sleeping bags, and they can crash on your sitting room floor," Philippa replied with a relieved laugh. "They can pretend that they're camping. A little rustic living here and there can be fun for children, don't you think?"

Maggie bit her tongue to keep herself from hurling an insult. *Rustic living? How dare you!* she screamed in her head. "When will you be picking them up?" she asked instead.

"Oh, sometime Sunday. After-dinnerish," Philippa replied as she took a step back towards the front door. "I'll drop them off right after school on Friday. You'll be here then, won't you? Oh, and I'll bring along some dresses you might want to wear to the recital. You always seem to wear the same outfit every year! Honestly, Miss Grayson, your pupils' parents do notice these things! Now don't try to stop me. I was going through my closet just yesterday and found several frocks that I have no use for anymore. They're still practically new, mind you, but I needed to make room for this season's clothes. I'm sure they'll look just lovely on you. I'll bring the dresses along with the children on Friday."

Philippa opened the door, stepped outside, and called over her shoulder, "You are a godsend, Miss Grayson!"

Maggie waved clumsily as Philippa climbed into her BMW and drove off.

*Did that really happen?* she asked herself, her cheeks blushing in humiliation. *Am I such a doormat that I just allowed that woman to walk over me completely?*

Maggie looked down at the square of all-weather carpeting resting on top of her doorstep and noticed the indentations Philippa had left behind with her stiletto heels.

*Yes,* she admitted to herself with a sigh, *I am.*

She walked back to her kitchen and picked up her mug of tea. It had grown cold. She poured the contents down the sink, opened her refrigerator, and pulled out her bottle of wine.

# Chapter Seven

## The Night Visitor

Jim woke at dusk from a deep and dreamless sleep, feeling groggy, numb, and sick to his stomach. The room around him was bathed in shadows, with only a faint glimmer of sunlight shining in through the small window. For a brief, terrifying moment, he couldn't remember where he was. But then his eyes fell on the black silhouette of the camping lantern perched atop his nightstand.

*The bastard left that for me to keep the darkness at bay,* he recalled.

He switched on the lamp, then examined the food Nessie had left for him—a puffed rice-cake perched atop a brown, earthenware plate, a beige gloppy substance that looked like applesauce in a matching ceramic bowl, and a banana. He had no appetite, but the bland selection nevertheless left him feeling somehow disappointed. He rested his head back on his pillow and reminisced about the lovely meal he'd shared with his friend Eddie just the day before in southern Ohio. His eyelids started drooping, and he drifted back to sleep.

But this bout of slumber was neither deep nor restful. Strange dreams wove in and out of his head—some frightening, some bizarrely sexual. At times he sensed he was half-awake, yet he was unable to control his thoughts. Visions of a mysterious creature with yellow eyes kept flashing before him. He felt it lean over him and lick his face with a cold, wet tongue. He woke with a start, panting and wondering if he was experiencing a flashback to a decades-old acid trip. But then he felt his injured foot being sucked into a deep hole, and he slipped back into his nightmare.

He woke again in the dead of night. This time, he knew exactly where he was. His room was dark, except for the dim glow cast by the lantern into its immediate surroundings.

He sat up and took a small bite of the rice cake, but as soon as he started chewing, he gagged. He searched frantically for a drink, but the moment he thought of the word "water," he was overcome by a powerful urge to urinate. He found the bedpan Nessie had left for him and flicked off his covers. Then he reached into his pajama fly to ready himself, and, *ahhhh*—relief.

"Oh my God! You went pee!" a woman's voice exclaimed.

The hairs on Jim's neck stood up on end, and his breath caught in his throat. His heart started pounding a rapid tattoo in his chest. "Who's there?" he gasped.

The woman laughed. "Don't worry. It's just me," she replied in a deep, sexy whisper. "I promise I won't tell a living soul what I just saw you do."

Goosebumps prickled the entire surface of Jim's body. "Who are you?" he called into the darkness. "Where are you?"

"I'm right here, by the foot of your bed," she replied calmly.

Jim focused his gaze in the direction of the voice. He could just barely make out the shape of a woman in the shadows. He squinted and saw the dusky trace of her face, surrounded by what looked like a profusion of long, wavy hair. She seemed to be wearing a pale, loose dress.

"Who are you?" he repeated.

"It's me, Cathy," she answered, her husky whisper gaining volume.

Jim took a deep breath and made a concentrated effort to still his racing heart.

*Don't panic!* he urged himself. *At least I sort-of-kind-of know who this woman is.*

He opened his eyes wider to get a better look at his visitor. "Come closer," he said. "I can hardly see you."

"I'd rather stay where I am," she replied. "I can see you just fine from here."

Jim continued scrutinizing the shadowy form of his surprise guest. But then he remembered that he had just used the bedpan, and quickly pulled his covers back up.

The woman laughed again. "You needn't be so shy," she said dismissively. "Pissing is a perfectly natural function. It's a part of life."

"But I usually prefer some privacy when I piss," Jim stammered, his voice skipping over the hard 'p' sounds like a flat stone skimming the surface of a still lake.

"Ooh, you're English!" she exclaimed. She started mocking his British pronunciation—*"The gentleman prefers his 'prih-vacy'!"*—then giggled. "I hadn't noticed your accent before. I'll bet you can make any American girl fall in love with you just by saying something funny and British."

"Well, not quite," Jim assured her. He leaned back against his headboard, instinctively pulling away from her maddening presence, and tried to think of something to say that wouldn't sound funny or British.

"Just look at all the yummy food you have beside you!" she cooed, interrupting his train of thought. "You should eat some of it."

He turned his face towards the nightstand. "I'm not hungry," he replied.

"When was the last time you ate?"

He sighed. "I can't remember. I'm pretty sure it's been more than a day."

"Well, you should definitely eat then. Try the applesauce. It looks delish."

Jim sat up a little straighter so he could address his guest more confidently. "Would you like some?" he offered. "I'd be happy to share."

"Oh no," she demurred. "I can't eat things like that anymore."

Jim furrowed his brow. *She must have quite a delicate constitution if she can't even stomach this bland crap,* he thought. He considered asking Cathy if she had an ulcer, but thought better of it.

"Take a bite," she urged him. "Tell me how it tastes."

Unable to think of an appropriate reply, he decided to oblige her. He found a spoon on the plastic tray, dipped it into the earthenware bowl, and brought some applesauce to his mouth.

"How does it taste?" she asked eagerly.

He swallowed his mouthful of glob. "It tastes—like applesauce," he responded dryly.

"Oh, come on. You can do better than that," she insisted.

"Seriously, I can't," he replied. "It's really quite ordinary-tasting. There's not even any cinnamon in it."

"Oh God, I used to *love* cinnamon!" Cathy exclaimed. Her low, sexy voice rose in pitch as she grew increasingly loquacious. "I used to make these spiced potpourris to put in my dresser drawers. I'd boil up orange rinds with cinnamon sticks and nutmeg, and let them soak overnight. Then in the morning, I'd prick the orange skins with cloves and lay them out to dry in the sun. Then I'd tie them up in sacks of lace with pink ribbons, and they smelled just—"

She broke off midsentence. Her voice grew deep once more. "I was just about to say they smelled 'heavenly,' but that's stupid, isn't it? How would I know what Heaven smells like?"

"It's just an expression," Jim replied. A growing sense of irritation was rapidly replacing his initial fear of his guest. "I say things smell 'heavenly' all the time."

Cathy offered no response. A long moment of silence stretched out between them. Then she blurted out, "Well, are you going to eat that banana, or are you just going to taunt me?"

*What the hell is <u>wrong</u> with this bird?* Jim thought. He made a face at her and crossed his arms in front of his chest. "I don't much fancy bananas."

"You're no fun!" she scolded. She backed away from him and retreated into the darkness.

Her gown made a soft rustling noise as she moved, like wind whipping through a tree full of dead leaves.

*What the hell kind of fabric is her frock made from?* Jim asked himself. He tried to think of the politest way to ask Cathy about her dress—*and* about her appearance in the room. But then he remembered that he was the guest here and had no business asking her to justify her presence.

*And yet,* he reminded himself, *Nessie said Cathy didn't live here anymore—*

"So did you find someplace dry last night?" he finally asked. "That storm was pretty wicked."

"Oh, rain doesn't bother me," she said dismissively. "I hardly even notice it."

When she failed to elaborate, Jim went ahead and blurted out a ruder question. "Nessie told me you don't live here anymore. So why did you come back?"

"To see *you*, silly!" she answered with another sexy laugh. "You were in a real bad way last night. I thought you might need someone like me to show you how to get where you were going." Her voice grew serious once more. "But it seems like you're just going to stay here for a while instead."

Jim tried to puzzle out her response but quickly gave up. "Cliff won't let me leave," he explained.

"Yeah, I can't break away from him either. He's got one of those magnetic personalities."

"That's not exactly what I meant."

"Well, what *did* you mean?"

Jim sucked in a deep breath. *This woman makes no sense,* he thought irritably, *and yet she's asking me to explain myself?*

"So, you don't live here anymore?" he repeated, not sure what else to say.

"No, I don't," she agreed.

"So you're just here for a visit then?"

"I suppose you could say I like to come back every once in a while and haunt the place."

Jim rolled his eyes and decided to stop beating around the bush. *Nessie answered my questions,* he reminded himself. *Why can't she?*

"Where *do* you live these days?" he blurted out.

Cathy chuckled softly. "Where do I *live?*" she echoed. Then instead of answering his question, she asked, "What is *life*, anyway?"

Jim leaned forward a few inches and attempted to glare at the faint traces of his shadowy companion. "Is there a reason why you're standing at the foot of my bed, talking to me?" he asked in a confrontational tone. "I mean, wouldn't you rather be talking to someone you know?"

"You're easy to talk to," she answered. "And I like chatting with sick people. They're so—vulnerable."

"Is there anything I can *do* for you?" Jim continued, hoping he didn't sound too "funny and British," like John Cleese ranting in exasperation on an episode of *Fawlty Towers.*

"Yes," Cathy stated bluntly, her voice dropping to an even lower register. "I asked you to eat some food and describe it to me, but you won't."

"Why do you want me to do that?" he challenged.

"I like watching people eat. And drink. And breathe. And—go pee."

"Whatever for?" he asked. He realized as he spoke that she had come a little closer to him. His goosebumps inexplicably returned. "They're just basic human functions."

"No, they're not *human* functions," Cathy corrected him, assuming the tone of a stern schoolmistress. "They're activities that *all* living creatures do."

She came a little closer still, once again making a noise like a whispering wind. The air in the bedroom settled around her as she moved and wafted towards Jim like a chill breeze.

He wrapped his blankets around him for warmth. "Well, um, yes, I do know that," he stammered, feeling chastised. "I mean, I did study biology in secondary school."

"Oooh, there you go again. *Secondary* school instead of *high* school. How veddy, veddy British you are!" Cathy taunted him.

Jim focused a steely gaze at Cathy's shadowy form and cast aside all pretenses of politeness. "What are you anyway, some kind of voyeur?" he asked in an accusing tone. "You get your jollies out of sitting in the dark and watching people?"

"I thought voyeurs just liked to watch people have sex," she countered in a smug voice.

"Well, that's another one of those basic life functions, you know," he spat back. "Sex."

"Mmmm," she replied with a seductive laugh. "I wouldn't mind watching that either. But you seem to be here all by yourself."

Jim brought his hands to his face and rubbed his temples. "You're making me very uncomfortable," he admitted, his courage slipping away once more. "If you want to talk to me, I'd really appreciate it if you would come closer so I could see your face."

"Excuse *me*, Mister-English-person-lying-in-my-favorite-bed!" she spat back at him. "If *that's* how you're going to be, then I'll just leave."

Jim stared at the foot of his bed. He saw a glimmer of Cathy's shadow as she started moving towards the bedroom door. Then he suddenly remembered what Cliff had whispered in his ear before he fell asleep.

"Wait!" he called out. "Cathy! Stop! Cliff wanted me to ask you—"

"Cliff?" she exclaimed. She was at Jim's side in an instant.

In the soft glow of the lantern light, Jim could finally make out the shape of Cathy's loose-fitting dress, but her long locks of pale blonde hair still shielded most of her face.

"What did Cliff want to ask me?" she said breathlessly.

"He wondered if you had a message for him," Jim replied.

Cathy withdrew from the circle of lamplight. Masked in darkness once more, she fell silent for several seconds while she considered her response. Then she started to laugh.

"Tell him to give you some better-tasting food," she said at length. "Succulent strawberries dripping with juice. Hot and spicy kebabs, slathered in curry sauce. A tender, boiled lobster tail dipped in drawn butter that just melts in your mouth. I want to watch you eat them. No. I want to watch you *savor* them."

Jim scowled at her. "I can't tell him that!" he scoffed. "He'll think I'm mad! He'll say I just made that up because I wanted some better-tasting food for myself!"

"Maybe you're right," she agreed with a soft moan of disappointment.

She fell silent again for such a long moment that she almost seemed to disappear into the darkness. The room grew so quiet that Jim could hear his heart beating. But then he heard the sound of her skirts rustling once more. Cathy leaned over his bed and whispered, "Tell him I'm getting tired of waiting for him."

Jim felt an icy chill pass through him as Cathy's hair brushed against his chest. He shivered and instinctively closed his eyes. Then he opened them rapidly, hoping to catch a better glimpse of his mysterious visitor's face.

She was gone.

# Chapter Eight

## A Wake-Up Call

An irritating sensation jolted Jim out of his slumber, as if someone were tickling him. He opened his eyes to the morning light and saw Cliff crouching at the base of his bed, examining his foot.

Jim clenched his hands into fists, preparing himself for a fresh wave of pain as Cliff poked at his wound. But neither Cliff's ministrations nor his injured foot caused him any real discomfort. The strange, tea-induced fug that had enveloped him the day before had lifted, and his fever seemed to have broken as well. He breathed a deep sigh of relief and wallowed in the exquisite joy of feeling like himself again.

He turned his head to the side and started examining his bedroom. He noticed for the first time that the walls were painted a soft shade of turquoise. Morning sunlight was streaming in through the window, lending the room an almost cheerful glow. Dust motes darted haphazardly in the rays of light like a dance troupe of drunken fairies.

He threw a quick, nervous glance at Cliff, then turned his head again and continued his survey of the room. A white crown molding encircled the top of the walls. Dark green curtains hung from a thin metal rod over the window. A framed picture of a black and white King Charles Spaniel hung on the opposite wall. It looked like it had been painted by a child. Beneath the painting stood an antique dresser with shiny brass knobs. It reminded Jim of an old chest of drawers he'd seen in his grandparents' house in Manchester.

Then he focused his gaze on the sturdy-looking captain's chair positioned beside the bed. A sapphire-colored cushion rested on top of its broad seat. It was tied with thin ribbons to the wooden spokes that ran along the chair's back.

*This room looks so ordinary,* he marveled. *It could be a bedroom in any old house. So why did it seem so creepy yesterday?*

He leaned back against his pillow and licked the surface of his front teeth. A thin layer of slime clung to his incisors.

*Christ, what I wouldn't give for a toothbrush,* he thought ruefully. Then he lifted his head to look back at Cliff again and mumbled, "Good morning."

"Mornin'," Cliff replied without raising his eyes. He finished rubbing ointment into Jim's cut, then started wrapping a fresh set of bandages around Jim's foot. When he was done, he walked to the side of the bed, sat down in the chair, and inspected the tray on the nightstand. "Didn't eat much, did ya?"

Jim propped himself into a more-or-less seated position and leaned his back against the headboard. "It was kind of bland," he apologized.

"Complain, complain," Cliff scolded him. "It's nourishment. This ain't no fancy Bed and Breakfast, you know."

"I know," Jim sighed. "And I am grateful to you for your help." He attempted to meet his host's eye, but Cliff was still staring at the barely touched food. "How does my foot look?"

Cliff turned his face back towards Jim. "It's healing. I want you to rest completely for one more day, but maybe tomorrow you can try using some crutches. Did you use the bedpan?"

"Yes," Jim answered, cringing in embarrassment.

"I'll take that then," Cliff said. He reached across the mattress and grabbed the pan.

Jim watched Cliff sniff the urine as he walked out of the room, but tried not to pass judgment on him. Pee-sniffing was probably just another procedure homeopathic doctors used to assess their patients, he guessed, like taking a temperature or feeling a pulse. The toilet flushed with a loud whoosh.

Cliff returned to Jim's side and held out the empty pan. Jim grabbed it and tucked it under his covers. Cliff curled his lips into a rude smile and sat back down in the chair.

"So how'd ya sleep?" he asked nonchalantly.

Jim shrugged. "Quite deeply at first. But then I had some very strange dreams."

"Not surprised," Cliff replied. He started picking absentmindedly at a hangnail while he added in a disinterested tone, "You smoked some pretty powerful shit last night. That blend I gave you often has that side-effect."

Jim cleared his throat in an attempt to redirect Cliff's attention. "Was it a hallucinogen?"

"Not precisely," Cliff answered. He crossed his arms in front of his burly chest, then furrowed his brow and stared directly at Jim. "Did Cathy stop by?"

Jim sucked in a deep breath and inched away from his host. "Yes," he replied after a few moments of awkward silence.

A strange expression washed over Cliff's face. Jim couldn't make out if he looked happy or sad, relieved or nervous.

Cliff closed his eyes and sank back in the chair. "What did she say?" he whispered.

"Lots of things," Jim answered. He tried to recall the details of their peculiar conversation. "She said—" Jim hesitated, then started to chuckle at his memories.

Cliff's cheeks reddened. "What did she *say?*" he blustered, his voice growing angrier.

Jim threw a loopy grin at Cliff. "She kind of rambled, you know? She said she couldn't eat much these days. She said the rain didn't bother her. She asked me if I knew what life was all about. She made fun of my English accent. She talked about making potpourris out of orange peels. And about breathing. And pissing."

Cliff twisted his mouth into a snarl and grabbed the handles of the chair, as if he were about to stand up. "Quite the conversationalist, isn't she?" he noted in a sarcastic tone. He turned his face to the window for a long moment, then added in a quiet voice, without looking at Jim, "Did you remember to ask her if she had any message for me?"

"Yes, I did," Jim replied.

"And?" Cliff shouted, his voice sounding both anxious and angry. He turned his face back towards Jim. The veins in his neck were pulsing visibly, and his cheeks were flushed red.

"She said—" Jim began. He considered relaying Cathy's entire message, but decided not to mention the part about bringing better food. "She said she's getting tired of waiting for you."

Cliff scowled at Jim, then stood up from his chair. "I'll send Nessie over with some breakfast for you," he announced without looking back at his guest. He stormed out of the room and slammed the front door of the cottage with such force that it shook the walls of the house.

\* \* \*

Nessie stepped into Jim's bedroom, carrying a new tray of food and a fresh pot of tea. She rested everything on top of his nightstand and offered him a kind smile. "It's still a little bland, but Cliff thinks you should be able to handle this."

Jim sat up straight against his headboard and eyed the buttered toast, fruit slices and scrambled eggs greedily. But then his eyes fell upon the teapot. He cast a nervous look at Nessie. "Is that the same kind I had yesterday?"

"Don't think so," she replied. "Why don't you try a little and tell me how it tastes?" She poured some tea into the same chipped smiley-face mug Jim had used the day before and handed it to him.

He took a quick sip, then smiled in relief. "Mmm," he mumbled. "Tastes like cherries with honey. I like it."

"Good," she said. "Sounds like the kind he usually gives me when I need a little pick-me-up."

Jim put down his mug and reached for the fork. He swallowed a bite of eggs and broke into a wider grin. "These are really good. Tastes like you put some salt on them."

"Well, it's not Morton's," Nessie countered. She sat down in the chair by Jim's side and crossed her arms over her large bosom. "Cliff keeps a collection of salts from all over the world to use in his potions. I think he sprinkled something from the Dead Sea on your food 'fore I brung it to you."

"I'll take it," Jim laughed. "It tastes pretty good!"

"Good," she replied, smiling broadly. Her gold-capped tooth sparkled in the late morning sunlight that flooded the room. "I sure am glad to hear you say that. Maybe when you're feelin' a bit better, I'll cook you up one of my om'lets. Folks say they're pretty fine."

"I'll look forward to that," Jim said. He picked up a triangle of toast and examined its shiny surface. "Is this butter or margarine?"

"Butter," Nessie replied. "But I think it's made from goat's milk. Or maybe sheep's milk. It's nothin' you'd find in the dairy section at Kroger's anyways. Cliff goes shoppin' a coupla' times a month at this health food store in Cleveland and buys all sorts of weird shit. I don't usually touch any of it myself."

"Well, it's not bad," Jim said, swallowing a mouthful of toast. "I suppose if you're hungry enough, anything will taste good."

"When was the last time you ate a proper meal?"

"I can't even remember," Jim answered, tucking greedily into his breakfast.

Nessie nodded. "Well, you sure look like you're feelin' better."

"I am," he agreed. "Cliff told me I shouldn't attempt to walk yet. But honestly, I don't think I could if I tried. My foot feels like a dead weight attached to the end of my leg."

"At least you're not in pain anymore," Nessie replied. She grabbed the chair's armrests to support herself as she stood up. "I'll be back in two shakes to pick up your dishes."

"No, please don't go!" Jim cried. He flushed in embarrassment at his emotional response, then offered Nessie a weak smile. "I'd appreciate some company, if you don't mind. It's rather lonely in here."

Nessie chuckled and settled back in her chair. "Oh, I s'pose I could sit for a spell if you'd like."

Jim brought another forkful of eggs to his mouth, then covered the lower half of his face with his free hand while he chewed. "Tell me more about Cliff," he mumbled. "You were talking about him yesterday, but then he interrupted us."

"I remember. But I forgot where I left off."

"He had just finished high school and left home."

"Oh, that's right. He took off. And didn't tell no one where he was goin'," she began. She shook her head at the memory and made a tut-tutting sound. "Cathy was beside herself, as you can prob'ly imagine. Oh, the tears! That girl was damn near hysterical. But then again, she always seemed like she was on the verge of a nervous breakdown, if you ask me. Lots of bats flyin' loose in her belfry."

Nessie stopped speaking abruptly and cast a nervous look at Jim. "Don't tell Cliff I said that. He don't like hearin' no one speak poorly of her."

"I won't," Jim promised, though he couldn't help but curl his lips into a conspiratorial smile. He had formed a similar opinion of Cathy last night.

"Well, Cathy moped around for a while, like the whole world was gonna end," Nessie continued. "But then Joe Lyndon came a callin' and asked her to go to some fancy-pants restaurant overlookin' Lake Erie, and she brightened up real quick. Started goin' out with him pretty steady after that. Least while she was at home, that is. She went away to college that fall, and somehow I don't think she spent too many Saturday nights sittin' alone in her dorm waitin' for the phone to ring. But if she had a boyfriend at school, she never mentioned him to me."

Nessie watched Jim take a bite of fruit, then reminded him to drink his tea.

"I will, don't worry," Jim said. He brought the mug to his lips and made a rolling gesture with his free hand to urge her to continue talking.

She smiled at him. "So now, Joe Lyndon, he kept on buyin' Cathy presents and takin' her to nice places, so she kept on goin' out with him and enjoyin' the free ride. But she never really cared for him, not like she did for Cliff. She'd still take those long walks whenever she was home from school. And most evenin's she wound up here at the Grange. I'd come home from workin' all day at the Heights, and find her sittin' here with Daddy, smokin' a fat one and listenin' to records."

Nessie rolled her eyes. "That girl sure liked her pot. No doubt about that. Though Daddy tol' me later all she ever wanted t' talk about was Cliff, and whether he'd heard from him.

"But, anyways, time went by. Cathy must a' got tired of waitin' for Cliff, cuz she went ahead and married that Joe Lyndon. Had a big, fancy weddin' with a big ol' dress. And the Lyndons went all hog wild with the reception, throwin' a party fit for a queen. Joe took Cathy on a Pacific cruise for their honeymoon. Lord help me, I don't know where his family got the money for that. Prob'ly took out a second mortgage. That's my guess."

She shook her head disapprovingly and refilled Jim's mug. "Then Cathy and Joe got back from their trip, and the bloom sure fell off that rose pretty quick. I never saw any pair of newlyweds look so damn miserable in all my days. But Joe's folks went on pretendin' everything was all right. They took Cathy to church with 'em every Sunday and showed her off to all their friends, like she was some prize heifer they'd won at the State Fair.

"And then, wouldn't you know, guess who came back to Ohio? Why, the devil hisself, my Daddy liked to say! And Cliff had pockets full of cash now. He started spendin' it everywhere, just to show off how rich he was. Soon as he came home, he and Cathy picked right back up where they'd left off as if nothin' had happened since. The two of them started shackin' up here at Daddy's place. I think Cliff figured she'd run away with him. But then she found out she was carryin' Joe's baby, so she decided to stay married after all.

"And that's when things got real ugly," Nessie added with a frown. "Cliff and Cathy got into another one of their knock-down, drag-out fights, and he stormed off and started datin' Joe's sister Beth 'fore Cathy even had a chance to say sorry. Swept Beth off her feet, he did, and eloped with her to Las Vegas. Mr. and Mrs. Lyndon were beside themselves, as you might imagine, though they weren't near as mad as Cathy was."

Nessie rolled her eyes. "I s'pose Cliff was just tryin' to show Cathy he could play games as well as she could. They had a few more fights, but then they made up and started hatchin' plans to run away together as soon as Cathy's baby was born. Beth found out and ran off to Florida so she could cry all over one of her rich ol' aunties' shoulders. Good riddance to her, was all I could say. Never did like that girl. Cliff divorced her 'bout as fast as he'd married her. He even tried to get their marriage annulled. But then it turned out Beth was pregnant too. She had her baby down in Orlando, an' never came back to Ohio again, 'cept for her parents' funeral. But I'm gettin' ahead of myself."

Nessie fell quiet for a moment, then clasped her hands together as if in prayer and started speaking in a sadder voice. "Well, now, as you can guess, all this stress wasn't good for a pregnant girl like Cathy," she said, looking into her lap and refusing to meet Jim's eyes. "She started havin' problems. Went into early labor. Then she had some kind of complications after the baby was born. Her daughter Katie— she was smaller'n a sack of sugar. Not even five pounds, she was. But she was strong for a preemie and turned out okay. But Cathy, well—"

Nessie's voice dropped off. Jim chewed quietly on his last bites of fruit and waited for her to continue. But when she said nothing else for several seconds, he prompted her.

"What happened to Cathy?" he asked as he set his fork back on the plastic tray.

Nessie stood up from her chair and started stacking Jim's dirty dishes. "She died. Allergic reaction to penicillin. She's buried out by that Episcopalian church the Lyndons used to go to."

# Chapter Nine

## A Voice in the Hallway

Maggie opened the door to her closet under the stairs, put away her Hoover, and gave her living room one last look. Then she lowered her head in embarrassment and laughed out loud at her own fastidiousness.

*Why am I worrying about presenting my best self to Clara and Robbie McCudden?* she chided herself. *They're just children, and they've been to my house countless times before. I don't need to make a good impression on them.*

They were good kids, Maggie reminded herself as she tried to shake off her nerves. At least they were always polite at their lessons and recitals. But she'd never seen them outside of her capacity as their piano teacher. She hoped she wouldn't have to discipline them when they were here this weekend. She wouldn't know how to face their parents afterwards.

She stepped into her kitchen and re-checked her refrigerator. Milk, cheese, apples—yes, everything she'd bought at the grocer's that morning was still there. She started closing the door, then spotted her bottle of Zinfandel.

*I'll just have a tiny sip,* she decided impulsively. *Just a little something to make me less nervous when Philippa arrives.*

She grabbed the bottle and poured an inch of wine into a small tumbler. She gulped it down quickly and rinsed the glass out in the sink to hide the evidence.

Then she returned to her hallway and gave herself a quick once-over in the mirror that hung beside her closet. She tucked a loose strand of hair behind her ear, then opened the closet back up and grabbed a duster to give herself something to do while she waited for the McCuddens to arrive.

"It is foolish to wish for beauty," said a voice from the top shelf.

Maggie jumped and reached for her heart. Then she closed her eyes and drew in a deep breath.

"Who's there?" she whispered nervously.

"You know who's here," the voice answered.

"Come out then," Maggie replied, struggling to remain calm. "You know I don't like how you talk to me without showing your face. It makes me very uncomfortable, having a conversation with a disembodied voice. I've told you that several times already."

"And you know I can't present myself to you," the voice retorted. "I've told you that several times too."

"Agnes," Maggie sighed, flexing her hands back and forth into fists and trying to make her heart stop racing, "this really isn't a good time for you to visit me."

"Why not?" Agnes replied. "You seemed lonely. I couldn't help but notice you were drinking by yourself again."

"I'm not lonely," Maggie insisted, her voice brittle with indignation. "As a matter of fact, I'm expecting company just now, so I'd very much appreciate it if you would just go away and leave me alone."

"Is it a gentleman caller?" Agnes asked in a teasing voice.

Maggie crossed her arms in front of her chest. "No," she stated emphatically.

"Well, I thought it might be," Agnes huffed. "Why else would you be checking your appearance in the mirror? Though you really shouldn't waste your time worrying about such trifles. I still recall how my father would chide me whenever he caught me glancing at a looking glass. *'It is foolish to wish for beauty, Agnes,'* he would say. *'Sensible people never either desire it for themselves or care about it in others. If the mind be but well cultivated, and the heart well disposed, no one ever cares for the exterior'.*"

"That's very nice, Agnes," Maggie replied irritably. "My dad used to tell me the same sort of thing."

"Well, it just goes to show you then, doesn't it?" Agnes said. "Good advice never grows old."

Maggie tapped her foot against the floor in vexation. "Agnes, I need you to go away this weekend. Or at least be quiet. I've got enough on my mind without dealing with you."

"Oh, stop being so ungracious," Agnes chided her. "Honestly, Margaret, you are one of the most self-centered people I have ever met. It's no wonder you're still a spinster. You need to work on becoming more friendly and welcoming."

Maggie rolled her eyes and leaned back against the wall. "Well, let's be honest here, Agnes, you haven't exactly *met* me. You just lurk in the hidden corners of my house and pop out as the mood strikes you. And you're not exactly friendly and welcoming with *me*. You've never even shown me your face."

"I will someday," Agnes promised. "But not yet. I don't think you're ready to handle me in the flesh quite yet."

"So, you'll just taunt me until then?" Maggie challenged.

"Now, now," Agnes said condescendingly. "I prefer to think of myself as your conscience, here to advise you in times of trouble."

"I am perfectly capable of making my own decisions," Maggie protested.

"No, you're not," Agnes countered. "If you were, you wouldn't have agreed to let that horrible woman drop her children off at your house."

Maggie puffed out her chest in defiance. "I like the McCudden children," she insisted. "And I'm sure we will have a lovely weekend together."

"You have no experience taking care of children."

Maggie's pulse began to race. "That's not true! I worked as a nanny when I was young!"

"I don't believe you. You're not made of strong enough stuff."

"How dare you say that?" Maggie shouted into the closet. "You know nothing about me!"

"I know you sometimes sneak sips of wine when you think no one is looking," Agnes countered. "But that's beside the point. Tell me about your experiences as a governess."

Maggie squared her shoulders and stared defiantly at her switched-off vacuum cleaner. "When I was eighteen, my dad arranged for me to live with some friends of his while I was earning my degree in music. I watched their two children whenever I wasn't in class. Or studying. Or practicing piano. Or busy in some other way."

"And how old were they?" Agnes asked impatiently.

"Three and one, when I started college," Maggie answered. "Six and four when I graduated."

"And how much were you paid?"

"Nothing!" Maggie boasted, her voice rising in triumph.

"Don't lie to me," Agnes admonished her. "I can always tell when you're lying."

Maggie slumped back against the wall and started twiddling the feather duster in her hands. "Well," she admitted sheepishly, "I received free room and board in exchange for helping out the family. And I got to practice my songs on their baby grand piano."

"Oh, please," Agnes laughed. "You call that a job? You watched two adorable children a few hours a week in exchange for a free bed and meals *and* access to an expensive pianoforte. I could have minded those babes in my sleep! Now, if you would like to learn a thing or two about the rigors of caring for children, let's discuss *my* first governess position—"

Maggie cut her off. "Actually, Agnes, I really don't want to learn a thing or two about—"

Agnes ignored her. "Now, at first glance, the Bloomfields of Wellwood Hall appeared to be a most respectable family. But as soon as I arrived at their home, I discovered they were the most ungracious of employers. Mr. and Mrs. Bloomfield expected me to mind all four of their children by myself, but offered me no support in my efforts to discipline them. Now, little Harriet wasn't too spoilt yet when I arrived, but her sister Fanny did nothing but whine, and Mary Ann instigated fights whenever she could. But none of the girls held a candle to Tom, the young heir to the estate. He modeled his behavior off the worst of the adults he had met, and was well on his way down the path to perdition by his seventh birthday. I still shudder when I recall the way he would steal baby robins from their nests and torture them—"

Maggie closed her eyes and took another deep breath. "Alright, Agnes, you win," she conceded. "My first babysitting job had nothing on yours."

"He'd twist their wings until they broke—"

"Yes, Agnes, I'm sure it was awful."

"And then pop them on the heads with rocks—"

"I see, Agnes. I see."

"Of course, the proper way to kill a bird is to wring its neck," Agnes went on. "Everyone knows that. But with a nestling so small, there isn't much of a neck to wring."

"No, I don't suppose there would be," Maggie agreed, gritting her teeth. "Though I take it your time with the Bloomfields did eventually come to an end, since you claimed it was only your first position."

"*Nine months* I watched those beastly children!" Agnes crowed. "And after that, the parents had the gall to sack me!"

Maggie bit back a smile. "Well, I'm sure it was all for the best," she said reassuringly. "I gather you weren't very happy there."

"Yes, but I had to bring in an income!" Agnes cried. "My family depended upon me!"

A knock on the front door interrupted their conversation. Maggie's face flushed with relief. "I have to go now, Agnes," she told the closet. "My guests are here. Now please stay out of our way this weekend."

"Oh, you're no better than Mrs. Bloomfield!" Agnes cried. "So high and mighty you are, thinking you're better than everyone else! Here I am, offering you some much needed advice on child-rearing, and you just—"

Maggie tossed her duster in the direction of the voice and slammed the closet door shut, then ran to her front door to greet her guests.

"Welcome!" she exclaimed with a nervous smile.

Clara and Robbie stepped into her hallway, carrying rolled-up sleeping bags in their arms and large rucksacks on their backs. Philippa followed at their heels, holding aloft three stylishly cut black dresses, dangling from wire hangers.

"You'll have to transfer these to proper wooden hangers," Philippa announced as she breezed into the living room. "Or better yet, padded satin hangers. I would have brought you some, but I didn't have any to spare. I'm sure you'll look quite smashing in any of these frocks. Why, the parents at the recital will hardly recognize the new you!"

Maggie took the dresses from Philippa with a polite, if not entirely sincere, word of thanks.

"Oh, it's nothing," Philippa insisted as she gently stroked the gowns one last time. "I do hate parting with my treasures, but I'm glad to know I'm sending them to a good home."

Maggie thanked her again and started draping the dresses over a chair so she could greet the children. Philippa cut her off.

"Oh no, Miss Grayson! Hang them up in your closet straight away! They're haute couture! I don't want that cat of yours to get near them!"

Maggie cast an exasperated look at Robbie and Clara and asked them to wait with their mother in the living room while she put away the clothes. For a brief moment, she considered hanging the dresses in the hall closet to save time, but immediately thought better of it.

She rushed up the stairs, threw the gowns on top of her bed, then hurried back to her living room so she could ask Philippa for a set of emergency phone numbers. But when she returned to the ground floor, she found Robbie and Clara standing alone, with only the cat for company. The BMW parked in front of the house made a loud whirling noise as Philippa started its engine.

Maggie sighed and tucked another stray lock of hair behind her ear. *We're off to a great start now, aren't we?* she thought ruefully. She turned towards the children.

"Why don't you two leave your bags where they are and go to the kitchen?" she suggested with a forced smile. "I'll make you an after-school snack. Or an early dinner if you'd prefer."

She watched Robbie and Clara tromp out of the room, then turned her gaze towards Percy. He leapt onto the window seat and started licking his front paws. Then he lifted his head as Philippa's car drove off, opened his mouth widely as if to yawn, and hissed.

\* \* \*

Robbie finished his last bite of macaroni and licked the cheese sauce off his spoon. "That was good, Miss Grayson. You're a much better cook than my mum."

Maggie smiled in secret triumph as she collected the children's plates and stacked them in her sink. "Does your mother like to cook?"

"She only cooks when we're between maids," Clara replied. "Which has been an awful lot lately. Mum says she's having a hard time finding good help."

Maggie plucked a tin of store-bought biscuits off her kitchen counter and brought it to the table. "Well, I don't usually prepare big meals for myself, but I like to cook when I have company. Maybe tomorrow we can make something together. What are you hungry for?"

Robbie threw a nervous look at his sister, then turned back towards Maggie, his eyes wide with fear. "You want us to cook for you?"

"No, no!" Maggie laughed as she sat back down. "I just thought we could do something together in the kitchen if you'd like. I don't know, maybe make a lasagna or bake a cake. I used to like to help my mother cook when I was your age."

Clara and Robbie squirmed uncomfortably in their chairs and looked down at the tabletop. They grabbed cookies from the tin and ate them in silence.

Maggie cleared her throat to redirect the conversation. "But first things first. What would you like to do this evening? Should we watch a movie or play a board game?"

Clara exchanged another anxious glance with her brother, then shrugged. "You don't have to play any games with us, Miss Grayson. Mum told us not to bother you while we're here. She made us promise to stay out of trouble."

Maggie smiled at the children indulgently. "I'm quite certain that neither of you will be getting into any trouble. You've always been two of my best students."

Robbie looked up at her and frowned. "We're not as good as David or Kim," he replied. "You always let them play last at the recitals."

"You'll play as well as they do when you're older," Maggie assured him. "Who knows? Maybe by the time you're their age, you'll be even better."

"Maybe Robbie will be," Clara countered. "But I won't still be taking lessons when I'm eighteen. Dad won't be able to make me anymore."

Maggie selected a ginger biscuit from the tin and smiled at Clara. "You never know. You might change your mind as you improve." She brought the cookie to her mouth and took a bite.

"How old were you when you stopped taking lessons, Miss Grayson?" Robbie asked as he reached for a second biscuit.

Maggie covered her mouth and finished chewing quickly so she could respond. "I was twenty-one."

"And how old are you now, Miss Grayson?" Robbie added.

Clara elbowed him. "Don't be rude!" she whispered. "Mum says you're never supposed to ask women over a certain age how old they are."

"How will I know if they're over a certain age if I don't know how old they are?" he whispered back.

Maggie stood up from the table and tried to hide her smile. "Why don't you two look through my videotapes while I tidy up? You can watch anything you like. And if you don't see a movie you're interested in, we can drive to Blockbuster and rent something."

The children jumped out of their chairs and ran to the next room. Maggie grabbed the biscuit tin and cautiously approached her pantry, projecting her thoughts into the dark recesses of the cupboard.

*Please don't speak to me, Agnes!* she begged the mysterious voice that had taunted her earlier. *Not while I have guests!*

She opened her pantry door and was met with a blissful silence. She sighed in relief, placed the tin on a middle shelf, and gently closed the door. Then she rinsed off the dishes and joined the children in front of the television set. She noticed they had pulled out her copy of *The Black Stallion* but had not yet inserted it in the VCR.

Clara offered her a polite smile. "We were waiting for you, Miss Grayson, since you said you wanted to watch the film with us."

"And since we couldn't figure out how to work your machine," Robbie added. "It's kind of old."

Maggie chuckled. She slipped the tape in to play and sat down to watch the film with her young guests. A few minutes into the movie, she cast a quick glance over her shoulder and projected her thoughts at the hall closet:

*I won't be needing any of your assistance with childcare this weekend, Agnes, so please don't bother me. If any problems arise, I'll just follow my sister's advice: 'When all else fails, feed them!'*

# Chapter Ten

## A Romantic Interlude

Jim spent the afternoon alone in his bedroom, fretting over Nessie's revelation and feeling increasingly like a sick terrier trapped in a cage with exotic zoo animals. Nessie's story made no sense to him. Cathy couldn't be dead. He had seen her with his own eyes.

Or at least he *thought* he had seen her. But when he tried to remember what she looked like, he could only envision a mostly formless shape standing in the shadows at the foot of his bed. Throughout their long talk, she had remained determinedly out of the lantern's reach. Even when she approached his side and whispered in his ear, her face had been obscured by her long curtain of hair.

But he had heard her. And he had spoken to her. He'd had a lengthy conversation with her, for Christ's sake!—even if it had been disjointed and rambling.

And he had felt her when she reached through the window that first night. She had grabbed his wrist and refused to let him go.

*There's no such thing as ghosts,* he reminded himself, over and over, as the long, lonely morning stretched into a longer and lonelier afternoon.

Nessie dropped by a few hours after her first visit to bring him a sandwich and a fresh pot of tea. He considered broaching the topic of Cathy's visit with her, but she had seemed terribly distracted. She'd told him Cliff needed her help in the greenhouse, then she'd left his side in such a hurry that she'd almost spilled the contents of his bedpan when she carried it out of the room.

*She's not the one I need to talk to,* he realized as he listened to her leave the cottage. *Cliff is the only one who can answer my questions.*

Jim thought about the cigarette Cliff had made him smoke the night before. God only knew what was in it. Jim had taken his share of drugs back in the Sixties and Seventies when he was living the pop star life. But he had never experienced a hallucination that was even remotely like his bizarre encounter with Cathy.

*It's no wonder that bastard brags about having dedicated customers all over the world,* Jim decided with a fresh wave of indignation. *He rolls the freakiest joints on the planet!*

Jim re-examined his bedroom as he ate his lunch. It seemed far more sinister than it had in the early morning light. The inside edges of the forest green curtains had been bleached by the sun to a paler, almost putrid, shade of green that reminded him of mold. One of the dresser drawers was missing a handle; a dark grey screw protruded menacingly from the hole where the brass knob should have been attached. The picture over the dresser no longer appeared innocently childish. The poorly painted, long-haired puppy looked deranged, like a creepy doll in a horror film. Even the strings that attached the cushion to the captain's chair seemed ominous. One pair was tied in a simple bow, but the other two ribbons were looped over each other in a strange pattern of knots that looked almost like a noose.

He swallowed his last bite of sandwich, then felt unaccountably thirsty. With considerable reluctance, he poured himself a mug of tea and took a small sip. It tasted different from the other two blends he'd been given. He took a larger sip and immediately started feeling tired. Before he had even finished his mug, he was drifting into another restless sleep.

He woke to the sound of a man's deep voice.

"Don't mind me," Cliff called up from the foot of the bed. "Just checking on your foot, then I'll be off. I brought you dinner. Eat it."

Jim tried to argue with him, but his throat felt too dry to speak. Cliff approached Jim's side when he was done applying a new set of bandages and switched on the camping lantern. He leaned over Jim and repeated, "Eat your dinner. And drink your goddamned tea." Then he left.

Jim propped himself up against his headboard with considerable difficulty and examined the meal Cliff had left for him—a bowl of soup, another rice cake, and a salad of strange-looking leaves and pointy-capped mushrooms that set off warning bells in his head. He considered leaving the entire dinner untouched, but his parched throat got the better of him.

He brought a spoonful of soup to his lips. It was weirdly delicious. He tasted hints of asparagus, onions and rosemary. He picked up the bowl and inspected its contents carefully. He couldn't see any diced vegetables or minced leaves—just a viscous blend of broth and cream. Despite his nagging reservations about consuming any more substances of unknown origin, he gave in to his hunger and finished the soup.

Then he glanced at the teapot, and before he even realized he was moving his hands, he poured himself a cup of tea.

*Damn, that bastard must have put some sort of mind-controlling agent in my soup,* he decided as he brought the chipped blue mug to his lips. *He's hypnotized me!*

Jim dozed off again after finishing the dregs of his tea, and this time he slept soundly. But in the dead of night, he woke once more with an urgent need to relieve himself. He pulled off his blanket and wished with all his strength that no hidden voice would congratulate him on successfully urinating. A welcome silence followed his last splash of pee in the bedpan. He smiled in relief, then pulled his covers back up and closed his eyes.

"Hey, English guy! You're still here!"

*Fuck!* he cursed in his head. He looked down at the foot of the bed and recognized Cathy's shadowy shape. His pulse began to race, and shivers started running up his spine.

"Go away!" he commanded her. "Don't come near me!"

"Well, that sure is a different greeting from the one you gave me last night," she rebuked him. "Yesterday, you couldn't stop asking me to come closer."

"Th-that was before I knew," Jim stammered, folding himself into the back corner of his bed.

"Before you knew what?" she asked in a mocking voice.

Jim started panting. "You know what I know."

"Ooh! We're playing riddles now, are we? Let's see, what do I think you think that I know?" she teased.

"You're dead!" he shouted.

"That would have been my second guess," Cathy replied with a raspy laugh. "I was going to suggest you found out I was Cliff's lover and decided it would be rude to ask your host's old lady to come closer to your bed."

Jim focused his gaze on the shadowy figure by his feet. "You're not Cliff's lover," he protested. "You're dead."

"What makes you so sure those two states are mutually exclusive?"

Jim shivered again and turned his face to the wall. "You're not making any sense," he whispered.

Cathy laughed and approached his side. Jim squeezed his eyes shut.

*This is just a dream!* he assured himself. *I'll wish her away. When I open my eyes, she'll be gone!*

He counted to ten silently, then turned his face and opened his eyes. Cathy was resting languidly on the chair by his side, staring at him with glowing yellow eyes. She smiled and tucked a strand of hair behind her ear.

*Goddamn her!* he cursed in his head. *Why won't she leave me alone?* He closed his eyes once more but sensed her presence leaning over him.

"Look at me," she whispered seductively. "I know you want to see me."

As the words slipped through her lips, Jim was overcome by a powerful desire to gaze up at her. He opened his eyes, then couldn't stop staring.

Cathy was exquisite. More beautiful than any woman he had ever seen in a film or cosmetics ad. But she looked nothing like the primped and polished pop stars and actresses he usually ran into at awards shows and benefit concerts. She was more like a hippie fashion model from the early Seventies. She had large, wide-set eyes, defiantly unplucked brows, and a straight nose with just a hint of a bump at the end. Her lips looked soft and full.

But she was as pale as—*Christ!* Jim thought. *So this is where the expression comes from!*—she was as pale as a ghost. Her skin, her lips, her hair, her fingers, her brows—her whole person—radiated a soft, off-white glow. And her eyes were otherworldly. The lantern was shining on her face, yet her eyes did not so much reflect the light as they seemed to cast a soft yellow incandescence of their own.

She wasn't translucent—Jim couldn't see through her. And yet she seemed to occupy no real space. Her form cast no shadow. She leaned forward and pushed her hand against the edge of the mattress, but she left no indentation on the surface.

"So, tell me, Englishman-lying-in-my-favorite-bed," she purred. "Have you ever had sex with a ghost?"

"No," he gasped, drawing in a sharp breath. He pulled his covers more tightly around him.

She drew nearer to him. "Oh, what a prig you are. Honestly. What are you so afraid of? It's not like you have to worry about getting me pregnant."

"Don't touch me," Jim begged. He started to sweat. "Please don't touch me."

"Why not?" she laughed. "Don't you think I'm pretty?"

Jim sucked in another deep breath and struggled to force his eyes shut. "The last time you touched me, it felt like a dagger of ice tore through my hand," he whispered.

Cathy flopped back onto the chair. "That's not very nice," she pouted. "I can't help the way I affect people. That's just the way I am."

Jim sighed in relief as she increased the distance between them. He watched her carefully. She was staring at the teapot.

"What did Cliff give you to drink tonight?" she asked.

"I haven't the faintest idea," he replied. His pulse started to slowly slacken. "He never tells me," he confessed in a resigned voice.

"Yesterday he gave you something to smoke, right?" she asked, focusing her gaze back at him. When Jim nodded, she smiled. "I could tell. It opened your mind. Made you more responsive."

Jim eyed her warily, his nerves still taut. But his curiosity started to push aside his fear.

*I spoke to her yesterday and came to no harm,* he reminded himself. *Why should tonight be any different?*

"What do you mean?" he asked hesitantly. "If I hadn't smoked that joint, would I not have been able to see you?"

"Oh, I'm not sure," she said. "You were already pretty receptive. You heard me at the window the night before and tried to speak to me. Most people can't make out my words when I talk. All they hear is a soft moan. Did you drop a lot of acid back in the Sixties?"

Jim squared his shoulders. "A little," he admitted.

"Well, that might explain it. LSD never entirely leaves your system, you know."

"Actually, I've heard that's a myth," he replied, eager to discuss the topic he had been pondering earlier that day. He tried to follow her line of reasoning. "So what are you suggesting then? Are you a drug-induced hallucination, or am I just having a flashback?"

"No, silly boy!" she laughed, flashing her golden eyes at him. "I'm quite real. As real as you are, only different. It's just that most people haven't learned how to open their minds to other types of reality like you have. They can't see me, so they don't believe I'm real. But *you*—you *know* that there's more to life than meets the eye. You went tripping when you were young and saw some really funky shit. And those visions you witnessed went through you—like water through wine—and they altered your ability to perceive. You can—"

She fell silent for a long moment, then smiled approvingly at him. "You know how to relax, turn off your mind, and float downstream."

Jim smiled back at her in spite of his reservations as she paraphrased the Beatles lyric. "You know what it's like to be dead," he replied.

"I know what it's like to be sad!" she countered, gazing at him mournfully.

Jim's smile slipped away. "You didn't get that lyric quite right either," he pointed out.

Cathy frowned. "What are you talking about?"

"You're quoting John Lennon, right? *Tomorrow Never Knows* and *She Said, She Said?*"

"I was quoting Timothy Leary's translation of the *Tibetan Book of the Dead*," she protested.

"Oh, right," Jim mumbled. "I think Lennon was referencing that in his songs too." He stared at Cathy for a long moment and tried to make sense of her inexplicable presence. "Can anybody else see you?" he asked at length. "Besides me and Cliff?"

"Of course!" she boasted, but then her brash attitude started to fade, and she sank back against the chair. "Well, Joe could. Sort of. But only at the very end. Sometimes I'd stop by to check in on him and the baby."

She turned away from Jim's penetrating stare and added in a defensive voice, "Not that I really cared about them, of course, but well, I mean—a lot of mothers gaze at their children while they're sleeping. It's a perfectly normal thing to do."

"Yes," Jim agreed. He sat up a little straighter against his headboard and offered Cathy a sympathetic smile. "I used to step into my kids' bedrooms at night when they were little to admire them too. They looked like such angels when they were babies."

"Yeah," she whispered, her voice soft and ruffled, like a breeze blowing through a field of tall grass. She sat up straighter, and her body seemed to take on a bit more substance.

"Katie's really pretty," she continued. "But Joe—I mean. God! It was so depressing watching him fall apart as the years went by. I could hardly bear it. So I usually stayed away from him. And even when I did stop by, he didn't recognize me. At least not at first. But towards the end, when he was really sick—sometimes his mind would kind of float in-and-out of the here-and-now, and he could *almost* see me."

Jim nodded. "So you talked to him then, like you're talking to me now?"

"Not exactly," she replied, her voice growing less wistful and more sultry. "But I visited him. I eased his pain, if you catch my drift. I took him out of his misery and helped him travel to a happier place. What can I say? He died with a smile on his face."

Jim stared at her in bewilderment. *She can't mean what I think she's suggesting*, he told himself. He pushed the disturbing thought aside and decided to throw caution to the wind and take Cathy to task.

"So why are you here, in this room, beside me? Is it just that you want company, and I can see you better than other people can?"

"Well, it *is* always nice to visit a person I can talk to," she agreed.

Jim pressed on. "Doesn't Cliff talk to you?"

Cathy turned her face and stared into the Coleman lantern. "He used to. Though mostly he just wanted to have sex. You know how it is. Men. Always thinking with their dicks."

"That's not possible," Jim scoffed.

"Yes it is! Here, let me show you," she offered, making a motion to get out of her chair. "Cliff and I figured out how to do it using blankets as protection against the cold."

"You're talking nonsense," Jim insisted, but he pulled his covers more tightly around himself nevertheless.

"No, I'm not. Really, it's fun!" Cathy assured him. "C'mon. Be brave."

Before Jim knew what was happening, Cathy had climbed on top of the bed and straddled him. She looked down on him and smiled.

"Maybe you should close your eyes," she suggested. "Pretend I'm the girl of your dreams, coming to you in a dream. In a very, very beautiful wet dream."

"Really, Cathy, I'm not so sure about this—" Jim protested.

"Don't be afraid," she urged him. "Embrace the unknown. You'll enjoy it, I promise. No coward's soul is yours!"

Jim sensed her form somehow pushing against him. The covers still separated them, and he couldn't exactly feel her weight pressing down on his body. Yet he was acutely aware of her presence. Intimately aware.

His heart started racing and his breathing became rapid. The sheets and blankets seemed to be acting as a sort of protective shield between them. *Just like she said they would,* he admitted to himself. And now, instead of making him feel cold, she was making him feel warm. Very warm. Almost hot.

"Cathy…" he moaned softly as he sensed her weightless presence rubbing against his crotch.

Soon he was no longer aware of the blankets separating them. She seemed to be touching him directly.

*How can this be possible?* he marveled with his last, fleeting grasps of rational thought. *She's right on top of me, but she doesn't feel like a ghost. She feels like a woman. This is crazy!*

"Cathy!" he cried out. A wave of excitement started building inside of him, filling him up. It rose from his crotch to his torso, then spread to his limbs, then flowed back again to his center. It gained strength and rose—slowly at first, then more rapidly as Cathy pressed herself against him with increasing urgency. The wave crested. He came into the sheet with a spasm of release. His entire body shook in an enormous, mind-blowing orgasm, and he cried out with joy.

Cathy slipped off the bed and returned to the chair. She gave Jim a few moments to compose himself, then leaned forward and whispered in his ear, "So tell me, English boy, how did that feel? Was it good for you?"

Jim rolled his face over the pillow and stared directly into Cathy's glowing eyes. "I, I—oh, Christ, Cathy—" he murmured in a hollow, almost broken voice. "Why did you do that?"

"I had my reasons," she whispered back.

Jim closed his eyes and tried to make sense out of what had just happened.

*That was not real,* he assured himself. *That did not just happen to me. There's no way in Heaven or Earth that this could have taken place. There's no way in Hell either.*

He opened his eyes once more to look at Cathy. She was gone.

# Chapter Eleven

## Bedside Manners

Jim woke with an ache. A dull pain throbbed in his right foot. He felt someone's hand roughly massaging his wound, and had to swallow hard to keep himself from crying out. He opened his eyes wider and was momentarily blinded by the intense morning light shining in through the window. He squinted and saw Cliff standing at the foot of his bed.

Cliff started singing the chorus to *The Witchdoctor* while he worked.

Jim summoned his courage and addressed him. "You have a gift for instilling confidence in your patients," he noted sarcastically.

Cliff looked up and grinned. "Yeah, I've gotten a lot of compliments on my bedside manner," he replied. Then he looked back down at Jim's foot and started rubbing his ankle.

"Oowww!" Jim cried.

"That hurts, huh? Which hurts more—if I do this? Or this?" Cliff asked, prodding two spots on Jim's heel.

Jim sucked in a deep breath and answered through clenched teeth, "The first."

"Thought so," Cliff said. He rested Jim's foot back on the mattress and walked over to his side. "It's a little inflamed. I'll brew you up some tea that should fight that.

And I'll put in a little something to help with the pain too. I don't think I made it strong enough last night."

"It was strong enough last night," Jim grumbled, turning his face to the wall.

Cliff sat down in the chair beside the bed. "So how'd you sleep?" he asked coolly.

"About as well as the night before," Jim answered, still not looking at Cliff.

"Any more nighttime visitors?" Cliff continued.

Jim slowly lifted himself into a sitting position, wincing as he moved his right leg, then turned his face towards Cliff and scowled. "What kind of drugs are you giving me?"

"I asked you a question first," Cliff answered.

"I don't want to take any more hallucinogens," Jim stated emphatically.

"I'm not giving you any hallucinogens," Cliff replied.

"Like hell you aren't!" Jim shouted.

Cliff fell silent for a few moments, then leaned back in the chair and rested his hands on the curved armrests. "So, did she say anything?"

Jim remained silent while he held Cliff's gaze, then looked down at his blanket and let loose a snort of bitter laughter. "Actually, she didn't seem in the mood to talk." He looked back at Cliff and winced.

Cliff's cheeks were flushed crimson with anger. His eyes brimmed over with hate.

"You bastard," Cliff hissed. "I should have thrown you out of my house the moment I found you."

"Throw me out then," Jim replied, his voice growing stronger. "I've told you all along I don't want to be here. Call me a cab. Shit, drop me off by the side of the Interstate, and I'll hitch a ride with a stranger. Just get me the hell out of here!"

Cliff continued to glower at Jim, his eyes boring into him like a sharp drill, and said nothing. The air between the two men grew so tense that Jim could almost sense an electrical charge as he drew in his breath.

After the silence had dragged past a minute, Cliff finally lowered his gaze. He kneaded the chair's armrests with such force that Jim feared the wood might split.

"Tell me everything Cathy said," Cliff demanded.

"I already told you," Jim replied, struggling to keep his voice steady. "She didn't feel like talking."

"How many blankets were between you?" Cliff asked, raising his eyes to meet Jim's.

"What the fuck does that matter?" Jim spat back at him.

"I wouldn't have asked you if it didn't matter, you brainless bastard!" Cliff shouted. "The number of goddamned blankets between you when you're fucking her matters!" The veins in his neck bulged and pulsed, and spit flew from his mouth as he spoke.

Jim cowered into his pillow and stared at his hands. They were shaking. He fell silent for a long moment while he struggled to regain his composure.

"Listen," he finally managed to squeak out in a marginally steady voice, "I don't know what the hell happened last night. I don't understand a fucking thing that has happened to me ever since I arrived here. I just want to leave. *Please*, will you let me *leave?*"

He looked back at Cliff.

Cliff's face remained contorted in rage. "You had no business touching her!"

"I didn't want to touch her!" Jim shouted back. "I was afraid she might hurt me again, like she did the last time! But I couldn't make her stop!"

Cliff lowered his head and covered his face with his hands. Then, visibly struggling to control his anger, he looked back at Jim and asked in a disturbingly calm voice, "When she touches you, does it hurt like ice, or like fire?"

Jim met Cliff's eyes and held his gaze, then leaned back against his headboard and sighed in frustration. "Like ice," he whispered in a hoarse voice. "Like sub-zero, mind-numbing, freezing-the-breath-out-of-my-lungs ice. But then—last night—" His voice trailed off.

"Last night was like fire," Cliff surmised.

Jim nodded and looked back at his hands. "Kind of like fire. Warm anyway."

"You had all these layers between you?" Cliff asked, grabbing the blankets in his fist and counting them.

"Yeah," Jim mumbled.

Cliff stood up from his chair and lowered his head once more. "Well, good then. It could have been a lot worse."

Jim furrowed his brow. "What the hell is that supposed to mean?"

Cliff walked to the foot of the bed and grabbed Jim's right ankle. A searing pain passed through Jim's body, but he bit back a cry and tried not to show Cliff how much agony he had just caused.

"Your foot is inflamed this morning," Cliff stated perfunctorily. "The first night, when Cathy touched you, she froze you up. Good thing she did too. Cold is good for an injury like yours. Heat's bad."

"I don't understand you," Jim said, clenching his teeth.

Cliff rested Jim's foot back on the mattress and returned to the chair. "Let's just say for the sake of argument that I had brought you to a hospital emergency room the night you got hurt," he began, his voice dripping with scorn. "What would your precious doctors have told you to do with that bad foot of yours? I'll tell you what they would have said. *'Put some ice on it.'* Now, the night you got hurt, you didn't have an ice pack. But you had Cathy. And she's better than ten ice packs. Better'n thirty."

He pulled the chair closer to the bed and locked eyes with Jim. "Now tell me, my little injured friend, what happens if you leave a wound exposed to heat? No. Don't reply. I'll answer for you. It festers."

Cliff leaned back in his chair and sneered at Jim. "If a hunter shoots an animal and can't eat the meat right away, he puts the carcass in his freezer to preserve it. If he leaves the carcass on his kitchen counter, it'll go bad."

Jim sneered back at Cliff. "I'm not a carcass."

"You would have been if your foot had gone untreated," Cliff replied.

Another heavy silence fell between the two men. Unable to think of an intelligent response to Cliff's last statement, Jim started to ask, "Is Cathy a——?" But he couldn't bring himself to finish his question.

"She's not a carcass either!" Cliff bellowed.

Jim flushed red and shouted, "I wasn't going to ask that!" Then he drew in a deep breath and let his voice drop to a whisper. "I was going to ask if she were a ghost."

"You know goddamned well she's a ghost," Cliff replied matter-of-factly. "Why would you even bother to ask me that?"

"Because I needed to hear you say that she is," Jim confessed, lowering his head and not daring to meet Cliff's eyes. "So I could know I'm not going mad. Because I don't believe in ghosts."

Cliff chuckled briefly, then broke into a full-throated, nasty laugh. "Well, I think it's about time you started to believe," he replied at length. "Cathy's a ghost. You've seen her. You've spoken with her. You've fucked her. And you're no madder than I am."

Jim sat up straighter in his bed and focused a steely gaze at his companion. "You're giving me drugs. Some weird kind of hallucinogenic, mind-blowing, reality-altering drugs."

Cliff arched his left eyebrow and smiled menacingly at Jim. "I'm giving you *tea*," he countered.

"And psychedelic soup that you mixed up in a blender, so you could mask its ingredients," Jim retorted. "You put fucking *mushrooms* in my salad last night! And some strange kind of leaves I've never seen before. God only knows what you meant for me to eat!"

Cliff threw a cursory glance at the wilted, untouched salad on Jim's tray, then leaned back in his chair. "I offered you Speckled Troutback. It's a gourmet lettuce. I grow it especially for a Five-Star restaurant in Cleveland that serves a particularly discriminating clientele. I've heard it's a nice place, though I've never been there myself. My girlfriend prefers to stay at home most nights."

Jim's growing frustration finally got the better of him. "Your girlfriend?" he taunted, his voice edged with sarcasm. "I heard she married some guy named Joe!"

Cliff leapt out of his chair and smacked Jim hard across the face. "Don't you *ever* say that name again in my presence!" he shouted. He let his fist linger over Jim's head for several seconds, threatening him like a boxer taunting his downed opponent during a long count. Then he stormed out of the room and slammed the cottage's front door with an ear-splitting bang.

# Chapter Twelve

## The Cat

Maggie peeked into her living room on Saturday morning and found Robbie sitting in her most comfortable chair, reading a comic book by the dim light of a small lamp. Clara was still fast asleep on the couch, with Percy curled up at her feet. Maggie whispered to Robbie to join her for breakfast. He jumped out of the chair and followed her into the kitchen.

Percy leapt off the couch and sauntered after the boy. When he reached the kitchen doorway, he rubbed his body against the frame a few times. Then he started walking back and forth between the kitchen and living room.

Maggie kept one eye on the cat while she placed a carton of milk, a box of cereal, and a bowl and spoon in front of Robbie. "Can't decide which child you want to pester, can you?" she teased her pet.

Robbie opened the box of cornflakes and filled his bowl. "Percy's all better now, isn't he?" he asked as he reached for the milk. "It's been a few months already, I think."

Maggie nodded and put a kettle on to boil. "He's fine," she replied. "Though he continues to make a nuisance of himself whenever the opportunity presents itself."

Robbie brought a spoonful of cornflakes to his mouth and chewed as he spoke. "Good thing Dad found him that day."

Maggie nodded once more, fighting back the urge to correct Robbie's table manners.

*It's not my place,* she reminded herself as she pulled a china mug and second bowl from her cupboard. Then she sat down at the table, poured herself a serving of cereal, and started eating while she reminisced about the day her former idol had rescued her runaway cat...

*Jim had looked so worried that afternoon when she'd told him Percy had escaped. He'd promised to walk around the neighborhood and search for Percy while she gave his children their lessons. And she had been so grateful for his offer that she hadn't acted flustered in his presence for once, or even asked him why he was dropping the children off instead of Philippa.*

*He'd returned an hour later and told her he'd heard a cat meowing on a rooftop a few blocks away, then led her and the children on a walk to the house in question. It had all seemed like a scene from a movie, she recalled as she pictured the small parade in her head.*

*When they reached the house, Robbie climbed a nearby tree and spotted Percy hiding behind a chimney. Then Jim knocked on the homeowner's door, borrowed a ladder, and climbed onto the roof. He returned to Maggie's side a few minutes later, clutching Percy to his chest. His face and hands were covered in scratches, and a small trickle of blood was running down his neck. He'd pointed out Percy's injured back leg as he handed over the cat, and urged Maggie to get her pet to a veterinarian's office straight away.*

*Maggie had begged Jim to step inside when they got back to her home, so he could wash his wounds and cover his cuts with plasters. But he had demurred, insisting the cat needed medical attention more urgently than he did. And so she had stood on her front doorstep, clutching Percy to her heart while she watched Jim drive off with his children, and wondering how Philippa ever could have let such a prince slip away...*

The kettle started whistling, jolting Maggie out of her reverie. She walked to the stove and poured some boiling water into her cup, then turned to face Robbie. "I trust your father's scratches are all healed now as well?" she asked with an anxious smile.

"Mm-hmm," Robbie mumbled as he finished his bowl of cereal. "I don't think he minded much. He likes cats."

Maggie rested the kettle on a back burner, then opened her pantry to fetch a tin of tea.

"Did I ever tell you about the time my Edward rescued Mrs. Nancy Brown's cat?" a woman's voice whispered from behind the oatmeal.

Maggie blanched. She threw a quick look over her shoulder at Robbie. He was pouring himself another serving of cornflakes and appeared oblivious to the voice.

Maggie cautiously reached her hand into the pantry.

"The gamekeeper had caught it poaching and was just about to—" the voice continued.

Maggie grabbed her tea and slammed the pantry door shut with a loud bang.

Robbie looked up at her with a shocked expression. "Miss Grayson? Are you okay?"

Maggie turned to face him. Her cheeks were flushed, and she was breathing rapidly. "Oh yes," she replied, tucking a small lock of hair behind her ear with her shaking fingers. "I'm just a little sleepy still. I need my morning cuppa to get me started for the day."

Clara stepped into the kitchen, yawning and stretching. As Maggie and Robbie turned to face her, Percy jumped onto the table and started lapping milk from Robbie's cereal bowl.

"Bad kitty!" Maggie exclaimed. She ran to the table, grabbed Percy, and dropped him unceremoniously on the floor. He dashed out of the room in a blur of grey and white fur.

"Do you have any other kind of cereal, Miss Grayson?" Clara asked as she took a seat at the table. "I don't much fancy cornflakes."

Maggie considered offering to make oatmeal, but immediately thought better of it.

*I have enough on my hands, managing Percy,* she thought. *I do not need to hear about Agnes' naughty cat too.*

She drew in a deep breath and turned towards Clara. "There's some bread and marmalade in the refrigerator," she said. "You could make yourself some toast if you'd prefer."

"Cool," said Clara. She stood up from the table and approached the refrigerator. "Percy slept with me last night," she added as she fetched the bread, butter and jam. "He's such a sweet boy. I wish Mum would let us get a cat someday. She says she's allergic, but I think she just doesn't like animals."

"But *you* like cats," Robbie said, offering Maggie a lopsided grin that looked remarkably like his father's smile.

"Well, obviously." Maggie laughed back.

Robbie nodded and brought another spoonful of cereal to his mouth. "Just like Dad," he mumbled as he chewed. "You two sure have a lot in common."

# Chapter Thirteen

## The Weary Blues

Nessie cast an anxious glance at the red mark on Jim's face when she stopped by the cottage with a late breakfast, but didn't linger by his side. She left a fresh tray of food on his nightstand and emptied his bedpan, then made to leave.

"Cliff'll be by later to look at your foot again," she promised as she walked to the bedroom door. "He tol' me to tell you to drink every last drop of tea in that pot."

She reached for the doorknob, then turned around and faced Jim once more. "I'll try an' sneak back here in a bit and bring you an ice pack for your cheek. Don' want you gettin' a shiner, now, do we?" She offered him a weak smile, then left the bedroom.

Jim's heart sank as he watched her leave. A fresh wave of loneliness and self-pity engulfed him. Then his foot started throbbing afresh, reminding him that his stinging jaw was the least of his problems. He turned his face to the tray on his nightstand and surveyed Nessie's offerings. Unbuttered toast, a boiled egg, a banana. More bland food.

*Fuck it all!* he cursed in his head. *I'm getting out of this goddamned prison if I have to crawl to the bloody motorway on my knees!*

He threw back his covers and swung his feet off the bed. But as soon as he placed his weight on his bad foot, he collapsed on the floor in pain. It took him all his strength to climb back on the mattress and slip beneath the blankets once more.

He wept for a few minutes, then looked back at his breakfast. He swallowed a few bites of toast and egg, and grudgingly filled his mug with tea. When he finished drinking his first cup, he poured himself a second and sipped at it slowly until sleep overtook him.

When he awoke, his room was dark, save for a flickering glow at the foot of his bed. His cheek felt damp. He rolled his head over the pillow and noticed a cloth ice pack at his side. He reached for it. It was warm to the touch and leaking onto his mattress.

*God bless Nessie,* he thought with a flush of gratitude. *She must have brought this to me hours ago.*

Then he lifted his head slowly and stared at the foot of his bed. Cliff was wrapping his foot in a new bandage. His callused fingers felt rough to the touch, but he seemed to be working with some small degree of gentleness.

Not wanting to speak to his tormentor, Jim lowered his head back to the pillow and pretended he was still asleep. But when Cliff finished his work, he walked over to Jim's side, rested the camping lantern on the nightstand, and sat down in the captain's chair.

"I brought you dinner," he said. "Eat something."

Jim opened his eyes slowly and met Cliff's gaze. He summoned his courage and spoke in the calmest voice that he could muster. "I don't want to eat any more of your food."

"I'm not poisoning you," Cliff replied. "Here, watch. I'll prove it." He plucked an uneaten sandwich off Jim's plate and took a large bite.

"I'm not hungry," Jim protested.

"You have to eat," Cliff insisted. "If you want to leave here, you've got to get your strength back first. Cathy drained a lot out of you last night."

"I don't understand."

"Eat while I explain," Cliff said, handing Jim the sandwich.

Jim sighed in defeat, then maneuvered himself into a more-or-less seated position and tore a crust off his bread.

Cliff waited until Jim put the food into his mouth before he resumed speaking.

"I want you to try to remember what your parents told you about sex when they first described it to you," he began. "Or what your teacher said. Or your big brother, or whoever the hell it was that first described sex to you."

Jim stared at him blankly and chewed on his bread crust.

"What did they tell you?" Cliff barked.

"They said, *Don't do it!*" Jim answered bluntly.

Cliff rolled his eyes and snorted, then looked back at Jim with a more serious expression. "I meant, what did they say that sex was all about? Why did you even want to know about sex in the first place?"

Jim thought for a long moment, but couldn't recall the first time he'd discussed sex with his father. But he did remember describing the sex act to his son. He hadn't shared any details with Robbie about how much fun it was or given him any pointers on technique. He had simply told his boy, *'That's how babies are made.'*

"I think maybe I asked my dad how my Auntie Miriam got pregnant with my cousin, and he explained it to me," Jim answered at length.

"Right," Cliff replied with a sigh of obvious relief. "Exactly. Sex makes babies. And even if a sexual coupling doesn't result in a pregnancy, it's still a life-affirming act. When a man and a woman have sex, they have the potential to create a new human life. It's an almost god-like power."

"It's not god-like," Jim countered. "It's just a natural act. Animals do it too." He took another bite of his sandwich and started chewing.

"But animals don't have souls," Cliff said. "Or at least they don't have the same kind of soul that humans have. We are created in the image of God and have dominion over the planet. And when we have sex, we have the potential to bring another soul into this world."

Jim swallowed his bite of food and considered Cliff's words.

"I always thought the man and the woman just did the physical part," he replied. "I mean, they contribute their sperm and egg and DNA or whatever, and the woman carries the fetus until it's ready to be born. But God puts the soul into the baby."

Cliff looked away from Jim and stared at his hands. "Well, maybe you're right. I don't know how or when God intervenes and gives the child a soul. Or why he even bothers to do it, for that matter. But I do know—"

His voice trailed off, and he fell silent.

Jim took another bite of his sandwich and chewed on a thick slice of ham while he waited for his exasperating host to continue.

Cliff took a deep breath and looked back at Jim. "Shit, man, you realize, don't you, that you're talking to a person who has spent more than twenty years communing with a ghost? I've learned a thing or two over the past couple of decades about how the soul and body are intertwined. They are *not* two separate entities. They're mixed up. It's hard to explain."

Cliff fell silent again, then reached over the bed and pinched Jim's arm.

"Ow!" Jim cried. "Why the hell did you do that?"

"What did I do?" Cliff asked calmly.

"You pinched me!" Jim exclaimed. "You deliberately hurt me! Just like this morning, when you punched me!"

"Right," Cliff replied. He leaned back in his chair and grinned. "That's what I hoped you would say. I didn't just 'pinch your arm' or 'punch your face.' I hurt *you*. You *are* your arm. You *are* your face. The part of your conscious mind that feels pain and is self-aware is *not* separate from your body. The soul and the body are intertwined."

Jim tried to follow Cliff's reasoning but noticed a flaw. "I'm alive," he said. "Of course my soul and body are somehow combined. But Cathy is dead. Her soul was supposed to go to Heaven, or—" He abruptly decided not to finish his sentence.

Cliff cocked his left eyebrow. "Or Hell, I believe you were going to say?" he surmised.

Jim fell back against his pillow and nodded.

Cliff looked down at the floor and cracked his knuckles. "Well, maybe so," he agreed. "But she didn't, did she? So, where does that leave us?"

Jim sighed in discouragement. "I have no bloody idea."

"Neither do I," Cliff confessed. He stood up, walked to the window, rested his hands against the sill, and stared into the darkness for several minutes.

Jim watched him in silence, but then his stomach growled loudly. He sat up straighter against his headboard and finished his meal.

When Cliff returned to Jim's side, he threw a glance at the empty earthenware plate and smiled. "It's good, isn't it? You're hungry, so you ate some food. And now you feel better. You're alive."

Jim eyed Cliff warily. "Cathy said something like that the first night she talked to me."

Cliff's nostrils flared. "What did she say?"

"I don't remember exactly," Jim admitted. He inched away from Cliff once more without even realizing he was moving. "Cathy said she wanted to—she wanted to watch me eat. And then she wanted me to describe how the food tasted."

Cliff nodded. "She's hungry, but she can't eat. She's thirsty, but she can't drink."

Jim met Cliff's steady gaze and sighed. "That really sucks."

Cliff laughed sardonically and sat back down in the chair. "I can see why you had your bandmate Eddie Rochester write the lyrics to your melodies. You don't exactly have a gift for words now, do you?"

"Well, all right then," Jim blustered, his irritation at Cliff rising afresh. "Cathy's situation is most *unfortunate*. She must find her lot quite *tiresome*."

"Wearisome," Cliff countered. "She's got the weary blues. She can't be satisfied."

Jim closed his eyes and called to mind his last visit with Cathy. He suppressed a shudder. "She can satisfy one of her desires, though, can't she?" he pointed out. "She can have—"

"She can have sex?" Cliff interrupted, scowling at his guest. "Yeah. She can. Sort of, anyway. But it's not quite the same experience as when two living, breathing people have sex."

"But it's still—life-affirming?" Jim suggested, remembering Cliff's previous words.

"One might say that," Cliff agreed. He looked down at the floor and steepled his fingertips in front of him. "I'm sure she would agree, at least. It makes *her* feel more alive."

Jim thought for a long moment, then furrowed his brow. "She draws life from it," he surmised.

Cliff looked back up at Jim and bore his eyes into him. "She draws *my* life from it," he stated succinctly. "And last night, she drew *yours*."

A sudden wave of coldness enveloped Jim. The air in his lungs stung, as if it had frozen mid-breath. "Christ," he whispered, his voice shaking. "I want to leave this place *now*!"

Cliff offered no reply. He simply closed his eyes and appeared lost in thought. But after a long moment of silence, he reached into his shirt pocket and pulled out a small parcel tied with string. He loosened the knot to open the brown paper wrapping, then handed Jim a small, black, gnarled piece of wood. "Chew this," he directed him.

Jim eyed the object suspiciously. "Why?"

"It will help you sleep tonight."

"I don't want to sleep," Jim protested. "I want to leave! Didn't you hear me earlier?"

"You're not well enough to leave," Cliff replied matter-of-factly. "Didn't you hear *me* earlier? Now chew this root."

Jim scowled at Cliff. "I don't want to."

"Do you want to see Cathy again tonight?" Cliff challenged.

"No!" Jim shouted.

"Then chew this root," Cliff repeated. "It will knock you out completely. If she comes into the room, you won't even notice her. You'll sleep like a rock."

Jim reluctantly put the root in his mouth and started to chew. It tasted bitter. He started gagging on his saliva.

"Keep chewing," Cliff commanded him. He offered Jim the napkin from the dinner tray to wipe the drool from his chin, then bore his eyes into Jim's face and watched him chew.

After several long and painful seconds had passed, he stood up from the chair and started walking to the door.

"You'll sleep like a rock," Cliff repeated as Jim started nodding off. "Or a man that's dead."

# Chapter Fourteen

## Evening Plans

Jim woke with a thundering headache. He rolled his head across his pillow, noticed it was damp with drool, and examined the wet spot. His spit was tinged brown by the piece of wood Cliff had made him chew. A brief wave of disgust coursed through him, but it vanished as soon as he turned his head toward the window. The sun was shining through the glass.

*I slept through the night!* he realized with an almost palpable sense of relief. *Cathy didn't come and see me!*

His good spirits lingered while he waited for Nessie to stop by with his breakfast. Of all his new companions, she was by far his favorite, and he wanted to continue their long-winded conversation. But Nessie appeared preoccupied when she visited him, and left as soon as she dropped off his meal and dumped his bedpan.

He nibbled at his food slowly, disappointed to have been left alone once more. Sipping his tea, he wondered what kind of mood Cliff would be in when he stopped by later to inspect his bandages. Jim wiggled his toes and realized with a begrudging sense of gratitude that his foot didn't hurt as much as it had the day before.

*Maybe Nessie was right when she said Cliff was a good man,* he considered. *He might not be a proper doctor, and Lord knows he's got one hell of a temper, but he certainly knows a thing or two about treating injuries.*

Jim eyed Cliff warily when he stopped by later that morning to examine his foot. But like Nessie, Cliff also had little to say. He knelt quietly by the foot of the bed, removed Jim's bandages, inspected the wound, and applied a new set of dressings. Then he stood up to leave.

Jim sat up as straight as he could and called out to him. "Talk to me! I hate lying here all by myself. I feel like I'm going crazy!"

Cliff threw him a look of disdain. "A sensible man ought to find sufficient company in himself," he snarled.

Jim ignored his remark and volleyed back a flurry of questions. "How much longer are you going to keep me here? Is my foot getting any better? Will I be able to walk again soon?"

Cliff rolled his eyes. "Your foot's much better today than it was yesterday," he answered impatiently. "I'll ask Nessie to look for her dad's crutches so we can get you back on your feet. But it'll be a while before you can drive your Jaguar again. Your foot's not strong enough yet."

"Where is my car, anyway?" Jim asked. "My suitcase is in the boot. If you could just bring me my—"

"Harry's still fixing it," Cliff interrupted. "It's a brand new car, and the Hanes Manual hasn't come out yet for the 1995 models, so he's working off last year's specs. But don't you worry. He'll get it working for you. He loves dinking with cars."

"Harry is—" Jim began, trying to remember the names Nessie had mentioned a few days earlier. "He's Ernie's son, right? That would make him your nephew?"

"Yeah, that's right," Cliff answered gruffly. "But he hasn't lived with his father for years now. I raised him myself."

"So he's like your son, then?"

"No, he's nothing like my son. He's worth ten of my son."

"Does your boy live here too? I mean the child you had with Beth? Nessie told me you were a father."

"Nope. Lyn's not here anymore."

"He's with his mother?"

"You could say that."

Cliff took another step towards the door, then turned and glowered at Jim. "Any more Shaw family gossip you want to discuss? Or would you rather I bring you my mother's Bible so you can read all about who begat whom while you're lying there, drooling brown spit on my sheets and pillowcases?"

"No," Jim answered, struggling to sound even-tempered. "I was just curious—I mean, if someone is working on my car—well, it's not even my Jaguar. It's a hire car. And I don't want to be held responsible if this boy starts playing with the engine and does something wrong."

"Harry won't do anything wrong!" Cliff bellowed. "I told you, he knows cars. And he's good with his hands. He can repair any broken thing that you give him. He has a gift."

"Right," Jim said with a shrug. "Sorry. I didn't mean to insult him."

"He's kind of sensitive," Cliff continued, his tone softening. "Can't blame him either. Kids used to tease him at school and say he was dumb. Stupid kids who weren't half as bright as he is. Harry's brilliant. Smarter than the entire faculty at that goddamned school his father sent him to. But he's dyslexic, so the damn-fool teachers didn't know what to do with him."

"But you did?" Jim asked, cocking his eyebrow.

"I did my best," Cliff sighed.

Speaking about his nephew seemed to knock the anger right out of Cliff, and his voice grew almost kind. "Didn't see much point in forcing him to read things he wasn't interested in. Wouldn't do anyone any good—just cause a lot of frustration. So I taught him to read with books he was curious about. He's been reading car manuals since he was eight years old."

Cliff took another step towards the bedroom door and rested his hand on the knob. "So don't you worry about your Jaguar," he added. "It's in good hands. Just like you are."

*The jury's still out on that point,* Jim said to himself, though he nodded a polite goodbye to his host.

He followed the sound of Cliff's heavy footsteps as he tromped down the hallway to the front door. But then he heard Cliff turn around and walk back.

"Oh, by the way," Cliff said, leaning his head through the doorframe, "I'm gonna spend the evening here with you tonight. Thought maybe we could try to have a little séance together. What'ya say to that?" He flashed a leering grin at Jim, then left once more.

# Chapter Fifteen

## The Manor House

"Onions really do make you cry!" Clara laughed. She wiped a tear from her cheek, then lifted her cutting board and poured her freshly chopped onions into the glass bowl Maggie had set out on the kitchen table.

"At least the onions are easy to cut," Robbie whined as he grated his slab of mozzarella into a second bowl. "This cheese is really messy."

Maggie offered him an encouraging smile. "But you can't have a lasagna without cheese," she said. She scooped a long noodle out of the pot on the stove to see if it was tender yet. "It's almost time to put everything together."

Robbie rested his grater on the table and threw an anxious look at his sister. "Do you think Mum's having a good time?"

"Of course she is, silly," Clara replied. "Mum *always* has a fun time at her parties."

"Then why does she always complain about the horrid people she had to talk to when she comes home afterwards?" Robbie protested.

"She won't be making idle chit-chat at this party," Clara retorted. "She's going to spend the whole weekend showing off Jean-Claude to her friends."

"Oh," Robbie replied. The corners of his mouth slipped into a frown. He leaned over the table and fell silent while he set back to work grating the cheese.

Maggie looked quizzically at Clara. "Your mother brought your French tutor along for her weekend in the country?"

"She brings him *everywhere* these days," Clara answered. "It's disgusting."

"You don't like him?" Maggie surmised.

"Oh, he's nice enough, I suppose," Clara replied with a shrug. "It's just that—well, he's kind of—"

"He's supposed to be our *teacher*," Robbie interjected, lifting his head and staring directly at Maggie. "Not her *boyfriend*. And he's not old enough to be her boyfriend anyway. He's only twenty-three! I asked him."

"Well," Maggie demurred, trying to tiptoe around the prickly topic, "maybe he's not really dating your mother. Perhaps they're just good friends. I'm sure she's very anxious to improve her French if she's going to be spending the summer in Saint-Tropez. And the only way to learn a language is to speak it with someone every day."

"They're dating," Clara countered. "He's practically moved in. It's really disgusting."

"Oh," Maggie replied, biting her tongue. She looked away from the children and re-tested the noodles, then announced in an overly cheerful voice, "Let's make the lasagna now, shall we?"

She tried to hold her young guests' attention while she demonstrated how to layer the ingredients, but Robbie remained focused on his mother.

"She said she'd call us when she got there," he reminded his sister. "Do you think something happened to her?"

"She's just busy," Clara assured him as she spooned some marinara sauce over the noodles. "Catching up with her old friends and all that."

"Well, I do wish she would have given me the phone number of the house where she's staying," Maggie said irritably as she reached for a tub of ricotta cheese.

Clara immediately came to her mother's defense. "Wes probably asked her not to. Dad doesn't like sharing his phone number with people he doesn't know very well, and Wes Von Alters is a *much* bigger star than Dad ever was."

Maggie rested her tub of cheese on the table and stared at Clara with a dumbfounded expression. "Wes Von Alters? Your mum is staying at *Wes Von Alters'* house this weekend?"

"Yeah, Mum used to work for him," Robbie explained. "She sang back-up on his first album, and Dad played keyboards. That's how they met."

"And then she got pregnant with me," Clara added with a mischievous grin. "And there went her big break."

Maggie continued to stare at Clara, agog. "I don't understand," she said.

Clara shrugged. "Mum was on bedrest for a couple of months before I was born, so she couldn't come to the studio when Wes recorded 'No Wings to Follow.' And after that song hit Number One, he married the girl who replaced Mum. Though they're getting a divorce now."

"I didn't know that," Maggie said softly. She grabbed a wooden spoon and scooped up some ricotta cheese. "Do you suppose your mother wants to start singing professionally again now? Is that why she went to Wes—to Mr. Von Alters' house for the weekend?"

"Nah, I think she just wants to see the inside of his mansion," Clara replied.

"She loves visiting those big houses," Robbie agreed. "She's got a National Trust card."

Maggie pursed her lips while she spread a layer of ricotta cheese over the lasagna, then started pulling more noodles out of the pot of hot water.

"Wes just bought an estate that hasn't been open to the public for a long time, and Mum wants to check it out," Clara added as Maggie worked. "It's called 'Thorp Green'."

Maggie blanched and reached for the edge of the table to steady herself.

Robbie grabbed her elbow. "Are you okay, Miss Grayson?" he asked.

Maggie stared at him with a dazed, wide-eyed expression for a long moment, then offered him a weak smile. "Yes, yes, of course. I just—I think maybe leaning over this pot of boiling water has made me light-headed all of a sudden. The steam, you know—"

"But the water's not boiling anymore," Robbie pointed out.

"Oh, yes, you're right," Maggie replied with a nervous laugh. She grabbed a paper napkin out of the rack on the corner of the table and started fanning herself. "I think I'll just sit for a moment. Why don't you two go into the other room and look for a movie we can watch while the lasagna bakes? I'll finish up in here and join you shortly."

"If you think you'll be okay—" Robbie said hesitantly.

"She'll be fine," Clara said. She grabbed her little brother's hand and started leading him away.

Maggie heard her whisper the words "hot flash" in Robbie's ear as they left the kitchen.

*If only!* Maggie thought ruefully as she rubbed her temples. Images of Thorp Green started filling her head, and she felt dizzy once more. She folded her arms on the table and rested her head on top of them while she surrendered herself to her memories of the magnificent Georgian manor house in Yorkshire...

*"You'd be perfect for the job!" Lydia Robinson assured Maggie in a loud, bright voice after the Sunday service had ended. She stepped closer to the organ, blocking Maggie's access to the exit. "You're far too gifted to be wasting your talents at this tiny little church. Why, most of*

the people at this service were so old, they probably couldn't even hear what you were playing!"

Maggie pulled her hymnbooks off the organ's music rack and placed them in her satchel. "But what would I do all day at your manor home?" she replied, hoping her father was too busy chatting with the departing parishioners to have heard the woman's rude remarks.

"Give my daughters piano lessons," Mrs. Robinson replied. "I have four of them, so they should keep you busy. And I give parties almost every night, so you'll be providing a lot of mood music for my guests. And then there's Padraig..." Her voice trailed off.

"Padraig?" Maggie asked warily.

Maggie's father cast an anxious glance over his shoulder at the woman who was pestering his daughter. Maggie caught his eye and gestured for him to look away.

"Padraig O'Pronntaigh," Mrs. Robinson continued with a gleam in her eye. "He's an extraordinarily talented young singer and the other artist-in-residence at Thorp Green. But our last accompanist just quit without giving notice, so I need to hire a good pianist to take her place immediately. Guests come from miles away to hear my prized Irish tenor sing at my soirées, and I'd hate to leave them disappointed. Do say you'll come work for me, Miss Grayson. I have a Steinway Grand in my ballroom that is calling out to you, just begging to be played!"

Mrs. Robinson then quoted a salary that far exceeded Maggie's wildest dreams.

And so it was that Maggie found herself living in a mansion just two months after graduating from college.

She quickly grew to love Thorp Green. She felt like a princess in a fairy tale each morning when she woke up in her elegantly furnished bedroom. She took enormous pleasure in playing her host family's Steinway Grand every day. She enjoyed teaching the Robinson girls. She relished the smattering of applause that the Robinsons' guests offered her at the end of their meals.

And then there was Padraig.

He was handsome, charming and caustically funny, and his voice seemed to reach directly into Maggie's soul. She had never met a person even remotely like him before in all of her sheltered twenty-one years. The dashing young Irishman quickly worked his way into her heart, and before long, found his way into her bedroom.

And thus passed five deliriously happy months at Thorp Green, until that harsh winter morning when Maggie awoke to discover she had been unceremoniously dismissed. The head butler who gave Maggie her notice icily informed her that Mr. Robinson had just discovered Padraig and Mrs. Robinson had been having an affair for the better part of a year. Divorce attorneys had been engaged, and the house was being put on the market immediately...

The sound of the television turning on in the next room roused Maggie from her reverie. She let her mind linger for one last bittersweet moment on her memories of Padraig's kisses. Then she gathered her wits about her and finished preparing the meal. She put the lasagna in the oven to bake, looked in on the McCudden children, and started cleaning up her kitchen.

She opened her refrigerator to put away the remains of the cheese. Her eyes immediately fell on her bottle of White Zinfandel.

*Not now,* she chastised herself. *I'm supposed to be watching the children.* She put away the cheese and closed the refrigerator door. *And anyway, red wine goes with Italian.*

She rinsed off her cutting board, then walked down the hall to fetch a tablecloth. She opened her closet door hesitantly. Hearing no voice, she reached for the top shelf.

"What were those children going on about?" the familiar voice called out. "That girl said something that really disturbed you, didn't she?"

Maggie rushed inside the closet and closed the door behind her. "Shh!" she hissed into the darkness. "Be quiet! I don't want Robbie and Clara to hear you. You'll scare them!"

"Me? Scare a child? What a ridiculous notion!" Agnes harrumphed. "Why, I have years of experience working as a professional governess. I know how to talk to children. And I can—"

"Stop it!" Maggie repeated. "They'll hear you!"

"I don't suspect they will," Agnes countered. *"You're the only one who can."*

"What do you mean by that?" Maggie challenged, but then she walked back her question. "Oh, never mind. You can tell me later. Just go away now, would you please? I'm very busy."

She switched on the lightbulb hanging from the ceiling, pulled a checkered tablecloth off the top shelf, and opened the closet door.

Robbie was standing in the hallway, staring at her.

"Are you sure you're okay, Miss Grayson?" he asked.

"Of course I am, dear," she blustered, meeting his puzzled gaze with a startled expression of her own.

"I thought I heard you talking in the closet just now, with the door closed," he added.

Maggie blushed. "Oh, pay me no mind," she said with an awkward laugh. "I thought I saw Percy in there, so I called to him, but I guess my eyes were playing tricks on me."

"Alright. Okay," Robbie mumbled uncertainly.

Maggie handed him the tablecloth. "Come now, love, let's set the table for our dinner. I'm sure we'll be eating just as grandly tonight in my little house as your mother will be in that pop star's giant mansion."

# Chapter Sixteen

## Tickling the Ivories

Nessie poked her head into Jim's bedroom.

"Oh, good, you're awake," she laughed. She rested a fresh plate of food on his nightstand and grabbed his bedpan. "I'll clean this out, then look for my daddy's crutches. They're in one of the closets, but I can't remember which one. I'll come back when I find 'em and show you how to use 'em. Now eat up while I'm gone. You need to get your strength back."

Jim wolfed down his sandwich and fruit while he listened to Nessie poking through the rooms on the other side of the house. When she returned to his bedside with a pair of wooden crutches, he broke into an enormous grin.

"Halleluiah!" he exclaimed. "I'm going to walk again!"

"Well, you can try anyways," she replied. "Here, watch me use 'em first, then I'll let you have a go."

Jim focused his eyes intently on Nessie as she swung her large body back and forth, gliding across the bedroom with ease on one foot while she leaned her considerable weight on the crutches. After she handed the crutches to him, however, his first attempts to move were clumsy at best. A trickle of sweat dripped down his forehead.

Nessie scrutinized his technique, then worked with him on his grip and leg positioning.

"Put your weight on your hands, not your armpits," she admonished him. "Then move the crutches first. Follow through with your gimpy foot, then step forward with your good leg."

She took the crutches back and demonstrated their proper use once more, then gave Jim a second try, coaching him all the way.

"Not bad," she said when Jim stopped to catch his breath. "You're gettin' the hang of it."

"I'd like to try to walk to the toilet," Jim panted. "I'm really getting tired of using that bedpan."

"I'll bet you are!" she laughed. She led him to the bathroom, then gave him a slow tour of the house.

"I'd forgotten there was a piano in here!" Jim exclaimed as he hobbled into the living room. "God, I wish I could have played that these past few days. I feel like I've been going mad, stuck in that little bedroom."

"Didn't know you could play," Nessie replied.

Jim straightened his back and stood up as tall as he could while still leaning on the crutches for support. "I was a member of the Pilots, m'dear. Do you remember the songs 'Yesterday's Girlfriend' and 'Too Much Trouble'? My band and I played on the Ed Sullivan show four times back in the Sixties."

Nessie put her hands on her hips and clucked her tongue. "Lordy! I didn't recognize you! You look kinda diff'rent now."

Jim chuckled, then bent his head to the side and attempted to rub his large bald spot while holding his crutches in place with his armpits. "Well, I'm losing my hair to be sure, but I daresay I've aged better than some of my peers. Have you seen a photo of Keith Richards lately?"

Nessie threw back her head and laughed, then asked Jim to play her a song. She helped him sit down on the bench and pulled up a chair for herself beside the piano.

Jim cracked his knuckles, then started banging out the chords to "Yesterday's Girlfriend," the first Number One song he had written for the Pilots, while he made a weak stab at intoning the lyrics. Nessie cocked a dubious eyebrow at him.

"That's why I sang backup instead of lead," he apologized with a grin. "Here, let me try something more contemporary." He started playing "Kiss from a Rose," singing the melody straight, but adding elaborate flourishes on the keys to approximate Seal's vocal gymnastics.

Nessie smiled and nodded in approval. "Why don't you play a song you don't have to sing along to?" she suggested.

Jim laughed and performed an impromptu, funky arrangement of Herbie Hancock's "Rockit." Nessie raised her hands and wiggled along to the beat in her chair.

"Lord bless me, you're good!" she exclaimed, offering him a round of applause as he brought the song to a close. "How'd you ever get that kind of sound out of this ol' upright? My daddy woulda' loved to have heard you play that. He always wanted to fill this house with music, but all he could ever do was pound out chords."

"I've done plenty of chord-pounding in my day too," Jim admitted, positioning his hands to form two C-Major chords and striking the keys in a rapid tattoo.

He played a few more requests for Nessie, but then she stood up from her chair.

"I hate to leave, but I think Cliff might need me back in the greenhouse soon," she apologized. She turned her head towards the old rotary phone and sighed. "Pity that's not workin' no more. Otherwise, I could just call 'im. Tell you what, I'll go check on his plans and come back with your dinner as soon as I get a chance."

"Could you—?" Jim began, but then he slumped over the keyboard and sighed.

"Could I what?" she replied, crossing her arms in front of her ample bosom.

"Could you please bring me some shampoo and soap and a towel?" he asked sheepishly. "I haven't showered in days."

Nessie waited for him to look back at her before offering a reply.

"You know, if you hadn't 'a asked for 'em, I might've brung you some anyways," she said, making a big show out of wrinkling her nose. "I'll see if I can't find you a toothbrush too. An' a razor and some shavin' cream."

She walked to the bedroom to collect his dirty dishes, then stepped out the cottage, leaving Jim to practice alone at the upright.

\* \* \*

Nessie returned a few hours later, carrying a tote bag filled with toiletries, a tray full of fresh food, and a wooden cane draped over her arm by its crook. She placed the tray on the coffee table in the middle of the living room and rested the tote bag beside it. Then she propped the cane against the wall with an almost religious show of reverence.

"This was Mr. Shaw's," she explained. "You ain't ready for it yet, but maybe you will be soon."

Jim smiled at her. "That cane is very precious to you, isn't it?"

"Any relic of the dead is precious," she replied in a solemn voice. "If they were valued livin'." She helped Jim stand back up and led him to the bathroom. Then she removed the bandages from his foot and turned on the shower tap.

"I'm gonna try to find another pair of my daddy's P.J.'s for you," she added as she pulled the soap, shampoo and towel from the tote bag. "And some clean underwear. I'll leave 'em on the toilet seat while you're washin' up. And I'll boil up some water so you can have a hot cup of tea with your meal. Now make sure you use them railings in the tub for support while you shower. Don't want you fallin'. And don't be shy 'bout askin' me for help if you need it. I used to bathe my daddy. I can help you too if you want."

Jim thanked her profusely, then undressed, climbed into the tub, and let the shower water flow over him until it ran cold. He managed to maneuver himself onto the rug in the middle of the tile floor without Nessie's assistance, then laughed out loud when he spied the chartreuse and fuchsia striped pajamas she had set out to replace the purple and orange pair he'd been wearing.

*Nessie's daddy had one hell of a sense of style,* he thought as he pulled on the clothes. He caught a glimpse of himself in the bathroom mirror, then laughed again. *I look awful, but I feel clean! Gloriously, wonderfully clean!*

Nessie helped Jim shuffle back to the bedroom, then brought his dinner tray in to him from the living room and sat by his side while he ate his cold meal. "Seein' you with those crutches sure brings back memories," she whispered almost inaudibly.

Jim reached out his hand and rested it on her knee. "Tell me about your father. I feel like I'm in his debt, using his old clothes and crutches." He threw a glance at the empty bedpan lying by his side and tilted his head in embarrassment. "And that too."

Nessie shrugged. "There ain't much to tell. Daddy didn't get around much. But I loved him. 'Most everyone else did too. He was quick with a laugh and said his prayers twice a day. When the walnuts started droppin' in the fall, he'd spend hours every day shellin' 'em for Mr. Shaw. Tried to make hisself useful, even though he couldn't work the fields no more. And he helped Mama make jars of jam with the berries Mr. Shaw grew too. He'd sell 'em at the farmers' market every summer, and Mr. Shaw let him keep the profits."

Nessie hung her head. "Daddy passed on about four years ago. After that, I moved up to the Heights, like I tol' you, so I didn't have to walk up that big ol' hill so much, and Cliff turned off the utilities in this place."

"But your father stayed here until he died, just like Mr. Shaw said he could?"

"He sure did," Nessie said, her eyes glistening. "He used the biggest bedroom—the one closest t' the livin' room. And I slept on a trundle bed beside him, so I could be there at night if he needed me. Mama used to use this room for sewin' back in the day, but after Mr. Shaw died, Cliff moved in here."

"He slept in this bed," Jim surmised.

"That's right. Till he moved back up t' the Heights, that is."

"And when was that?"

"Oh, 'bout a year or two after Cathy died." Nessie slid her chair to the side so she could open the nightstand drawer. She pulled out a large embroidered bag and poured its contents on top of the table. Dozens of gold and silver coins with Asian markings tumbled out.

"When Cliff came back to Ohio, he had pockets full of these." She picked up a coin and offered it to Jim. "I don't think they're worth very much. Cliff used to use these as poker chips when he played cards with Daddy. But he had other money too. Real money. And lots of it. That man was filthy rich. And just between you and me, that's what everyone said about Cliff's money, too. That it was dirty money—ill-gotten gains."

Nessie clucked her tongue. "Nobody knew how he made his fortune, and Cliff never told a soul—not even my daddy. But rumors went a flyin'. Most folks figured he got it sellin' drugs, though some guessed he robbed a bank. Others said he killed a man. My favorite story is that he married some rich ol' widow and talked her into givin' him all of her worldly goods. But I don't know. I just don't know."

She slipped the coins back into the pouch one by one as she continued talking. "So, anyways, Cliff was doin' all right for hisself. But you couldn't say the same for anyone else 'round here. Ernie, well, like I tol' you before, he was always a jerk. His wife got sick of him pretty quick and run off with one of her old boyfriends. Left little Harry without so much as a goodbye. And she never came back. Don't know what ever happened to her. Can't say I care much either, but Ernie took it hard. Real hard. That's when he turned to drink."

Nessie returned the coin pouch to the drawer and closed it shut.

"Though Ernie wasn't doin' so hot even before she left him," she added with a harrumph. "He'd been losin' money on the farm for years, but he couldn't swallow his dumb pride and ask Cliff for help. Cliff found out though, and started clearin' Ernie's debts behind his back without tellin' him. But he made sure the *banks* knew who was puttin' up the cash. 'Course, Cliff's name had been on the deed to the property ever since Mr. Shaw died. So things bein' the way they was, it didn't take long 'fore everything started shiftin' Cliff's way. And it didn't take long for Ernie to throw in the towel either. He started lettin' Cliff do *every*thing. The plowin', the plantin', the reapin'. He stopped lookin' at the books too. An' while Cliff was mindin' the family business, Ernie went off with his buddies, drinkin' anything they could pour in a glass and smokin' big ol' heaps of weed.

"Then one night, Ernie got drunk, went out drivin' and killed a man." Nessie closed her eyes briefly and shook her head, then looked back at Jim with an irritated face. "The other driver was drunk too, but that ain't no excuse. Cliff pulled some strings with the judge and got Ernie's charges reduced, but that fool still had to do some time.

"Cliff moved back to the Heights then, while Ernie was locked up. An' after Ernie came home, Cliff made sure that worthless jailbird knew he done sunk to th' bottom of th' totem pole. Cliff made me feed the *dog* first, 'fore I laid out Ernie's dinner. From that day forward, Cliff made *all* the decisions 'round the house and farm, and Ernie, well, he just slunk off to a dark corner and drunk hisself blind."

Nessie cocked her head towards the window, in the direction of the Heights. "Now Ernie's son Harry, he started havin' a hard time at school, as you can well imagine. All that awfulness goin' on, no wonder the kid couldn't learn nothin'. But when he came home from school one day with a note from his teacher sayin' he'd have to repeat a grade 'cause he couldn't read right, Ernie just let into him. Beat that boy somethin' awful. But Cliff heard Harry screamin', thank the Lord, and run in from the field to pull that worthless bastard off the chil'. He smacked Ernie so hard across the face he knocked out two of his teeth."

Jim rubbed his own cheek instinctively, remembering the strength of Cliff's blows. *I'll bet that bastard earned his fortune prizefighting!* he thought with a fresh wave of anger.

Nessie ignored Jim's gesture and continued her story. "After that, Cliff pulled Harry out of school and taught him at home, just like Mrs. Shaw used to do with him an' Cathy. And he wouldn't take no lip from Ernie 'bout anythin' havin' to do with that boy either. Harry pretty much became Cliff's kid then."

Jim watched Nessie closely and noticed her eyes were moist with tears. *She told me earlier that she'd been like a nanny to the boy when he was a baby,* he recalled. *After Harry's mum left, she no doubt became like a mother to him completely.*

"You mean, Harry pretty much became Cliff's and *your* kid then," he corrected her.

Nessie looked away from him as if embarrassed and grabbed a napkin off his tray to wipe her face. She took a few moments to settle her nerves before resuming her tale.

"Now mind you, things weren't goin' so well over at the Lyndons' place either," she said once she had composed herself. "All those years of livin' high on the hog finally caught up with 'em, and they ran up some big ol' debts. Joe took all the money Cathy's daddy had left her, and lost the whole kit and caboodle in one of them get-rich-quick pyramid schemes. Then he and his folks paid a call on Cliff, sayin' they'd be willin' to sell him back Cathy's share of Mr. Shaw's land, since it was technically Joe's property now. They needed cash real bad.

"Lordy, did *that* ever piss Cliff off! But he wrote out a fat check to Joe, and threw him one of his shit-eatin' grins when he handed it over. Then he kept his ear to the ground, and whenever he heard the Lyndons were auctioning off another tract of their land, he bought it on the sly through a broker. He ended up takin' title to everything they owned, 'cept their house and a quarter acre of land around it."

Nessie folded and unfolded her paper napkin absentmindedly and shook her head at the memory. "Then those damn-fool Lyndons got this idea in their heads that they should turn their home into a Bed and Breakfast. Figured maybe *that* might bring in some money from folks comin' to the Cuyahoga Valley, after the government named it a National Recreation Area. But you can prob'ly guess how well their idea panned out."

Jim repositioned himself in his bed and imagined how lovely it would have been if his car had stalled in front of a cozy B&B instead of this abandoned cottage. But Nessie knocked him out of his pleasant reverie with her next revelation.

"The family had hardly finished hangin' up their sign, when Mr. and Mrs. Lyndon died in a car crash," she stated in a flat voice. "Beth came home from Florida for the funeral, and finally introduced Cliff to his son. She'd named the kid 'Lyndon' after her family, and called him 'Lyn' for short. Claimed it was a manly name, 'cause of that football player, Lynn Swann. But Cliff just laughed at her and told her it was a damn fool name for a damn fool child. She flew right back to Orlando after the funeral and left Joe to run their parents' business by hisself. And guess what?—he started losin' money hand over fist. So Cliff stepped in *again*."

Nessie flashed Jim a knowing smile. "Cliff knew from his judge friend that the Lyndon family had gotten a liquor license, 'case they ever wanted to serve fancy cocktails to their guests at the B&B. So he tol' someone he knew—who knew someone who was good friends with Joe—to put a bug in

Joe's ear 'bout usin' that license to open up a bar. An' Joe fell right into Cliff's scheme.

"He remodeled the bottom floor of his house to look like some cozy ol' English pub, and renamed his place 'The Black Bull.' I'm sure he figured he was gonna bring in some high rollin' customers for wine tastin's. But the very first day Joe opened up his bar for business, Cliff drove Ernie and his buddies over there and set up accounts for each one of 'em. Cliff promised to pay all their tabs ev'ry month—no questions asked. They took over the place right quick, an' before Joe knew it, his whole livelihood depended on servin' that crowd of losers every night.

"Joe couldn't figure out how to dig hisself out of his hole without sellin' his childhood home, but he didn't have the heart to do that. So he just kept on playin' Cliff's game. 'Fore long, Cliff decided he was sick of lookin' at Ernie during the day. So he offered Joe some rent money to let Ernie move in to a room above the bar. An' Joe didn't really have no choice. He needed the cash. Then, after a while, Joe started drinkin' too."

Nessie frowned. "You should see that old Lyndon place now. What a dump!" Then she noticed Jim had finished his sandwich and salad but left his dessert untouched.

"Eat that," she directed him. "You could use some fat on your bones."

Jim picked up the dark brown muffin she was pointing to and took a bite. Then he looked back at Nessie. "Finish your story while I eat. I want to know what happened to the Lyndons. Don't leave me hanging."

"Alright then," Nessie said, settling back in her chair. "Beth Lyndon died 'bout six or seven years back. Skin cancer. That Florida sun ended up bein' the death of her. So Cliff flew down to Orlando to fetch his chil' an' bring him back to Ohio, to live with him and Harry."

She let loose a mirthless laugh. "But Beth done poison her boy 'gainst his daddy. When Lyn moved in to the Heights, all he did was complain about how he didn't wanna be there. So Cliff shipped him off to military school right quick. Hah! But that didn't last long. Lyn got hisself expelled for smokin' rollies and drinkin' beer, and came back to the Heights with his tail 'tween his legs. He lived with Cliff and Harry for a spell. But then he started hangin' out with a bad crowd at school and gettin' into all sorts of mischief. Vandalism, shopliftin', that sorta thing.

"Cliff couldn't care less, but Joe Lyndon took pity on the kid and offered to take him in. So Cliff sent him right over. Joe tried to raise him right, but all Lyn wanted to do was hang out with the drunks at the bar. He was drinkin' pretty heavy by the time he was sixteen, and started doin' hard drugs not long after that. Ended up overdosin' at his eighteenth birthday party and dyin' the next mornin'. Joe felt guilty 'bout the whole thing, but I don't think Cliff shed a tear.

"And then Joe died last year. All things considered, it's kinda surprisin' he hung on for as long as he did. His and Cathy's daughter Katie took over the bar then. Cliff's tried to talk her into lettin' him help, but she won't have nothin' to do with him. She knows how bad he screwed her daddy over, and she's got too much of her family's dumb pride to ever forgive him."

Nessie stood up from her chair and started stacking Jim's dishes. "So that's how it stands now. Katie Lyndon's the only thing Cliff has left of Cathy. But that girl won't even speak to him. Cliff sometimes sends Harry over to pay her a call. They're kissin' cousins on her mom's side, so Katie's a little more willin' to put up with him. He'll fix whatever's broke 'round her house, an' throw a drunk out of the bar for her. He keeps an eye on his mis'rable ol' daddy too. Makes sure Ernie don't get into too much trouble. I sometimes get the feelin' Harry's kind of sweet on Katie, though I don' know if she likes him back. She oughta, though. He's a good'un."

Jim searched for an appropriate response. But before he could say anything, he heard the front door of the house open and a deep voice he didn't recognize calling Nessie's name.

Nessie stepped out of the bedroom to greet the visitor, then came back a minute later with a tall young man by her side. He wore a loose-fitting jean jacket and a red baseball cap with a black brim that partially obscured his face. His frame was muscular, but his shoulders were slumped and his eyes were downcast. Jim got the distinct impression that he was nervous.

"This here's Mr. Harry Shaw," Nessie announced. "He done fixed your car."

"Thank you," Jim said, breaking into a grateful smile. "I very much appreciate that."

"T'weren't nothin'," Harry mumbled.

"My name's Jim McCudden," Jim said, reaching out his hand in greeting.

"I know," the young man replied. He shoved his own grease-stained hands into his pants pockets and started rocking back and forth on his heels.

Harry and Nessie stood silently beside Jim's bed for a few awkward moments, then Nessie shrugged her shoulders. She collected the tray of dishes and walked out of the room. Harry started to follow her, but then he turned and faced Jim.

"I found some shoes not far from where your car was parked. Think they might be yours?" he asked in a hesitant voice.

"Probably," Jim replied.

"I'll bring 'em to you," Harry mumbled. "I polished 'em. Nice shoes."

"Thank you very much," Jim said. "That was very kind of you."

"T'weren't nothin'," Harry repeated. He stood in the door frame for a few more silent seconds, then lifted his head and announced, "My Uncle Cliff asked me to remind you he's stopping by later this evening. He said he's gonna bring you somethin' new to smoke."

Harry turned and walked away, leaving Jim alone once more.

# Chapter Seventeen

## Photographs

"Who's this?" Robbie asked, pointing to a curly-haired woman in a wizard costume.

Maggie pulled the framed photograph off her dining room wall so he could see it better. "That's my friend Ellen Nussey. We went to school together. This girl in the fairy costume is my friend Mary Taylor. And I, as I'm sure you can tell, am the frog."

Clara giggled. "I wore an outfit like that to a fancy dress party once. The fairy costume, I mean. Not the frog." She turned to her teacher with a curious expression. "Do you still keep in touch with your old friends?"

"Ellen, yes. Mary, not so much," Maggie answered. "She wanted to see the world, so she became an airline hostess. We exchange letters, but I haven't spoken to her in a long time." Maggie hung the picture back on her wall and pulled down a larger photograph. "This is my family at my sister's wedding. Can you tell she was an Eighties bride?"

Clara took the photo from Maggie and giggled once more. "Oh my God, look at those shoulder pads! And everyone's big hair!"

"It is rather embarrassing to look at the styles now," Maggie agreed. "But back then, we thought we looked very beautiful."

"You should see my parents' wedding pictures," Clara said, handing the photo to her brother. "My dad had so much mousse in his hair that it stood straight up. He looked almost like a punk rocker."

Maggie swallowed hard. *Don't let these kids see how I feel about their father,* she reminded herself. She felt foolish even admitting her feelings to herself. *I'm a thirty-nine-year-old spinster with a crush on a man who used to be a pop star. I'm pathetic!*

She took her sister's wedding portrait from Robbie and hung it back on the wall. "Well, I should wash up the dinner plates now. Why don't you two practice your recital pieces while I'm in the kitchen? I promise not to interrupt you or offer any critiques."

Clara and Robbie exchanged frustrated looks. Then Clara turned back to Maggie. "We could help you with the washing up instead, if you'd prefer."

Maggie rested her hand on Clara's shoulder. "Thank you, love, but I don't mind doing it myself. And you need to practice. What would your parents think if they found out you never rehearsed your pieces the entire time you were staying at my house?"

"Mum wouldn't care," Robbie replied without missing a beat.

Clara grabbed him by the elbow. "But Dad would. C'mon." She ushered her brother into the next room and left Maggie to her task.

Maggie collected the dinner plates, silverware and glasses, and brought them to her sink. She listened with half-an-ear to Clara's practicing while she covered the leftover lasagna with cling film. Then, as she rinsed off the dishes, she let her mind wander back to her history of awkward meetings with Jim McCudden...

*He was wearing a simple suit and tie when she first met him two years ago, and he looked very much like every other dad at the reception following her students' annual piano recital. But she had immediately recognized his face from the albums she'd collected when she* was young. He was that rarest of pop stars—a classically trained pianist! From the moment she first spotted her former idol standing by the punchbowl, she couldn't stop staring at him, and she literally froze in her tracks when he walked up to her and introduced himself.

"Hello. I'm Jim McCudden. Robbie and Clara's dad," he said, holding out his hand.

"Yes, I know!" she exclaimed, trying and failing to contain her excitement. "I mean, yes, of course, I know you're Robbie and Clara's father," she blustered as she shook his hand. "I saw you standing with them just now."

He smiled at her then, with a lop-sided, goofy grin that looked just like his children's smiles, and unwittingly set her insides all aflutter. "Thank you for working so hard with my kids. You've done wonders with them."

Too nervous to think of a polite response, she blurted out, "I've often wondered if you named your son and daughter after Robert and Clara Schumann." Then she winced, fearing that she'd come across as a nerdy classical music snob.

But Jim hadn't seemed upset by her query. He just smiled at her more broadly and leaned closer to her ear. His breath felt hot against her skin. Her knees started to buckle.

"Yes, I did," he whispered. "But don't tell Pippa. She thinks they're old family names."

Maggie had shared a conspiratorial smile with him after that, but their tête-à-tête was cut short when another student's mother interrupted their conversation.

"I must take your picture to show my friends!" the woman squealed. She draped her arm around Jim's waist and thrust a camera into Maggie's hands. "The four of us all skived off school one day when we were fifth formers to buy tickets to a Pilots concert! They'll just die when they see me standing right next to you!"

Maggie watched Jim's back stiffen at the stranger's request, but he forced a smile when Maggie called out, "Say 'Cheese'!" As soon as Maggie returned the camera to the bothersome intruder, he made a hasty retreat to the other side of the room. Maggie's heart had sunk.

But she'd managed a slightly longer conversation with him at the following year's reception. He had asked about her musical training, then confessed that he'd always regretted dropping out of university before finishing his degree in music. "But what could I do?" he joked. "Opportunity knocked!"

Maggie tried to sound like an intelligent piano teacher when she responded to his remark, though she suspected she came across as more of an overgrown fan. Jim steered their conversation to the topic of a newly released Glenn Gould recording. But then another student's mother interrupted, this time asking Jim to snap of photo of Maggie with her and her daughter.

Jim had complied with the request but then wandered off to speak to his ex-wife. Maggie couldn't help but notice that he left the reception shortly afterwards, looking irritated.

Convinced that she would not hear from him again for another year, Maggie had been stunned when Clara brought a copy of the Glenn Gould CD to her next lesson. Jim had attached a yellow post-it-note to the jewel case, inscribed with the hand-written instruction, "Enjoy!"...

"Miss Grayson?" Robbie called to her from the kitchen door. "Is once enough, or do you want me to play my song two times?"

Maggie looked up from her sink full of dishes and blushed. She'd been so lost in her memories that she hadn't even heard Robbie play his piece. She shook off her soapy hands in the sink and wiped them on a tea towel.

"Once is enough," she assured him. "Now, why don't you and your sister find another video to watch, and I'll join you two in the living room when I'm done here?"

Robbie nodded and turned to leave, then looked back at her once more. "I think you and your sister both looked very pretty in that wedding picture. Your dress was much nicer than the green one my Aunt Lucy wore when she was Mum's maid-of-honor. She looked like a frog in her frock, just like you did in that photo with your friends from school."

Maggie stared at him for a long moment, unsure of how to reply. Then she smiled.

"Thank you, love," she managed to say. "I think my sister picked out lovely gowns for both of us too."

Robbie nodded and scooted out of the kitchen.

Maggie finished rinsing off the plates, then stacked them in a rack by her sink. The soundtrack to "E.T." started wafting into the kitchen from the next room. She hung her wet tea towel over the handle of her oven, then filled her kettle with water so she could enjoy a cuppa while she watched the film with the children. She opened her pantry to grab a tin of tea.

"I posed for a daguerreotype once," said a clipped voice from behind the canister of flour. "It turned out rather nice. My Edward kept it in a frame on his desktop."

"Not now, Agnes!" Maggie whispered into the closet.

"Oh, don't be such a spoilsport," the voice replied. "I'm just trying to give you a little friendly advice. So tell me, Margaret, have *you* ever posed for a portrait to present your beau?"

Maggie grabbed her tin of tea and shut the pantry door with a loud clap. She spread her arms out over the kitchen table and drew in a few deep breaths to calm her nerves. Then she stood up straight, pulled a clean china cup from her cupboard, and waited for her kettle to boil.

# Chapter Eighteen

## The Hookah

Jim sat cross-legged in the middle of his bed and watched the pale smoke rise and fall in the hookah's glass jar. It reminded him of a stubborn morning fog back home in Manchester, lifting briefly for a short, tantalizing moment, then settling back down to earth and hanging in the air like a land-locked cloud.

Cliff handed him back the long, black hose he had set aside. "Take another hit."

"Christ, I'm so tired," Jim protested. He continued staring bleary-eyed at the large hookah sitting on his nightstand. "It's got to be four in the morning already. I just want to sleep."

"Take another hit," Cliff repeated, squaring his eyes at Jim.

Jim ran his fingers over the mouthpiece at the end of the hose and hesitated. "This is giving me a headache. I've never smoked anything like this before."

"I'm well aware of that," Cliff replied. "It's my own unique blend. Now take a hit."

Jim brought the mouthpiece to his lips and reluctantly inhaled. A small ripple of bubbles danced in the jar's liquid. Then he released his breath in a stream of pale mist. "It's weird how this feels so cool," he whispered hoarsely. "Smoke is supposed to be warm."

"That's because I put ice in the water jar," Cliff explained.

"Fire and ice," Jim murmured, shifting his gaze to the etched flame pattern wrapped around the hookah's brass stem. "Just like Cathy."

"Yes," Cliff agreed. He walked away from Jim and stared out the bedroom window into the night.

Jim straightened his back and watched Cliff in silence for several seconds, then cleared his throat, "Does she only ever visit this house?" he asked. "Or does she come to your other home—the one Nessie calls 'The Heights'?"

Cliff glanced back at Jim. "She'll come to both, but she prefers this room," he replied bluntly.

"How often do you two, umh—?"

Cliff scowled. "How often do we have sex?" he bellowed. "Damn, you're an impertinent bastard!"

Jim recoiled into the pillow he had propped against the wall. "I wasn't going to ask that. I was just going to say 'meet'."

Cliff looked back out the window and gazed into the darkness for almost a full minute. Then he returned to Jim's side and sat down in the captain's chair.

"We don't meet as often as we used to," he confessed. He grabbed the hookah's shorter hose and took a puff, triggering another ripple of bubbles inside the glass jar.

Jim scooted forward and met Cliff's eye. "When was the last time you saw her?"

Cliff looked down at the floor. "It's been almost a year," he whispered.

Jim's drooping eyelids bolted wide open. "But Cathy's been coming to see me almost every night! What's going on between you two? Did you have a fight?"

"You could say that," Cliff admitted with a slump of his shoulders.

"What did you argue about?"

Cliff looked back up at Jim. "That's none of your goddamned business!"

Jim's face flushed as his indignation rose. "It's my goddamned business *now!* You're holding me prisoner in this house, and your dead girlfriend's been haunting me night after night. I don't know what kind of game the two of you are playing with me, but whatever it is, I know one thing for damned sure—this *is* my goddamned business!"

Cliff lowered his head again and sighed, then whispered, "She killed Joe."

Jim dropped the hookah's hose into his lap and blanched. "She did *what?*"

Cliff looked back up and stared directly at Jim. "You heard me. She took his life."

Jim stared back at him. A thousand questions raced into his head at once. But then he remembered what Cliff had told him earlier about Cathy drawing life from her sex partners—and Cathy's odd remark about Joe dying with a 'smile on his face.' He shuddered.

A long silence settled between them. The soft, dull buzz of the Coleman lantern burning through its propane echoed through the room. Jim picked up the hookah's mouthpiece and twiddled it absent-mindedly between his fingers. He tried to push away his memories of his last encounter with Cathy, but they kept rushing back to his head. He sighed in frustration, then looked back at Cliff. "Explain that to me. I think I know what you're implying, but I'm still confused."

"She fucked him!" Cliff lashed out, the veins bulging in his thick neck. "She fucked him till he died!"

Jim shrank back against his pillow once more, preparing himself for another blow from his irate host. But Cliff simply lowered his gaze and took another hit from the hookah.

Jim swallowed hard and summoned his courage. "But Cathy told me Joe didn't even recognize her when she visited him. She said he only ever saw her at the very end when he was dying. But even then, he didn't seem fully aware of her presence."

"Dammit, she sure does like to talk to *you*, doesn't she?" Cliff cursed. He flung himself out of the chair again and returned to the window. "She's a regular little Miss Chatterbox with our bedridden English Patient!"

Jim eyed Cliff warily. "Doesn't she talk to you too?"

"Sometimes," Cliff replied haltingly. He tugged at the curtain and crinkled a handful of fabric in his fist. "Sometimes she does. But it's been a while."

Jim stared at Cliff's back. The dim light radiating from the lantern illuminated only a small portion of Cliff's figure. The rest of his body was sheathed in shadows. He looked almost like a ghost himself.

*God, this place is so fucking weird,* Jim thought, cursing his bad luck afresh. *I cannot wait to get the hell out of here!*

A tsunami of conflicting emotions started racing within him—fear, confusion, frustration. But then, from out of nowhere, a new and entirely unexpected feeling began to form inside him as he watched Cliff stare out the window:

Pity.

He summoned his courage and broke the silence once more.

"What exactly did Cathy do to Joe?" he asked in a hesitant voice. "And why did you two fight about it?"

Cliff let go of the curtain and walked back to Jim's side. He sat down in the chair and took another hit on the hookah, then stared blankly into space while he spoke in short bursts of jumbled speech. "Cathy and Joe—I mean, Cathy and I—Shit, man!—where the hell am I supposed to even begin?"

Jim fell back against his pillow and tried to hide his rueful smile as he prepared himself for another long story. He cleared his throat, then asked in what he hoped was an encouraging voice, "When did she first appear to you? Was it right after she died?"

"Almost," Cliff replied. He dropped the hookah's hose into his lap, clasped his hands together between his knees, and hung his head low. "Not long after that, anyway. I used to go out walking every night and think about her. I'd follow the paths we took when we were kids, and curse myself the whole while for everything that I did wrong. Sometimes I'd walk all the way to that goddamned church where the Lyndons had fucking buried her and lie down on her grave until the sun rose. And then one night, just before dawn, I—I saw her. I called out to her, but she didn't answer. I thought maybe it was just my imagination running wild. But then a couple of weeks later I, well—one night when it was snowing too hard for me to go out walking, I started smoking a spliff, and she came to me again. Right here in this room. I saw her a lot more clearly this time, but we still couldn't speak to each other.

"I figured maybe it was the joint that'd helped me see her, so I started experimenting with different blends of dried leaves. I rolled myself all sorts of cigarettes. I brewed myself teas. I chewed on herbs and roots and mushrooms, and I smoked anything I could think of in the hookah. And after a while, it got so I could break through to her layer. I'd leave this world behind for an hour or two and be with her again. We'd talk and laugh. But we couldn't touch. She was too cold. We couldn't even hold hands. So I kept trying out new concoctions, and I finally found a mix that allowed us to— that let me touch her without getting frostbitten. And then I tinkered with the blend some more and found a combination that let us have sex."

Cliff took another hit on the hookah and exhaled his breath slowly before continuing his story.

"After a few trysts, though, I started growing weaker. I felt drained. But Cathy got stronger. More solid, like she had more substance to her body. She became more, I don't know—more real. I realized then that she was drawing my life out of me, and I knew I couldn't go on like that. So we started trying different techniques and positions. We kept blankets between us. And I kept experimenting in my greenhouse—growing things that I thought might make me stronger, more resilient. After a while, we got into a groove. We could do it—fairly often, even—and things were good. Things were good for years.

"But we couldn't do it every night. I needed to regroup afterwards and prepare myself for our next meeting. So on the nights when she wasn't visiting me, she—well, I'm not sure where she went *every* night. She was always pretty vague about her habits. But she told me she used to look in on little Katie sometimes. And I was cool with that, so long as she didn't scare the poor kid. But she always swore to me that she didn't visit Joe."

Cliff's cheeks burned red, and his hands started to tremble. He let go of the hookah's mouthpiece and rested his hands on his knees to steady them.

"But of course, how could she look in on Katie and *not* see Joe?" he asked in a cruel voice. "I started getting on her case about that, and she finally admitted that she saw him sometimes. But she insisted that she hated the sight of him. She said he just depressed her. And like a fool, I believed her.

"But then one night when we were cuddling after—after sharing an intimate moment, she let it slip that she'd been looking in on Joe quite regularly. I flipped out. She got all defensive and claimed it didn't matter, since he couldn't see her. But it mattered to me. We got into a huge fight. She argued that Joe was still her husband, so she was within her rights. But I reminded her that her vows were only good until 'death did them part.' Then she got all snitty with me. Really pissed off. And, hell, I've known her since we were kids. She used to get like that a lot, so I didn't think too much of it at the time. But she stopped coming to see me.

"So I started dropping by the Black Bull in the evenings for a drink, hoping to catch a glimpse of her there. And I'd always bring along one of my special spliffs, just in case she saw me too and wanted to make up. Then one night I mislaid it. I'm not sure how—maybe one of Ernie's cronies picked my pocket. But it doesn't matter how it got there. What matters is, I left one of my cosmic joints behind at the bar—and Joe found it."

Cliff sneered and let loose a dry, mean-spirited laugh. "I never took Joe Lyndon for a pot-smoker. Or for someone who would find a loose, hand-rolled cigarette of unknown origins lying on his bar, and just pick it up and take a toke. But this was towards the end of his life. He was hitting the sauce pretty hard by then, so he probably wasn't thinking very clearly."

Cliff shrugged and rolled his eyes at Jim. "That bastard smoked some of my best shit and saw Cathy that night. And afterwards, she started visiting him all the time for a month." He fell into a deep, brooding silence once more.

Jim turned his gaze back to the hookah while he waited for Cliff to continue his story. Feeling restless, he impulsively decided to take another hit. But then his head started pounding, as if he'd been smacked between his temples. He stared vacantly at the hookah's glass jar and felt himself being drawn towards the vapors by a force beyond his control. He brought the tube back to his mouth again and took a bigger hit. A buzz traveled through him like a tree sprouting inside his body, shooting branches of dead-feeling cork into his veins and capillaries. He exhaled his breath slowly, then, with a shaking hand, rested the tube on his mattress.

"So that's how Joe died," Jim surmised, his numbed lips somehow managing to form the words. "Cathy—"

"She fucked him to death!" Cliff shouted, spitting out his words. "After the funeral, she came back to see me and told me everything. She said she'd found a stash of weed that my son had stolen from me and left behind at the Black Bull—and she somehow convinced Joe to smoke it. It was old, and not nearly as potent as a fresh blend would've been, but it still did the trick.

"And that's when I let into her. I told her she'd as good as murdered Joe. Then she said I'd screwed Joe over so badly that I'd fucked him to death too! And then she said if I really cared about her and wanted to be with her, I would—that I should be willing to—she said I was afraid to d—"

Cliff swallowed hard and left his words hanging in the air. A long silence followed, but then he spoke again in a hoarse whisper. "It doesn't really matter what she said. All that matters is that she hasn't come back to see me since that night."

Jim gazed blearily at Cliff and tried to think of an appropriate response, but his mind was reeling from the hookah. "She's been coming to see *me*," he eventually replied.

Cliff shot him a look of contempt. "Yes, I damn well know that."

A vision danced before Jim's eyes of Cliff peering into the window like a Peeping Tom while Cathy was straddling the bed. Jim squared his shoulders and attempted to match Cliff's scornful expression.

"Is that why you won't let me go?" he asked. "You're hoping that if I stay on here indefinitely, you'll be able to see her again somehow?"

Cliff looked back at the floor. "Draw your own conclusions," he answered curtly.

Jim's head was pounding now. He watched Cliff lift his head and turn it towards the window, searching for a visitor who seemed unlikely to come. Then he sighed irritably.

"Why do you even care if Cathy killed Joe?" Jim challenged. "I thought you hated him."

Cliff turned back towards Jim. His face looked bereft. His eyes were filled with ache.

"I don't want her to go to Hell," he said quietly, the words almost catching in his throat. "People who commit murder go to Hell. My father taught me that. I don't agree with everything Dad told me about religion, but he was a good man. A God-fearing man. And he was right on that point. I'm sure of it."

Jim sighed once more. He tried to think of a logical argument to Cliff's remark, but the combined effects of hookah smoke and encroaching fatigue were making it very hard for him to think straight.

"But Cathy's not really a person anymore, is she?" he ventured at last. "I mean, are the penalties the same for ghosts as they are for the living?"

"I don't know," Cliff admitted. He shut his eyes and buried his head in his large hands.

Jim stared at Cliff for a long moment, feeling completely exasperated, then blurted out recklessly, "What about what *Cathy* said? She accused you of contributing to Joe's death, and she was right. You trapped him in that awful situation—"

Cliff lifted his head and flashed Jim a contemptuous look. "I did nothing of the sort!" he retorted. "If Joe was half a man, he would have fought back. Or he would have sold his parents' goddamned house and gotten the hell out of town and started a new life for himself. It's not my fault that he was a spineless jellyfish who didn't have the strength to walk away. He was weak. And I have no tolerance for weak people."

Jim stared back at Cliff in bewilderment. "But, Cliff, you're in the business of helping the weak," he pointed out. "You sell medicinal herbs to sick people. You took care of me when I was injured. And Nessie told me you used to look after her crippled dad."

"That's different!" Cliff barked. "Helping the sick is a noble undertaking. But hurting a man who's too much of a schmuck to even notice he's being hurt is an entirely different matter."

Jim sucked in a deep breath and started rubbing his throbbing temples. "Calm down, would you, please? You're giving me a headache. Or maybe it's the hookah that's giving me a headache. I'm not sure. Why aren't you smoking from it anymore?"

Cliff cast Jim another spiteful look, then grabbed his hose and inhaled through the mouthpiece. He exhaled his smoky breath in a cool stream directly at Jim's face. "There," he said. "Are you happy now?"

Jim shrugged and fell back against his pillow.

The two men sat quietly for another long moment and watched the smoke rise and fall in the hookah's icy water jar.

"Some say the world will end in fire, some say in ice," Cliff noted at length, breaking the silence. He looked up at Jim and sneered. "That's Frost."

Jim threw him a puzzled look. "What's frost got to do with fire?"

Cliff laughed at him. "Robert Frost, you moron! You know, the poet who read at Kennedy's inauguration? Sorry, I seem to have mistaken you for an educated man."

"I'm educated!" Jim said defensively. "I went to uni before I joined the Pilots. I studied music composition and French literature. I didn't just skip town when I finished high school."

Cliff scowled at him, then grabbed Jim's hose, held up both mouthpieces, and started speaking in a mock-British accent. "One side will make you grow taller, and the other side will make you grow shorter."

Jim stared back at him and crossed his arms defiantly over his chest. But then the corners of his eyes began to crinkle up, and a bubble of unsolicited laughter started forming deep inside his gut. Before he could stop himself, he erupted into a fit of uncontrollable giggles.

"Right," Jim said when he finally managed to stop laughing. "I *do* know that one. Lewis Carroll. *Alice in Wonderland*. And then Grace Slick pinched the line for 'White Rabbit'."

Cliff shook his head in bemusement, then rested both hoses on the bedside table. He stood up from his chair, returned to the window, and cursed under his breath. "Fuck it all. She's not coming. She only wants to visit *you*. She probably saw me here and left."

Jim picked up his hose and started wrapping his fingers around the mouthpiece. "Have another hit," he suggested. "I think maybe I'm finally starting to like this shit."

Cliff looked back at Jim. "Be careful. It's potent."

Jim ignored him and brought the mouthpiece to his lips. "What's in it?"

"You don't want to know," Cliff answered. He turned back to the window.

"Thanks a lot," Jim replied in a sarcastic voice. He took another long drag on the hose and held his breath, then started coughing. "Ah, Christ. I think I'm gonna be ill."

"Well, use the goddamned bedpan!" Cliff shouted. "Don't puke on my blankets!"

Jim grabbed the bedpan and retched. Cliff looked away while Jim vomited, then picked up the dirty pan and carried it into the bathroom. He returned to Jim's side a few minutes later, carrying a large glass of water.

"Drink this," he commanded him.

Jim took a sip from the glass and sloshed the water around in his mouth.

"Feeling better?" Cliff asked in a disinterested voice.

Jim sighed. "I think so," he mumbled.

Cliff walked back to the window. He opened the curtains wider and stared into the dark, empty distance.

Jim watched Cliff in silence. After a while, he noticed that Cliff's shoulders were shaking. Then he heard a small, muffled sob.

*Christ,* Jim marveled. *He's crying! I didn't think that bastard was capable of tears!*

The first glimmer of dawn broke through the darkness and shone down upon Cliff's face. Cliff whispered under his breath. "Haunt me, Cathy. Take any form. Drive me mad. But don't leave me alone in this abyss, where I can't find you. I cannot live without you."

The bedroom took on a grayish hue as the sun started filtering through the window.

Cliff walked back to Jim's side and switched off the camping lantern. "She's not coming," he announced, his voice ringing hollow.

Jim grunted in agreement and lowered his eyes. "Where do you suppose she goes on the nights when she doesn't come here?"

"Haven't the faintest idea," Cliff mumbled.

"Do you think she visits other ghosts?"

"Like who?" Cliff challenged. He furrowed his brow in an irritated expression.

"I don't know," Jim replied. "Maybe your parents. Or that baby you were named after who died from polio. Or Nessie's parents. Or, I don't know, maybe even—Joe?"

Cliff glowered at him. "I thought I told you not to say that man's name in my presence."

"But we were just talking about him," Jim protested.

Cliff turned his back on Jim. He picked up the hookah and started walking towards the bedroom door. "Joe's not a ghost, and neither are any of those other people you mentioned."

"How do you know that for sure?" Jim challenged.

Cliff turned around and glared at him. "Cathy told me!" he barked. "They all went to Heaven!"

# Chapter Nineteen

## The Sermon

Maggie crouched down beside Clara and gently shook her shoulder. "You need to wake up now, love," she said. "It's almost time for church."

Clara rolled her sleeping bag away from Maggie and mumbled an incoherent response.

Maggie turned her attention to Robbie. "C'mon, lamb, it's time to get up. It's Sunday morning. We don't want to be late for Mass."

Robbie sat upright and rubbed his eyes. His nylon sleeping bag slipped down his small chest and pillowed around his waist, revealing his Thomas the Tank Engine pajama shirt. "What are you talking about, Miss Grayson?" he asked in a sleepy voice. "We don't go to church."

"But I do, and you're in my care for the weekend," Maggie replied. "So you're coming with me." She stood up straight and clapped her hands. "I'll give you a choice. You two can wake up on your own, or I can sit at the piano and play you a thunderous rendition of Chopin's 'Polonaise' to get you moving."

Clara propped herself up on her elbows and focused a bleary gaze at Maggie. "Dad usually plays Rachmaninoff's 'Prelude in C-Sharp-Minor' when he's trying to rouse us."

Maggie chuckled. "Well, I can play that instead if you'd prefer. Nice, big, pounding chords in that one. It'll have you running to the next room in seconds."

"We're up, we're up," Robbie groused. He unzipped his sleeping bag and stood up. "But can't we eat breakfast first?"

"If you get dressed in a jiffy, then yes," Maggie replied. "If you diddle-dawdle, then no."

Clara dropped her head back on her pillow. "I'm old enough to stay home by myself alone. I'll just wait for you two here."

"No, you won't," Maggie insisted. She walked to her piano and lifted the cover off the keys. "Actually, I know Khachaturian's 'Sabre Dance' by heart. I don't even need to pull out the sheet music."

"I'm up, I'm up!" Clara whined. She unzipped her sleeping bag and tucked a small stuffed animal into her pillowcase. "But I didn't bring a frock with me. I only have jeans and tee-shirts."

"Jeans are fine," Maggie assured her. She started walking to the hallway. "A lot of people don't dress up for church anymore. But you can't wear pajamas."

"What church are we going to?" Robbie asked as he pulled a clean shirt out of his backpack.

Maggie looked back at him. "Manchester Cathedral, on Victoria Street. They have quite a lovely choir at the High Mass. You might even enjoy singing along with them." She headed towards the kitchen.

"But we won't know the words," Robbie protested.

"There will be hymnbooks in the pews that you can use to follow along," Maggie called over her shoulder. "Now let me put the kettle on so we can all have some tea before we leave. It will help us wake up."

\* \* \*

"Woah!" Robbie exclaimed loudly as he stepped into the magnificent gothic cathedral. He tilted his head back as far as he could and gazed in awe at the high vaulted ceiling. "This place looks like a *castle*!"

Clara elbowed him the ribs. "It's a church, stupid," she whispered. "You're supposed to be quiet in here."

Maggie stepped between the quarreling siblings and took each of them by the hand.

"You're supposed to be quiet *and* kind," she reminded Clara in a soft voice.

She led the children down the wide main aisle and guided them into a wooden pew in the middle of the church. Then she directed them to kneel while they waited for the first hymn.

The organ breathed to life with a loud G-major chord that echoed back and forth between the enormous stone arches lining the nave, and the Mass began.

Maggie stole occasional glances at each of her two charges throughout the opening rites. Clara stood and sat when she was supposed to, Maggie noted with relief, and remained respectfully silent as the priest intoned the blessings. But the child's cross expression betrayed her clear irritation at being forced to endure the dreary service. It also accentuated her strong resemblance to her mother.

Maggie scolded herself for thinking such an uncharitable thought at a Mass and focused her attention on Robbie instead.

He appeared strangely mesmerized by the spectacle unfolding before him. As soon as the opening hymn ended and the priest started speaking, he picked up a prayer book and made a sincere effort to follow along with the Mass. He even tried to sing the refrain of the psalm.

Maggie directed the children to stand for the Gospel reading, then motioned for them to sit back down for the sermon. Clara closed her eyes and pretended to fall asleep as soon as the priest started delivering his homily. Maggie offered her an indulgent smile, remembering the many times she had drifted into a daydream herself during a tedious sermon. Then she threw a quick glance at Robbie and noted with a smile that he still appeared to be paying attention.

The priest repeated a long verse from the morning's Gospel reading—the parable of the foolish virgins—and Maggie soon found her own attention wandering away. She closed her eyes and folded her hands as if she were in prayer, and let her mind drift back to her memories of another minister preaching on the same passage from Matthew, more than fifteen years ago…

*"At midnight there was a cry made: 'Behold, the bridegroom cometh! Go ye out to meet him!"* the Reverend Theodore Sutherland intoned from his pulpit. He turned his face towards the organ and threw Maggie an admonishing look while he continued reciting the Gospel. *"All the virgins arose, and trimmed their lamps. And the foolish said unto the wise, 'Give us of your oil, for our lamps are gone out'."*

*Maggie held the curate's gaze defiantly until he looked back at the congregation.*

*I won't be angry with him, she swore to herself as she squirmed on her bench. That would be beneath me.*

*But she had every reason to dislike the arrogant cleric.*

*Teddy had courted her ardently for months, almost from the moment she first arrived in County Offaly, Ireland. Her heart still broken from Padraig's betrayal, she had fled England to assume a governess position at the home of a wealthy Irish family.*

*The Catholic O'Malleys left Maggie on her own on Sunday mornings, and she initially found solace at the local Church of Ireland services presided over by the handsome young minister. She even volunteered to fill in for the parish's regular organist on a substitute basis.*

*Teddy sought her out after she played her first service, and chatted her up in an awkward, painfully polite, and very nearly charming way. He was learned and witty. And while his soft brogue and bright blue eyes initially reminded her of Padraig, his penchant for discussing spiritual topics and the moral issues of the day set him squarely apart from her last Irish suitor. He dropped by the O'Malley's* stately home on a regular basis to visit Maggie, and within four months of their first meeting, proposed marriage.

But Maggie had demurred. She liked Teddy. She liked him very much. But she didn't want to rush into matrimony while her heart was still on the mend. And she didn't want to dismiss her dreams of living the artist's life and settle down at such a young age into marriage with a clergyman. She turned him down—quite courteously, she believed—insisting that she needed to know him better before she pledged her troth to him.

He took her refusal badly. He shunned her after the following Sunday's service and soon began courting a wealthy, childless widow who had recently moved to the area. They were engaged within *two* months of their first date.

Maggie would never forget the triumphant expression on Teddy's face when he asked her to play the organ at his hastily planned wedding, scheduled for the following month. Nor would she ever forget the way he singled her out in his sermon that week, when he preached on the parable of the foolish virgins.

*"I'm no more a virgin than your fiancée is!"* she had wanted to tell him.

But she held her tongue, and played the organ with exceptional finesse that morning, ending the service with an impromptu performance of the Presto movement from Bach's "Sonata Number One in G Major." Then she handed in her notice to the O'Malleys, so she could return to England as soon as possible...

"You were a fool," said a voice from an overhead speaker.

Maggie shook herself out of her reverie and threw a terrified look at the vaulted ceiling.

"You heard me, Margaret Clementine Grayson," the voice continued. "You were a fool to let him go. So full of pride you were—thinking you were somehow above marriage to a common curate. And now look where your stubbornness has brought you. You're almost forty years old, and you haven't a romantic prospect in the world."

Maggie looked frantically to the left and right to see how the rest of the congregation was reacting to Agnes' interruption. But no-one else seemed to have noticed it.

"Don't worry about the other parishioners," Agnes chided her. "No one can hear me but you."

Maggie squirmed uncomfortably in her pew. *That weirdo can read my thoughts now!* she realized with chagrin. She darted her eyes between Robbie and Clara, then looked up at the angelic minstrel statue that was staring down at her from the ceiling and drew in a deep breath to calm her nerves.

*Read this thought, Agnes!* she beseeched the sculpture. *Go away!*

"I'm not going anywhere, Margaret," Agnes gloated from on high. "I've got you where I want you now. I can say whatever I please and don't have to worry about your pestering me with silly questions or slamming a door at me. I am going to tell you about my beloved Edward now. And don't think that I'm going to feel guilty about interrupting this service. I know perfectly well that you weren't paying attention to the sermon anyway.

"Now, where should I begin? Oh yes, after I left my position at the Bloomfields' residence, I took another job, working as a governess for the Murrays of Horton Lodge. They had four children—two unruly sons and two unprincipled daughters. But I won't bother you with details about the three youngest offspring. It was the eldest child who concerned me the most.

"Rosalie Murray was sixteen, and as beautiful a young woman as I had ever seen. She was too old to need a governess anymore, but her mother hoped I would serve as Rosalie's companion, and guide her through that difficult transition between childhood and marriage. Rosalie was quite the matchmaker, however, and when she noticed me blush in the presence of our parish's new curate, Edward Weston, she made a point of pushing the two of us together.

"I treasured my blossoming friendship with the Reverend Weston. He was everything a man should be.

Noble, pure-hearted, God-fearing. I considered it an honor to walk beside him on my way home from church and discuss religious topics. However, I did not have many opportunities to nurture my secret love because Rosalie was engaging in several clandestine romances of her own.

"She met a very suitable young squire named Sir Thomas Ashby at her coming-out ball, and soon became engaged to him. But she was a prodigious flirt and continued to enjoy dalliances with several other beaux. I was at my wit's end, trying to steer her away from her indiscreet gentleman callers. However, monetary considerations ultimately succeeded where my moral arguments failed. Sir Thomas was Rosalie's richest beau, so she married him.

"I quitted from Horton Lodge not long after the wedding, to visit my ailing father. I returned after Papa's death with a heavy heart. My only joy lay in seeing the Reverend Weston again, yet our visits remained achingly infrequent. But then fate stepped in. My mother called me back home to help her establish a girls' school, and I re-dedicated my life to educating England's fairer sex. My livelihood was no longer dependent upon serving the whims of the landed gentry. I could now earn an honest, if meager, living working as a teacher."

Maggie glanced at the pulpit and noticed with profound relief that the priest had started walking back to the altar. *Thank heavens,* she thought. *Now that woman will finally shut up.*

"Not yet, my dear," Agnes continued. "My story isn't finished. Though you're right, I must hurry. The Eucharistic Prayer is about to begin. I shall sum up the rest of my tale in a nutshell. The Reverend Weston was reassigned to a parish very close to my mother's new school. We renewed our acquaintance and were married shortly thereafter. So it just goes to show you—a poor clergyman's daughter is not doomed to a life devoid of romance."

Maggie sighed. *Well, good for you, Agnes,* she thought begrudgingly. *Go ahead, flaunt your good fortune in front of me. But* your romance didn't seem particularly romantic to me. You seemed far more interested in describing your coquettish pupil than 'your beloved Edward!'

She closed her eyes, lowered her chin, and pretended to pray. Agnes remained blessedly silent throughout the Consecration. *Well, thank God for that,* Maggie thought uncharitably.

Robbie tugged at the sleeve of her dress. "Miss Grayson," he whispered. "Everyone else is leaving their seats. Should we be going too?"

Maggie opened her eyes and saw two lines of congregants forming on either side of the aisle. *I've missed the Lord's Prayer!* she chastised herself. *I can't remember the last time I was so distracted during a Mass!*

She blushed and turned towards Robbie. "No, dear," she whispered. "People are just lining up for Communion. But you and Clara haven't had the proper catechism yet, so you should stay in the pew. I'll sit here with you."

Maggie picked up a prayer book and read a few verses silently in her head, hoping to atone for her blatant inattentiveness. When the organist started playing the closing hymn, she sighed in relief. She sang the first verse of the song, then joined hands with Robbie and Clara and led them out of the cathedral.

"So how did you like the service?" she asked them with a nervous smile.

"It was kind of cool," Robbie answered. He threw a quick glance at his sister's cross face, then shrugged his shoulders and hung his head. "I mean, it was okay, I guess."

"It was long," Clara added.

"Yes, it certainly was a long service," Maggie agreed as she looked at her watch. "What do you say we three go out for a nice lunch, then take a walk in the park? I could use a little fresh air after spending so much time in that stuffy old church."

# Chapter Twenty

## The Lament

The afternoon sun was already high in the sky when Jim woke from his long night of smoking from the hookah. His bedroom stank like rancid, ashy mildew. His head throbbed, his throat hurt, and his fingertips felt tingly and swollen. But he somehow found the strength to swing his legs out of bed and hobble to the bathroom on his crutches. When he returned to his quarters, he opened his window a crack to let in some fresh air. Then he climbed back under his covers and closed his eyes.

When he opened them next, his bedroom was completely black. He had no memory of having drifted off to sleep, yet somehow night had already fallen. A primordial fear of the dark sprang up from a place deep within him and pushed aside all of his other terrors. His skin broke out in a sweat and his heart started to pound. He plunged his hand through the darkness and fumbled blindly for the lantern on his nightstand. When he finally managed to switch it on, he fell back against his pillow and sighed loudly in relief.

*I've slept all day,* he realized as his pulse slowly slackened. *Or maybe I've been sleeping for a day and a half. Who the fuck knows anymore?*

He threw a quick glance at the window and noticed it was closed again. Then he sat up straight against his headboard. His right foot felt different. He reached under the blanket and felt a stiff cloth brace wrapped tightly around his ankle. His bandages were gone.

*Cliff must have stopped by while I was sleeping to check on me,* Jim marveled. *How the hell did he find the strength to do that? He was taking almost as many hits on that goddamned hookah as I was!*

An unexpected outpouring of affection for his irascible host started welling within him, catching him completely off guard.

*He's a bastard,* Jim reminded himself as he slipped his hand out of the blanket and rubbed his cheek. *A sad and pathetic bastard perhaps, but still a bastard.*

Once his breath and pulse returned to normal, Jim turned his attention to the tray of food sitting on his nightstand. He picked up an apple and bit into it with a loud crunch.

"It was *so* cool watching you throw up last night!" a familiar voice called out to him from the foot of the bed. "I can't remember the last time I saw someone do that!"

Jim gagged on his fruit. The hairs on the back of his neck stood immediately on edge. He counted to five silently in his head while he gathered his wits, then swallowed his mouthful of apple and attempted to project a mask of indifference as he replied, "I'm so glad I was able to provide you with an evening's entertainment, Cathy."

"You *are* very entertaining," Cathy agreed. "Though you didn't introduce yourself to me properly before, you rude boy. Why didn't you tell me you were one of the Pilots? I used to have all of your records when I was a kid. Or some of them anyway. I know I had that really good one Eddie Rochester did by himself, with all those beautiful love songs."

Jim took a deep breath to calm his rattled nerves, then focused a steady gaze at the shadowy figure at the foot of his bed. "I'll be sure to pass along your compliments to Eddie the next time I see him. That is, I will if your boyfriend ever allows me to leave this house."

"Cliff's not my boyfriend," she replied curtly. "Not anymore."

Jim sat up a little straighter against his headboard and rested his apple back on the tray. "If you saw me throw up last night, then you were here in the room," he noted. "Why couldn't Cliff and I see you?"

She drew closer to him, her diaphanous gown rustling softly as it brushed against the side of his bed.

"I didn't want you to see me," she answered in a smug voice. She slipped into the captain's chair and smiled at him. "I can change my form to suit my purposes, you know. I can make myself very small, or spread my body out so wide that it almost fades into the air. It's a useful talent. Makes it easier for me to spy on people. And to travel."

"You can travel?" Jim gasped. His goosebumps returned as a new fear popped into his head. *She can keep haunting me even if I manage to escape from this place!*

His cool, brittle mask of indifference shattered. "How far can you go?" he whispered.

"Oh, I don't know. Anywhere I want to, I suppose," she boasted. "I get around."

Jim looked into Cathy's glowing eyes and held her gaze. Her expression looked just the face his daughter Clara always made when she was lying to get out of trouble. His terror dissolved as quickly as it had arrived, and a more surprising sensation took its place:

Sympathy.

Pale, shadowy and almost formless, Cathy suddenly seemed more helpless to him than frightening.

*Damn, how old was she when she died?* he tried to remember. *She couldn't have been much out of her teens!*

"Why didn't you want Cliff and me to see you?" he asked, his voice growing softer.

"Because I wanted to hear what you two had to say about me," she replied, straightening her shoulders in what looked like a defiant gesture of pride. "I thought it might be interesting. But it wasn't. Honestly, quoting Robert Frost and

Lewis Carroll to each other! You guys were as boring as Mr. Lockwood, my old English teacher from high school."

Jim offered her a wary smile. "Come closer," he said, swallowing back the last of his trepidation. "I want to see your face more clearly."

She rose out of her chair and leaned over him. "How close do you want me to come, piano man?" she asked in a mocking tone. "Do you want to do the nasty with me again?"

"No," he replied in as calm a voice as he could manage. He pulled his covers more tightly around his chest, but attempted to project an aura of fearlessness.

*Did she hear me playing the piano the other day?* he wondered as he considered his next words. *Why did I assume she wasn't here in the daytime? I know so little about her.*

Cathy sat down on the edge of his mattress and sneered at him. "You know, for a rock star, you sure are a prig. I thought musicians were always humping their groupies."

His patience snapped. "I prefer groupies with pulses," he retorted.

"Fuck you!" she spat at him.

"I'll fuck whomever I please, Cathy," he replied coolly. "I just don't want to fuck you." He glared at her and forced himself not to look away when her amber eyes started glowing more brightly.

She let loose an angry, howling moan, and before Jim was even aware that she had moved, she was straddling him once more.

"Don't *do* that!" Jim shouted, kicking at her from beneath the blankets. "I've *told* you, I do *not* want to have sex with you!"

Cathy recoiled from his harsh voice and curled herself into an undulating shape inside her diaphanous gown. "But you enjoyed it the last time," she protested.

"That's not the point," he replied. "And anyway, I most definitely did not like the way I felt afterwards."

"Well, I can't help that," she whined. "It's not my fault. That's just the way I am."

Jim sighed and allowed his voice to grow gentle once more. "But it's more than that, Cathy. I know you don't really want me. You're just using me to try to get to Cliff, and I don't want to get involved in your messed up relationship. I have enough on my hands already, dealing with an ex-wife who likes to play games with me. The last thing I need is to hook up with another woman who gets her jollies out of manipulating people."

Cathy curled her lips into a taunting, seductive smile. "I'm not really a woman."

"You're close enough," he replied, then added in a haughty tone, "but you're certainly not a lady."

"That was rude!" she shouted. "I should slap you!"

"Go ahead," Jim said. "I'm getting used to that. Cliff's been smacking me ever since I got here."

Cathy tilted back her head and moaned. Her voice echoed off the ceiling and seemed to almost take shape. It spun around the room like a tornado, then slowly thinned out into a soft, diminishing wail of ache. The hairs on the back of Jim's neck stood up once more, and an electric shock pulsed through his body.

Cathy lowered her chin, then looked up at Jim with a sad puppy dog expression. She slipped off his mattress and slunk back into the chair. Her shoulders slumped to a disturbingly low angle. "What am I going to do about him?" she moped.

Jim eyed her warily for a long moment while he chose his words. "You know, I have a hard time believing that you really care about him," he ventured at length. "When you were alive, you left him for Joe. And now that you're dead, you keep trying to have sex with me."

"You don't understand!" she cried. But then her shoulders slumped down even further into her quivering, increasingly shapeless nightgown, and she started to sob.

"Crocodile tears," he chided her.

"No, they're not!" she shouted, flashing him an angry scowl. Her body immediately solidified into a more human-like form. "I have no tears at all! I can't cry anymore. Just like I can't eat or drink or pee anymore. And to tell you the truth, I can't even feel the sex very much either."

Jim gazed into her unearthly yellow eyes for several seconds, then sighed. "Can't you go to Heaven or something?" he asked gently. "I mean, are you cursed to walk the earth as a ghost forever, or is there some other place where you can go?"

"I'm stuck here," she grumbled. "This is my Heaven. And this is my Hell."

He stared at her in silence, then offered her the faintest hint of a smile.

"So what happened?" he asked in the voice he always used with his children when they were upset. "Do you want to talk about it?"

Cathy stifled a sob. She made a noise that sounded like a deep inhalation of breath, but Jim noticed that she didn't exhale afterwards.

"It's kind of a long story," she began.

"That's okay," he replied. He leaned back against his headboard and crossed his arms in front of his chest. "You know as well as I do that I'm not going anywhere."

"Well, it all started when—" She fell silent briefly and cast Jim a sad, side-long glance. "I'm not really sure when it all started. I guess it was the day I first had sex with Cliff."

"And when was that?" he asked, hoping he wasn't sounding like a dirty old man.

"We were both about fifteen. It was right after we came back from spying on the Lyndons. We went for a walk in the woods and got into this *huge* fight. He got all mad at me for spending the night with Joe's family, and accused me of having a crush on Joe. So I started beating his chest, and he started pulling my hair, and the next thing you know, we were having sex."

She made a dismissive snorting sound, then looked down at the floor. "But, I mean, it was wrong, right? Because Cliff and I were really too young to be doing that. And he was technically my brother too. I know we were both adopted, but we lived together in the same house and called the same man 'Dad.' We were kind of like Marcia and Greg Brady, you know? So it sort of bothered me. But it didn't bother *him*. After that afternoon in the woods, all he ever wanted to do with me was have sex. Sex, sex, sex. I mean, honestly! Whatever happened to romance? A jug of wine, a loaf of bread, and thou?"

Jim cocked his head to one side. "Well, teenage boys are generally pretty horny."

Cathy looked back up at him with an earnest expression. "I know," she agreed. "And I was hot for him too. But—Urrgh! I mean, a bouquet of daisies every once in a while would have been nice, you know? And then Joe started being really nice to me. He came to check on me after I'd spent the night at his house, and *he* brought me flowers. Then he asked me to a movie, so I said yes, just to show Cliff that there were other things a couple could do on a date besides fuck in the forest. Then when Joe brought me home, he kissed my cheek, and it was so sweet. The sort of kiss a girl dreams about. But Cliff saw him kiss me through his upstairs window, and, oh Lord, it was just another huge fight!

"Things got worse after Dad died. Cliff moved in to this house with Nessie and her father so he wouldn't have to deal with Ernie any more. But that meant Joe could visit me without having to deal with Cliff. Then Ernie's wife took a shine to Joe and started inviting him over for dinner sometimes, and before you know it, Joe had become a big part of my life.

"But I still loved Cliff. He knew that. And we talked about getting married someday. And we kept on having sex too. Most of the time, we'd do it right here in this bed."

She reached out her hand and lovingly stroked the mattress, then offered Jim another sad smile. "Nessie told you what happened next, I think. I got into Baldwin-Wallace. I was gonna major in art. Cliff begged me not to leave, but I told him he should go to college too. I thought maybe we both needed a little time apart so we could just breathe for a while. But Cliff didn't understand what I meant about giving each other some space. He just up and left! I woke up one morning in this very bed and reached out for him, and he was gone.

"He sent me a few postcards at first. Notes from Hong Kong and Singapore and Japan. But he never gave me an address where I could write back to him. Then after a while, the postcards stopped coming."

She leaned back in the chair and fluttered her fingers in a strange, twisting pattern, as if she were trying to wring her hands.

"I got tired of waiting for him," she confessed in an irritated voice. "And Joe was so sweet. He kept taking me out to nice dinners and buying me roses and chocolates and all that. Then one night, we were at this fancy restaurant in Cleveland, and Joe hired a violinist to serenade me at the table. Then he dropped down on one knee and proposed, and offered me this *huge* diamond ring. I freaked out. I mean, come *on!*—Joe hired a *violinist!* When did Cliff ever do anything like that for me? And everyone at the restaurant was staring at me with these eager expressions, so even though I really didn't want to marry Joe, I didn't know how to say no. So we got engaged.

"But I kept hoping Cliff would ride back home on a white horse and sweep me off my feet and carry me away."

Cathy turned her gaze towards the Coleman lantern and stared at it forlornly for a few moments. Her pale hair glimmered in the lamplight. Jim couldn't decide if it looked more like a halo or a cloud of hot fire.

"He never did," she finally added in a hoarse whisper. She looked back at Jim and smiled wistfully. "It was kind of fun being engaged, I suppose. Ernie let me take some money out of my inheritance, and I bought this gorgeous wedding dress at Higbee's that made me look like a princess. Joe's parents planned the reception and offered to pay for everything too, and God knows Ernie was cool with *that*. So we had this super-elegant party at Pier W overlooking Lake Erie, with real French champagne and stuffed truffle mushrooms. It was *très chic*."

Cathy's smile faded, and her voice grew brittle. "While we were engaged, Joe and I used to make out a lot, but he never took me to bed. He thought we should wait until we were married. And that was okay with me, 'cause I was still in love with Cliff, and I knew Joe couldn't hold a candle to him. So every evening after Joe kissed me goodnight, I went back to my bedroom and reread my postcards from Cliff and tried to figure out where the hell he was. I knew if I could only tell him that I was engaged to Joe, he would come right home and stop the wedding. But he never sent me his address. He was *such* an asshole!"

Cathy's lovely features briefly morphed into an angry scowl. Her face took on a terrifying, elongated shape, like the ghoul in Munch's famous painting. But she quickly regained her composure, and with it, her unearthly beauty. Jim flinched as he watched her rapid transformations, but he did his best to hide his reaction behind a blank, expressionless face.

"Joe let me pick our honeymoon destination," Cathy said at last, breaking the awkward silence. "So I told him I wanted to take a slow boat to China. I wanted to look for Cliff, of course, but Joe thought I was just being romantic, like the singer on that old record."

She met Jim's eyes and started singing the opening lines of the Frank Loesser standard.

Jim joined her in singing, "*Leave all your lovers weeping on the faraway shore!*" Then he smiled at her and confessed, "I've always liked that song."

"Me too," she replied, lowering her gaze. She ran her fingers through the folds of her gown. Her hands seemed to dissolve into the fabric. Then she turned her head back to the lantern and continued speaking.

"So anyway, our wedding was cool, but our wedding night was a major bummer. Joe didn't know what he was doing, and I didn't want to let on that I did, so it was all very awkward. Then we flew to San Francisco and boarded our cruise boat, and that *really* sucked, 'cause our cabin was so small, and Joe got seasick. So I started walking the deck at all hours of the day, just to get away from him. Then the first mate started flirting with me, and before long, he took me to *his* cabin. He was a lot more fun than Joe was, and he managed to get us a place at the captain's dinner table most nights."

Jim snorted out a laugh. "You little minx."

Cathy threw him a dirty look and blew an ice-cold stream of air into his face.

Jim flinched again, remembering how Cliff had blown cool smoke at him the previous night.

*They're so much alike,* he marveled. *They're practically cut from the same cloth!*

He lowered his gaze, apologized for his remark, and asked her to go on with her story.

Cathy laughed in triumph, then leaned a little closer to him. "Okay. So we *finally* got to Hong Kong. And as soon as we disembarked, I left Joe with a tour group and hired a taxi to take me to this herbal medicine shop that Cliff had mentioned in two of his postcards. I left a message with the owner that 'Mrs. Catherine Shaw Lyndon was looking for Mr. Clifford Shaw.' Then I went back to the boat. Joe got *really* mad at me then, 'cause I wouldn't tell him where I'd gone. But I didn't care.

"The rest of the cruise was pretty miserable," she summed up dismissively. "Except for when we docked in Hawaii, and I drank a bunch of Mai Tais at a luau and managed to slip away with the first mate again. Then we got back to Ohio, and I waited for Cliff to respond to my message. When he finally came home, he was *sooo* mad at me. But I didn't care. I knew he'd get over it. He moved back in to the Grange, and I snuck over to see him whenever I could.

Joe found out, of course, and tried to make me go to marriage counseling, but I just blew him off.

"And then—major bummer—I found out I was pregnant. The doctor gave me a due date, so I counted the days backwards and—I couldn't believe it—it was too late to be the first mate's kid and too early to be Cliff's. It was Joe's! And that *really* sucked. Cliff said he didn't care. He promised to raise the child as his own if I would just run away with him, and I thought, okay, I can do that. But still, I had to tell Joe what was going on before I left. I mean, I'm not entirely without a conscience, you know? But then Joe said he wouldn't hear of our getting a divorce until after the baby arrived! He wanted his child to be born in wedlock."

Cathy started to tremble at the memory. She lifted her hands from her lap and clasped them together to stop them from shaking. Then she started speaking in a softer, sadder tone.

"Everything went downhill from there. Cliff and I started fighting again. And then, just to show me how much I'd hurt him, he decided to hurt me too, and started screwing Joe's sister Beth. And man, did he ever lay it on thick with her! Every romantic thing he never did for me, he piled up on her like extra whipped cream on a giant hot fudge sundae. And that little bitch gobbled it all up like candy!

"My in-laws couldn't stand the thought of their precious, lily-white daughter sleeping with a man who looked like Cliff. So they cut off her allowance to try to make her break up with him. So Cliff gave Beth a big wad of *his* cash, just to taunt them. So then they told Beth they wouldn't pay for her wedding if she married Cliff. So Cliff bought two First-class tickets to Las Vegas and married Beth at one of those cheesy little casino chapels. When they got back home, they rented a big house in Maple Heights, a few miles northeast of here. It was one of those tacky new model homes with wall-to-wall shag carpeting and a sunken living room and mirrored walls in the bedroom."

Cathy rolled her eyes dismissively at the vulgar décor, casting brief flashes of yellow light across Jim's face. Then she hung her head and continued her lament.

"*Finally*, after a couple of weeks of looking at Beth's ugly face every morning, Cliff decided he'd had enough of his stupid game. He called me up and asked me to meet him here at the Grange while his little missus was out shopping for furniture in Cleveland, so we could try to figure out how to clean up the mess we'd both made. And wouldn't you know it—Beth found out and came after us! She caught us here, together. We weren't even doing anything, 'cause I was 'great with child' by then, you know? But she assumed the worst and went home crying to her parents. They gave her that old line, 'You've made your bed, now sleep in it,' and that pissed her off even more. So she threw everything she owned in the back of her green Ford Gremlin and drove down to Orlando to live with her rich Aunt Eunice. She took Beth in with open arms and made a big fuss over how badly Cliff had treated her."

Cathy furrowed her brow and made a snorting sound. "Eunice Lyndon is such a two-faced, meddling old maid," she scoffed. "And a cheapskate too. All she ever gave Joe and me for a wedding present was a goddamned blender!"

She focused a steely gaze at Jim. Her nostrils flared, and her yellow eyes turned chartreuse with envy as she continued speaking. "Cliff filed suit against Beth for desertion and asked the court to annul their marriage. But then Beth found out she was pregnant too. That little bitch was carrying Cliff's baby! So the judge said he had to pay her child support."

Cathy fell silent for a long moment and rocked back and forth in the chair while her anger cooled. Her skin pulsed bright white with diminishing flashes, like a dying strobe light. When she finally returned to her usual soft glow, she looked back at Jim with a pitiable expression.

"Cliff kept trying to talk me into running away with him after Beth left. But I started having complications with my pregnancy. So I told him I didn't want to leave until the baby came. It's not like I wanted to stay with Joe—"

She released a sad sigh that sounded almost like another moan, and lowered her voice. "It's just that I knew I'd never be able to make a clean break from Joe if I took the baby with me. He'd come after me. So I started thinking maybe I should leave the kid with him instead. But, you know—my birth mother gave me up when I was a baby too, so, I mean, like—"

Her voice drifted off, then she added in a hoarse whisper, "I loved my mom and dad, I really did. But it still hurt sometimes, knowing that my real mother abandoned me."

Jim instinctively extended his hand towards her in a gesture of comfort, then remembered that he shouldn't touch her and quickly withdrew it. Cathy watched him in silence, then lowered her gaze. She slipped her hands back under a fold in her gown and resumed speaking in a sad voice.

"My water broke a month before the baby was due. Joe rushed me to the hospital, and—from this point on, things get really fuzzy in my memory. The doctors gave me an emergency C-section, and I got some sort of infection from that. So then the doctors gave me some medicine that just made everything much worse, and before I knew what was happening, I heard some nurse say that I was dying. And the next thing I knew, Cliff had snuck into my room, dressed up in a surgeon's scrubs. He climbed into my hospital bed and cuddled me, and I died in his arms. And you know, that was the most romantic thing that ever happened to me."

Cathy smiled wistfully at the memory. She closed her eyes and started radiating a glow of almost palpable joy. But then she drew her knees up against her chest, hugged them tightly, and started speaking in a hollow, dry voice.

"As I lay in Cliff's arms, I started to sense that I was floating. I wasn't in my body anymore—I was looking down at myself, lying beside Cliff in the hospital bed. And we looked so good together. But I couldn't stay and enjoy the view, 'cause this weird blobby thing suddenly appeared at my side and started talking to me. It kept saying my time was up and I had to go.

"I looked away from my body and asked the blob if it was an angel or a devil. But it wouldn't tell me. It just took me by the hand and led me down this long tunnel. It said I really wasn't supposed to go to Heaven, 'cause I'd behaved so horribly on earth. But my parents had put in a lot of good words on my behalf with God, so I just had to do a little time in Purgatory, and then I'd get to join them."

Cathy smiled weakly. "I guess it helps to have friends in high places," she joked, her voice cracking. Then she turned her face towards the lantern and continued her story.

"The blob started describing Purgatory to me, and it sounded pretty vile. So I stopped walking down the tunnel and said I didn't want to go there. Then the blob got really pissed off and said Purgatory wasn't nearly as bad as the place where I was supposed to go. Then it pushed me to the side of the tunnel and told me to look out this little window, and I got to glimpse Hell. Then it made me walk to the other end of the tunnel and gave a peek at Heaven.

"Heaven was—I don't know—kind of weird. Pretty, I suppose. And bright—though the light was soft and warm, like sunlight after a rainstorm. The angels and saints all looked really happy there. But I started crying. I told the blob I didn't want to go to Heaven without Cliff. I begged it to send me back to earth. I said staying on earth would be kind of like Purgatory for me, because I'd be stuck between Heaven and Hell there too. It would be like Heaven for me to see Cliff every day, but like Hell to never actually be with him.

"Then the blob got *really* angry at me. And the angels got all cheesed off too. A couple of them slipped through the pearly gates and whispered something to the blob. Then the blob took me by the hand and led me back down the tunnel again. It opened up a little side door that I hadn't noticed before and flung me out. I fell into the middle of a meadow right by the Heights and started sobbing for joy. And I've been here ever since."

Cathy looked back at Jim and released a sad, soft moan.

Jim stared at her incredulously, hardly daring to reply for several seconds. Then he said, "That has to be the strangest story anyone has ever told me."

"Yeah," she agreed with a wobbly shrug of her shoulders. "Being a ghost really sucks. I wish I'd known more about it before I told the blob this was what I wanted. But I just made a blind leap of faith." She lifted one of her hands to her hair and started twisting a few tendrils into a coil around her fingertips. "Though I suppose it's still better than Hell."

Jim gazed into her eerie yellow eyes. "Is there no way out for you?" he asked gently. "Is this an eternal thing? Or will you someday move on to Heaven?"

"I'm not sure," she replied, her voice tinged with sorrow. "The blob wasn't very clear about that. But I do know one thing for certain—my soul is tied up with Cliff's."

She looked back down at her lap. "Every now and then, the blob comes back to check on me. It tried to explain my fate to me once. I couldn't follow most of what it said—it got all philosophical and used a lot of big words. But I understood this much: Cliff and I are soul mates. But Cliff's soul is living, and mine is in some sort of weird, between-stages-of-life dimension. But that doesn't matter, because whatever our souls are made of, his and mine are the same.

"So I don't know what's going to happen to me in the long run. I only know that I'm not going anywhere without Cliff. But Cliff has this stupid hang-up about not wanting to die. So, here I am." She looked back up and locked eyes with Jim.

Jim stared long and hard at Cathy's sad, beautiful face and struggled once more to find an appropriate response.

*She's a world-class bitch,* he thought. *She makes my ex-wife look like a bloody saint! Yet I once loved Pippa, and Cliff still loves this mysterious, wretched creature.*

"Does Cliff know about this?" he asked at length. "That you're trapped in this miserable ghost state for as long as he's alive?"

"Are you kidding?" she replied with a bitter laugh. "He's as single-minded as he was when he was a teenager. All he ever wants to do with me is have sex. He's too impatient to talk."

Jim nodded at her. "I'll have a word with him," he offered. "I'll see if I can help."

Cathy smiled then, and bent down to kiss Jim's hand. A momentary rush of coldness seeped through his body. Then Cathy lifted her lips and disappeared.

Jim's heart started pounding. A warm rush of blood coursed through his arm and brushed away the icy sensation. Then he lifted his hand to the lamplight and saw the frosty, ice-blue traces of a woman's lips on his skin.

# Chapter Twenty-One

## A Wish List

A loud, shattering crash roused Jim from his deep slumber. He opened his eyes to the morning light and heard a low, muffled voice cursing on the other side of the house.

He propped himself up against his headboard and listened to the small cacophony of noises transpiring outside his bedroom. Heavy footsteps tromped down the hallway and back. A broom started swishing back and forth against the hardwood floor in the cottage's front room. A delicate chinking sound followed, as pieces of whatever it was that had broken were brushed into some sort of receptacle. Jim chuckled under his breath and imagined he was listening to an old-time radio show, laden with sound effects.

Then he remembered his visit from Cathy the night before. He threw a quick glance at his hand. The frosty, azure mark of her kiss had faded to a barely perceptible, pale blue shadow. He sat up a little straighter and waited for his new visitor to join him.

Cliff's nephew Harry stepped into his bedroom a few moments later, clutching a breakfast tray tightly in his hands. He left it on Jim's nightstand without saying a word, then started walking out of the room.

"Thanks!" Jim called after him.

Harry shrugged and muttered an incoherent response. But when he reached the door, he slipped off his baseball cap and turned to face Jim. "Dropped your toast. Sorry. I can bring you more if you want," he mumbled as he fiddled absentmindedly with his hat.

"That's alright," Jim assured him. "I'm not that hungry."

Harry nodded in response. His mop of dark hair flopped over his forehead, obscuring his eyes. "Nessie washed your clothes," he added in a slightly more audible voice. "She'll bring 'em by when she comes back for your plates." He hurried out of the bedroom without waiting for a reply, and dropped his hat in his haste.

Jim called to mind the words Cliff had used when he'd first described the boy—*"He's kind of sensitive."* He chuckled again, then tucked into his breakfast. He wondered why Nessie had sent Harry in her place, but figured she would tell him when she stopped by later that morning to collect his dishes. He finished his food, then grabbed his crutches and hobbled to the bathroom, picking up Harry's hat along the way and resting it on top of the chest of drawers.

He fiddled with his new brace when he reached his destination, and practiced taking it on and off. Then he placed it on top of the toilet tank so he could take another long, hot shower before returning to the living room to while away the afternoon at the old upright.

\* \* \*

Jim knelt in front of the piano bench, lifted its lid, and examined the songbooks Nessie's father had stored inside. He looked up when he heard the front door opening.

Harry stepped into the cottage, with Jim's laundered clothes draped over one of his arms.

Jim pulled out a yellowed paperback with a torn binding and pointed excitedly to its cover. "*Fifteen Top Motown*

*Hits for Easy Piano!* There's some great sheet music stashed away in here!"

Harry shrugged. "I brung you your clothes," he mumbled. "I'll put 'em in your closet."

"Thanks," Jim replied. He closed the bench's hinged lid and carefully maneuvered himself into a seated position in front of the keys.

Harry stepped back into the living room a minute later, gripping the plastic tray of dirty dishes tightly in his hands.

Jim rested the songbook in his lap and met eyes with the young man. "You dropped your hat when you stopped by earlier. I left it on the dresser in the bedroom."

Harry sighed, then tightened his grip on the tray. "I'll get it later. I don't wanna drop this and break any more plates."

Jim nodded and cleared his throat. "Is Nessie busy this morning?" he asked, hoping he wasn't sounding too rude.

"She's helping my uncle in the greenhouse," Harry replied. He took a step towards the door, then looked back at Jim. "I like driving your Jaguar," he added. "It's a good ride. I adjusted the steering column and suspension when I was done fixin' the engine. It handles better now."

"Thanks," Jim chuckled. "That was very kind of you. But you really didn't have to do that. It's just a hire car."

"I like workin' on cars," Harry replied. He glanced down at the dirty plates for a few seconds, then looked back up at Jim. "So how long are you plannin' on stayin' here?"

Jim stared back at him, dumbfounded. "I thought that all depended on your Uncle Cliff."

"I don't think he wants you around anymore," Harry said. "He seemed pretty upset with you when he came back to the house the other mornin'."

Jim sat up a little straighter on the piano bench. "I'd like to leave as soon as possible. But I don't think I could work the pedals of a car yet with my right foot. It's still pretty weak."

Harry threw a quick glance at the wooden cane propped beside the front door. "Maybe you should practice walkin' with my grandpa's old cane instead of them crutches," he suggested. "That might help you get your strength back."

"I plan to," Jim said. "But even if I master that, I don't think I'd trust myself to drive on the motorway quite yet."

Harry shrugged and took another step towards the door, then turned and faced Jim once more. "I suppose I could drive you," he proposed. "Where is it you wanna go?"

Jim's stomach dropped. A warm wave of relief started flooding through him, and his skin tingled with joy. He had to catch his breath before he could respond to Harry's question, and even then, his words came out in an excited, rapid patter. "I was planning to meet someone in Cleveland. But I've obviously missed my appointment. So maybe you could just take me to the airport and drop my car off at the Hertz office there?"

Harry repositioned the tray in his hands and assumed a thoughtful expression. "Okay. Sure. But how would I get back here then?"

Jim's spirits immediately sank. He closed his eyes and tried to think of a solution.

Harry broke his reverie. "Maybe your friend in Cleveland could drive me home?"

"Maybe," Jim replied, opening his eyes and casting Harry a dubious look. "Though she's not really a friend. She's just a curator from the Rock and Roll Hall of Fame that I was supposed to meet. I was going to advise her on an exhibit they're installing."

"Mmm," Harry mumbled. "I heard that place was gonna open up soon."

Silence enveloped the two men as they considered possibilities, then Harry spoke once more. "Maybe I could hitch a ride with one of Katie's beer distributors from Cleveland."

Jim offered Harry a hopeful smile. "That would be wonderful. I'd really appreciate it if you could ask around."

"I can call your friend at the museum too," Harry offered. "If you still wanna meet her, that is. Then maybe she could drive you to the airport when you're done talkin'."

Jim's face brightened. "Her number's on her business card. I left it in an envelope in my glovebox."

Harry furrowed his brow. "Your what?"

"My—um, you know, the little drawer on the car's dash," Jim said. "The place where you keep your maps and papers. And gloves too, I suppose."

"Oh," Harry said, the faintest of smiles forming on his lips. "You mean the glove compartment on your dashboard."

"Yes, yes," Jim replied, almost laughing in relief.

"I'll call her for you," Harry promised. "Then I'll come back and tell you what I worked out."

He turned and walked away as Jim called out an enthusiastic, "Thank you!" Then he stood on the doorstep and repositioned his grip on the plastic tray so he could use one hand to grip the front doorknob.

Jim heard the door click shut. Then he heard another dish fall from the tray and shatter with a loud crash on the concrete step just outside the house. Harry's curse resounded through the thick wooden door.

Jim shook his head and chuckled.

*I'll be home soon!* he thought, a wave of joy filling his heart. *Maybe even in time for Robbie and Clara's recital!*

He lay the Motown book on the music rack and scanned the titles listed on its cover. Then he put his fingers to the keys and pounded out an impromptu arrangement of the Temptations' classic hit "Get Ready."

"Fee, fi, fo, fum," he sang along in his reedy voice. "Look out baby, 'cause here I come!"

\*\*\*

Jim was still sitting at the piano when Harry returned a few hours later, wearing an orange and brown baseball cap and carrying a fresh tray of food. He left Jim's lunch on the low-slung coffee table, then pulled a cloth bag off his shoulders and extracted two leather loafers. "Got your shoes," he said. "I'll leave 'em in the bedroom closet with the rest of your stuff."

"Thank you so much," Jim said with a grateful smile.

Harry hesitated for a long moment, then offered Jim a hesitant smile in return. "You play real good," he said, his voice growing bolder. "I heard you when I was walkin' down the hill. Nessie told me you used to be in a band."

"That's right," Jim replied. "I was one of the Pilots. You ever heard of us?"

Harry's jaw dropped. "You're one of the Stone Temple Pilots?"

"No!" Jim laughed. "Different band. My group was just called 'The Pilots.' We broke up in the early Seventies."

"Oh." Harry shrugged in disappointment. "Still. That's kinda cool."

"I agree," Jim laughed. "It was kinda cool."

Harry looked down at his feet for a long moment and rocked back and forth on his heels, then drew in a deep breath and looked back at Jim.

"So I called your friend at the museum, and she said she'd still like to see you. She asked me to drop you off tomorrow morning. She promised to get you to the airport after that. And I talked to Katie's Budweiser guy. He said he could pick me up at the Hertz office, so long as I'm willin' to help him with his beer run."

Harry looked back down at his feet and sighed, as if his long speech had taken the wind out of him.

"God, you're amazing!" Jim exclaimed. "I can't thank you enough!"

"It's no big deal," Harry replied. He looked back up and locked eyes with Jim. "I like drivin'. Some mornings I just get in my truck, drive to the highway and see where the road takes me. I need to get away every once in a while. This place kind of gets to me sometimes."

Jim nodded thoughtfully. "So, we'll both be springing the joint, eh?"

Harry shrugged once more. "Nah. It's not that bad. It's just—it just sometimes seems like there's a lot of bad karma floatin' around here. Like some sort of restless spirit is hauntin' the place."

"I think I know what you mean," Jim agreed, struggling to hide his grin.

"So whatd'ya want for dinner this evening?" Harry asked. "You should have somethin' nice for your last meal."

Jim thought for a long moment, then remembered his first conversation with Nessie. "Could you please ask Nessie to make me one of her omelets? I've heard they're pretty fine."

"You heard right," Harry agreed. "They are pretty fine. Anything else?"

Jim started to shake his head, but then a slight breeze drifted in through the open front door, carrying with it the scent of honeysuckle. He breathed in the intoxicatingly sweet smell. Then his eyes fell on the faint blue mark that still lingered on his hand. He looked back at Harry and smiled.

"Could you also please bring me some strawberries?" he asked. "Big, fat, juicy strawberries?"

"Well, I dunno if we've got any fat and juicy ones in the garden yet, but I'll see what I can round up," Harry replied.

Jim's mind started to race. "And a chocolate bar?" he added. "Something sweet that melts in your mouth."

"You sure are hungry, huh?" Harry noted.

Jim laughed. "And something spicy too. Salsa with jalapenos maybe, or a bowl of curry sauce."

Harry eyed Jim dubiously but promised to ask Nessie to put some spicy condiments on the tray. He started walking towards the bedroom, but Jim called out to him once more.

"Do you have anything soft to the touch in your house? I don't know—maybe an angora sweater, or a velvet pillow?"

"You want an angora sweater?" Harry retorted, casting Jim a suspicious look.

Jim threw him a loopy grin and raised his hands in a self-deprecating gesture. He knew he sounded like a complete fool, but he'd gone too far to back down from his plan now. "It doesn't have to be a sweater. Just something that feels good against your skin."

Harry stared at Jim blankly for a long moment, then offered him a sad smile. "I got my mom's old winter coat with a fur collar and cuffs. That's pretty soft. I used to like rubbin' my face against the fur when I was little. Dad tried to throw it away after she left, but I pulled it out of the trash when he wasn't lookin' and hid it in the back of my closet." He looked down at his feet. "But you pro'bly wouldn't like it. I think it smells like mothballs now."

"That would be perfect!" Jim exclaimed. "Bring some other smelly things too! Garlic cloves and a bottle of ammonia. And something that smells really good, like perfume or aftershave. And some scented candles."

"This is gonna be one hell of a last meal," Harry noted. He brushed back his bangs and threw Jim another dubious look. "Are you plannin' on havin' company?"

"Yes, actually," Jim answered. "I would like you to ask your Uncle Cliff to stop by around midnight. There's something I want to say to him before I go."

"I don't think he wants to talk to you no more," Harry replied. He shifted his gaze away from Jim and looked out the front door. "He told Nessie and me that he should'ah just left you for dead when he found you."

Jim sat in silence, offering no reply until Harry turned back towards him. Then he gazed directly into Harry's eyes and spoke in a calm, measured voice. "Then please tell your uncle that his presence has been specifically requested by a person who should be dead, but isn't."

Harry gave Jim another funny look and asked him to repeat his sentence.

"I'll write it down," Jim replied. He grabbed the note pad and pencil he had found inside the piano bench when he was searching for sheet music, then scribbled down his invitation and handed it to Harry.

Harry bit his lip, but promised to deliver the note to his uncle.

"Thanks," Jim said. "You really are a fine young man."

"That's what my grandpa used to say," Harry mumbled. He turned and walked into the bedroom to drop off the shoes. Then he left the cottage, shutting the front door behind him.

Jim threw a brief glance at the tray of food Harry had left for him on the coffee table. He noticed the usual earthenware plates had been replaced by plastic dishes, and smiled to himself. Then he cocked his head and let his gaze fall upon the wooden cane propped against the wall by the front door. He grabbed his crutches and hobbled over to it, then picked it up by its crook, leaned his weight against it, and took his first small step.

# Chapter Twenty-Two

## The Closet by the Door

Maggie sprang up from her chair at the sound of the doorbell. "That must be your mum," she told Robbie and Clara. "Collect your things. I'll let her in."

"But the movie's not done yet," Robbie whined.

Clara stood up from the sofa and grabbed her backpack. "It's way past tea time," she reminded him.

Maggie opened her front door and welcomed Philippa into her hallway. "They're packed and ready to go," she said.

Robbie glanced over his shoulder. "Can't we finish watching this movie, Mummy?" he pleaded. "It's almost over!"

Philippa squinted at the small television screen. "But you've seen *Jurassic Park* already in the cinema."

Robbie focused his eyes back on the television. "Miss Grayson rented it for us at Blockbuster after church this morning. Please, Mummy, it's at the good part!"

Philippa arched an eyebrow at Maggie. "You took them to church?"

Maggie met her gaze. "You left them in my care for the weekend. That's where I go on Sunday mornings." She threw a quick glance at the television, then looked back at

Philippa. "I've seen this film already too. There's only about ten minutes left. Come to my kitchen, why don't you? I'll make you a cuppa while we wait, and you can tell me all about Thorp Green."

Philippa eyed her warily. "You sound like you know the place already."

Maggie shrugged. "I've seen it before, many years ago."

Philippa furrowed her brow, but then a flash of insight washed over her face. "Oh, right. Wes told me one of the previous owners showed it to the public through the National Trust."

Maggie bit back a laugh. "Yes, that's right. Though I suppose your friend has put an end to all that. Can't say I blame him. Celebrities need their privacy. Though I *am* curious to learn what he's done to the house since I was last there."

Philippa's mask of cold reserve started to melt, and she offered Maggie a rare smile. "I'm sure you wouldn't recognize it. Wes brought in this Belgian designer who did the whole place over in a sort of 'boho-chic-meets-the-Raj' décor. There's a giant stuffed tiger standing in the foyer in front of a portrait of one of the home's original owners. It almost looked like a Gainsborough. The painting, that is. Not the tiger."

"I think it was by Joshua Reynolds," Maggie replied. "If it's the portrait I'm remembering."

"Miss Grayson, we can't hear the telly!" Robbie shouted over his shoulder.

"Mind your manners, Robbie!" Philippa shouted back at him.

"C'mon, let's go to my kitchen," Maggie whispered.

"Okay," Philippa agreed reluctantly, but then she eyed the door to the hall closet and rested her fingers on its knob. "This is a walk-in, right?"

Maggie flinched. "Um, yes, though it's rather small," she replied hesitantly.

Philippa's eyes sparkled mischievously. "Come in here with me instead. I want to tell you a secret!" She threw open the door and pulled the string hanging from the ceiling to switch on the light.

Maggie threw an anxious glance at the top shelf. "I don't understand," she protested.

"C'mon," Philippa whispered, grabbing her arm. She pulled Maggie into the closet and shut the door behind her. "I want to tell you something without the children hearing, but you have to promise me you won't tell *anyone*!"

"Well, um, okay—" Maggie stammered. She leaned against her winter coat and tried not to look worried.

"So, the party was going just swimmingly," Philippa began, flashing an impish look at Maggie. "But then last night, right before midnight, Wes got into a row with his manager Jack Straub. I don't know what they were fighting about. They were both drunk—practically legless! It looked like they were about to come to blows. Then Maria Gerard— that gorgeous Reggae singer Jack just signed up—threw a glass of champagne in Wes's face to shut him up! Wes stared at her for a few seconds, all beady-eyed, champagne dripping off his nose. Then he let loose a torrent of insults—my God, Miss Grayson!—he called her every racial slur in the book! It sounded like a pack of skinheads had crashed the party! But all of those vile words were coming right out of *Wes Von Alters'* mouth!"

Philippa laughed so hard that her eyes watered. She put her hand to her heart. "Jack made us all sign papers before we left, swearing we would never leak the story to the press! But I just had to tell *some*one!"

Maggie chuckled nervously. "I don't know what to say. I don't know much about Mr. Von Alters, but I always thought he had a rather squeaky clean image, almost like Cliff Richards."

"I'm so glad I didn't stay with him after his first album," Philippa confessed, wiping a tear from her cheek. "I'd hate to be working for such a bigot." She smiled brightly, but then immediately frowned. "You won't tell a living soul what I just told you, will you? Promise me?"

Maggie darted her eyes to the top shelf, then offered Philippa a conspiratorial smile. "Don't worry. Your secret is safe with me."

A knock on the closet door interrupted their exchange. Maggie turned the knob and saw Clara standing in the hallway with her mouth agape.

"What are you two *doing* in there?" she asked.

"Never you mind," Philippa scolded, her face resuming its familiar stern look. "The film has ended. I hear the title song. Now fetch your things so we can drive home."

Philippa followed Maggie out of the closet. "Thank you so much for watching them," she said in the kindest voice Maggie had ever heard her use. "You really are a lifesaver. I promise I'll write you a nice big check next month after my ex comes back from the States and pays me my alimony."

Maggie nodded and turned to Robbie and Clara. They each allowed her to hug them briefly while they mumbled their goodbyes. Then they clutched their sleeping bags to their chests and followed their mother out of the house.

Maggie walked to her front window and watched the taillights of Philippa's BMW recede into the distance. Then she glanced at the television set and let her mind wander back to her own memories of Thorp Green for a few seconds while the movie credits rolled by in a blur.

*There must be something about that house that brings out the worst in people,* she decided. *Perhaps it's haunted by the ghost of that man in the painting by the door!*

The videotape came to an end with a loud clap, then made a high-pitched whirring noise as it started to rewind. Maggie glanced over her shoulder and realized she had forgotten to close her closet door. She walked into her hallway and approached the closet cautiously.

"Agnes? Are you there?" she called up to the top shelf.

Hearing no response, she put her hand to the string hanging from the ceiling and shut off the light.

"That woman is a dreadful gossip," called a voice from the darkness. "I imagine she'll be blabbering her secrets to the newspapers before you can say 'Bob's your uncle'."

Maggie sighed and took a step backwards. "Perhaps you're right, Agnes. Though I think not. If Philippa McCudden ever wants to sing professionally again, she'll need to keep in Wes Von Alters' good graces. He's a very big star. I imagine he has the power to make or break any aspiring singer's career."

"Why would she want to return to the life of a wanton strumpet, performing on a stage?" challenged Agnes. "She found herself a wealthy husband, who gave her two handsome children, and he continues to support her, despite their estrangement. Most men I know would shun a divorcée. My father always preached that marriage was an indissoluble union."

"Well, things have changed a lot since your father was a preacher," Maggie said irritably. "Nowadays, a woman can do almost anything she wishes."

"Wishes are like tinder," Agnes replied. "My father used to say that too. He was such a wise man."

Maggie stared into the dark closet for a long moment, then slumped her shoulders in defeat. "I have no idea what you're talking about. Now, if you'll excuse me, I'm going to tidy up my house and go to bed."

"You'll thank me someday," Agnes called back. "For all the advice I've given you."

Maggie tightened her grip on the doorknob and fought back the urge to scream at her unwelcome intruder. "I hardly think so, Agnes," she said instead. "You're not giving me advice at all. You're just haranguing me with tedious stories about your own life."

"That's not true," Agnes protested. Her clipped voice grew soft and took on a surprisingly gentle tone. "I am a woman very much like yourself, my dearest Maggie. I was a teacher, just like you are. I had no great prospects, and faced the daunting likelihood of life-long spinsterhood, just like you do. But I did not give in to loneliness. I sought love, and found it. And you should too."

Maggie flushed. She fiddled with the knob and considered slamming the door shut, but a nagging twinge of curiosity got the better of her. "Explain yourself," she demanded.

"Wishes are like tinder," Agnes repeated. "The flint and steel of circumstances are continually striking out sparks. But they vanish immediately, unless they chance to fall upon the tinder of our wishes. Then, they instantly ignite, and the flame of hope is kindled in a moment."

Maggie closed her eyes and breathed rapidly through her nose to assuage her growing impatience. "I'm not following you, Agnes," she said. "You're not making any sense."

"What do you wish for?" Agnes asked. "What do you hope for?"

Maggie opened her eyes and reached for the string. "Well, for one thing, I wish you would reveal yourself to me," she said, giving the string a sharp tug. The lightbulb flashed on.

A small, thin woman stood before her, dressed in a long, grey, Victorian gown. Her hair was brushed back smoothly from her forehead. Her heart-shaped face looked strangely familiar, but Maggie was too shocked by the woman's sudden appearance to make any guess as to where she might have seen her before.

Agnes reached out her gloved hand towards Maggie. "Don't forget me," she whispered. "And don't forget the things that I have told you."

Maggie stood frozen on her feet. She stared wide-eyed at the apparition with an overpowering and deeply unsettling mixture of wonder and fear. Then she slowly, hesitantly, lifted her hand off the knob of the closet door and touched Agnes' glove. A chill ran through her.

Agnes' body started to shimmer. Her eyes glowed a soft golden hue. She curled her thin, pursed lips into a half-smile. Then she dissipated into nothingness, like a glow worm fading into the night.

Maggie swallowed hard. She staggered backwards and almost fell against the opposite wall. Then she took a long, deep breath, and ran to her kitchen to grab her Zinfandel.

# Chapter Twenty-Three

## A Fantabulous Night

Jim sniffed each of the scented candles Harry had dropped off at dinnertime, then scattered them strategically around his bedroom, creating small, pungent pockets of floral, spiced and woodsy aromas. He lit the wicks with the plastic cigarette lighter he had found on his first night in the cottage. Then he sat down in the chair beside his bed, rested his hands on the crook of his cane, and let the hot, waxy fragrances fill the room while he waited for his guests.

Cliff was the first to arrive. He slammed the cottage's front door shut with a loud bang, stormed into the bedroom, and started hollering at Jim. "You've got a hell of a lot of nerve writing that note for Harry to see, you bastard! What kind of game do you think you're playing?"

"I'm not playing any game," Jim replied, meeting Cliff's eyes with a preternaturally calm gaze. "I'm just doing what Cathy asked me to do. So calm down. You're killing the mood." He gestured to a cluster of flickering candles and smiled.

"*She* invited me here?" Cliff challenged, cocking his bushy eyebrows in disbelief. "You didn't just make up that message?"

"She told me to ask you to bring me some tasty food," Jim said.

"You're fuckin' crazy," Cliff cursed. He threw a glance at the tall bayberry candle flickering on the nightstand beside a bowl of strawberries, and snorted. "And you're kinky too. You want me to sit here and watch you eat strawberries by candlelight with my dead girlfriend."

"No," Jim replied in a steady voice. "I want *you* to eat the strawberries."

"You're full of shit!" Cliff yelled. He turned away from Jim, then stopped dead on his feet. Cathy was standing in the bedroom doorway, scowling at him.

"*You're* the one who's full of shit!" she howled. "You're so fucking mean! You haven't got one decent bone in your body. You're a selfish asshole! You screw people over just for fun, then run away and leave everyone else to clean up your messes!"

Cliff stared at her incredulously. "*I* screw people over just for fun? What the hell are you talking about, woman? *You're* the one who plays games with people's lives! *You're* the one who ran off with Joe just to see if you could get a rise out of me!"

"Well, *you're* the one who ran off to begin with!" she retorted. "*You* started it!"

"*I* didn't—" Cliff protested, but before he could finish his sentence, Jim stood up and stuffed a strawberry into his mouth.

"Take a bite," Jim commanded him. "And tell her what it tastes like. She misses eating."

Cliff spat out the strawberry. "Screw you!" he barked.

"You just wasted a perfectly good strawberry," Jim replied coolly. "Please don't do that again. You're going to cheese her off. And Cathy is a woman who doesn't like being cheesed off. Trust me. I know a thing or two about women who don't like being cheesed off. Now take this food that your nephew brought me. Cathy wants to watch you eat it. She wants you to describe how it tastes. And she wants you to be nice to her. She wants you to make her feel special."

Cliff clenched his right hand into a fist and lifted it towards Jim's face. But before he could throw a punch, Jim looked away and grabbed the lantern off the nightstand. Then he clutched his cane with his free hand and faced his two companions.

"Now if you'll excuse me, I have a musical engagement to keep. I'm going to serenade two hopeless romantics who don't know how to romance one another."

He limped out of the bedroom, assuming all the dignity that a man wearing a pair of chartreuse-and-fuchsia striped polyester pajamas could hope to project, and hobbled to the piano in the living room.

He placed the lantern on top of the instrument and lifted the cover off the keys. Then he sat down at the bench and started playing the first song he had planned—his former bandmate Eddie Rochester's biggest hit, "Dreaming Tonight"—since Cathy and Cliff had each complimented Eddie in previous conversations. When he finished playing, he rested his hands in his lap and listened for a response. Cathy and Cliff's voices were audible in the next room, but muffled.

*Well, at least they're not arguing,* he thought with relief. He cracked his knuckles and started playing a trio of tunes about true love—Paul McCartney's "I Will," Irving Berlin's "Always," and the Platters' "Only You." He considered polishing off his medley with Diana Ross and Lionel Richie's chart-topping duet "Endless Love," but imagined Cliff would probably hate the song and segued instead into the Righteous Brothers' "Unchained Melody."

He pounded the last chords of the power ballad in a drawn-out coda, then stopped playing once more. He could no longer hear voices in the bedroom. He glanced out the cottage's front window and saw a full yellow moon hanging low in the sky. Smiling to himself, he brought his hands back to the keyboard and played the jazzy syncopated opening to Van Morrison's "Moondance" while he imagined Cathy singing about the night's whispering magic.

*This is such a sweet little song,* he thought as he worked his way through the verses and chorus. But then he considered the intensity of Cliff and Cathy's passion. Their love defied all standards of human decency. It defied even the constraints of death. It was operatic. So he impulsively shelved the pop ballads he had rehearsed earlier that day and started playing Puccini arias instead. From there he branched into Chopin's dramatic "Prelude in C Minor." Then he remembered how Barry Manilow had used the opening measures of that opus as the intro to his smash hit "Could It Be Magic?" and chuckled to himself.

*Well, Cliff and Cathy were lovers back in the Seventies,* he reflected. *Maybe they liked that song.* He started weaving Manilow's melody over the chords, and softly intoned the lyrics about a spirit moving like a cyclone in the mind.

He finished the song and considered his next number. A vision of Cliff shaking a maraca and singing "Copacabana" danced in front of his eyes. He bit back a laugh. *Cliff's probably not a Fanilow,* he promptly decided. He tried to imagine what song Cliff might sing to Cathy in his deep, gravelly voice, and immediately thought of Joe Cocker's "You Are So Beautiful." He put his hands back to the keyboard and started playing Cocker's heart-rending ballad.

The night wore on. Jim kept up a steady stream of melodies, playing all the classic love songs from the Sixties and Seventies that he could remember, and hoping that a few tunes might strike a chord with the haunted lovers in the next room. Then he rested his fingers on the keys and stole another glance out the front window. The dawn was breaking.

He stood up from the bench, picked up his cane and lantern, and limped back to the bedroom as unobtrusively as he could.

The tangy smell of melted candle wax hit him squarely in the face as he approached the open door. He peeked inside and saw a plastic plate resting on the floor. It was covered with discarded strawberry hulls, jalapeno pepper stems, and a half-eaten bar of chocolate.

He stepped into the room and stole a glance at the bed. Cliff was sleeping naked on top of the blankets. Cuddled up in his arms, wrapped tightly in Harry's mother's fur coat, was Cathy. Her eyes were closed in ghostly slumber; her sultry lips were curled into a contented smile.

A dim glow from the muted dawn filled the room. Then a sunbeam burst through the window and landed directly on the foot of the bed. It lingered there for a moment, then started climbing towards the headboard along with the arc of the rising sun. It passed across Cliff's right shoulder, then settled upon Cathy, bathing her pale face in an intense bright light. Blinded by her radiance, Jim turned his head away.

When he looked back, Cathy was gone.

# Chapter Twenty-Four

## A Farewell

Jim collected his clean clothes from the closet, hobbled into the bathroom to change, then returned to the bedroom to put on his shoes. He approached the door cautiously, not wanting to disturb Cliff, and was met by a malodorous cloud of fresh cigarette smoke. He knocked on the wooden doorframe and peeked inside the room once more.

Cliff was sitting upright in the bed, his back resting against the headboard. He had pulled the blankets up to his waist and thrown a shirt over his shoulders, though he hadn't bothered to button it. Harry's red-and-black baseball cap was perched on top of his head, its wide brim casting a shadow over the top half of his face. He took a long drag on his cigarette and asked Jim if he'd like a smoke too.

"No thank you," Jim said. He limped into the room and draped his striped pajamas over the back of the captain's chair. "I just came to get my shoes so I'll be ready when Harry arrives."

"Suit yourself," Cliff said indifferently.

Jim slipped on his left loafer with ease. Then he sat down in the chair, squeezed the brace on his right ankle, and maneuvered his injured foot into his other shoe with considerable difficulty. He winced at the snug fit, then gripped the arm of the chair and stood back up.

Cliff chuckled. "Don't take that brace off. You still need it. Ask Harry to find you a bedroom slipper to wear instead of your shoe before you leave. It'll fit better."

"I have one in my suitcase," Jim replied. "I'll pull it out when I get to the car."

Cliff nodded, then offered Jim a sly smile. "Nice touch, the Barry Manilow. She always liked that song."

Jim grinned back. "So did my ex-wife. Cathy reminds me a lot of her."

"Really?" Cliff laughed. "I always thought Cathy was one of a kind."

"Well," Jim said hesitantly. "I didn't say they were *entirely* alike."

"Mmmm," Cliff mumbled. Jim grabbed his cane and started hobbling towards the door, but then Cliff called out to him. "The ammonia was good too. She really liked that."

Jim looked back at him. "No kidding?"

"Yeah, she kept making me inhale deep whiffs of it and try to describe the scent. I nearly puked. But just when I thought I was gonna pass out, she took it from me and sniffed it herself." Cliff hesitated a moment before adding, "And she smelled it."

Jim cocked his eyebrow. "Really? She could smell the ammonia?"

"Yeah. She could," Cliff replied with a shrug. He turned his face away from Jim and stared at the glowing tip of his cigarette. "And then she cried."

"She cried?" Jim asked incredulously. "She told me she couldn't cry tears anymore."

"She cried tears last night."

"Oh," Jim mumbled. He took another small step towards the door, then turned and faced the bed again. "You know, she may be a ghost, but I think she's almost more real to me than you are. I feel like I know her. But everything about you is shrouded in mystery."

Cliff snorted. "No it's not," he said defiantly.

"Nessie told me no one even knows where you come from," Jim countered.

Cliff took a last puff on his cigarette and crushed the stub out in a dish on the nightstand. "*I* know where I'm from," he said without looking up at Jim. "I remember what my life was like before I came to live with the Shaws. I just don't like talking about it."

Jim immediately called to mind what Nessie had told him about Cliff's mysterious origins. He tried to picture the crooked "preacher man" who had used Cliff as a prop in his revivals, then abandoned him into the hands of strangers. He tried to imagine the horrors Cliff must have faced at that tender age—abuse, public humiliation, criminal neglect, desertion. "Maybe you should talk to someone about that," he suggested gently. "It might be good for you."

"I have," Cliff replied. "Cathy knows all about it."

"Oh," Jim whispered.

*Of course he told her,* Jim realized with a flash of insight. He felt like a fool for not suspecting it earlier. He took another step towards the door, then stopped and turned one last time. "Can I ask how you made your money when you ran away from home?"

"I didn't run away from home," Cliff retorted. "I just left home when I finished high school. Like a lot of people do."

"But most people don't fly to Hong Kong and break off all contact with their family," Jim argued.

Cliff shrugged.

Jim frowned at Cliff. "Nessie told me you studied traditional Asian medicine while you were there."

"Yeah," Cliff agreed. "But that's not exactly a lucrative line of work."

"Right," Jim replied. He sighed and clutched the crook of his cane, then started turning towards the door.

"You got a Walkman?" Cliff called up to him.

Jim furrowed his brow. "A portable cassette player? Of course I do. But not with me."

"I invented them," Cliff said, his lips curling into another shrewd smile.

Jim stepped closer to the bed. "No you didn't. Sony invented them. I remember when they first came out."

"But I came up with the idea. I met a guy who worked for Sony when I was studying Kampō with a botanist in Yokohama, and we created the prototype together. The engineers perfected the design, but I did all the original drawings. I got a big cash advance in the mid-Seventies, and a percentage of the company's profits once they started selling the machines. The money's been rolling in ever since."

Jim eyed Cliff dubiously. "How did you come up with the idea?"

"Oh, I'd been thinking about it for years," Cliff boasted. "Ever since I was a kid and Cathy used to make me take all those long walks with her. She was such a flower-child. She'd stay outside for hours in a storm so she could listen to the wind whistling through the trees. Some days she literally wanted to lie down in the meadow and watch the goddamned grass grow. I'd get so fuckin' bored. So I'd stretch out on the ground beside her while she was communing with the cosmos and think about how nice it would be if I could pass the time listening to music. I had a transistor radio, but I hated listening to deejays and stupid commercials and songs I didn't like. And I had a cassette player too, but it was too big to carry around on long walks. I wanted something small that would fit in my shirt pocket, but with earphones, so I could listen to my tapes without disturbing Cathy. I think I was about twelve when I first came up with the idea."

Jim chuckled. "I don't believe you."

"Last week you didn't believe in ghosts either, did you?" Cliff replied.

Before Jim could think of a response, he heard Harry opening the front door. "I'm gonna go now," he said. "Thank you for tending to my foot and feeding me."

"Anytime you're in the neighborhood," Cliff replied nonchalantly.

"Please give my best to Nessie," Jim added. "I'm sorry I didn't get the chance to say goodbye to her."

"I will," Cliff mumbled.

Jim called out to Harry that he'd be ready in a minute, then took another step towards the bed and said, "Goodbye."

Cliff offered no response.

Jim looked squarely at Cliff's face. "Thanks again."

Cliff lifted his chin, bringing his face into the light at last, and murmured a quiet, "Bye."

He met Jim's gaze for only a moment, but in that brief glance, Jim could see that a faint yellow cast had crept into his eyes.

# Chapter Twenty-Five

## The Frenchman

Maggie's temples throbbed. Her mouth felt like someone had stuffed it with cotton balls. She opened her eyes slowly and glanced at the clock on her nightstand. It was almost noon.

"Oh God!" Maggie moaned. She sat up straight in her bed and felt a rumble in her stomach.

*I'm hungover,* she realized. *I haven't woken up hungover since I was in my twenties. Lord help me, how much wine did I drink last night?*

Her mind trailed off. She felt too sick to think.

She threw a glance at the three black dresses lying in a heap on her floor and let loose a dry, mirthless laugh. It had seemed like such a good idea to try them on last night, she vaguely recalled. She'd felt like she was playing dress-up with a fashionable friend. And even though the gowns all looked hideous on her, they had come from Philippa. And she had felt such a strange rush of affection for Philippa last night.

Jim's ex had been so nice to her when she'd come to collect the children. A little creepy, perhaps, Maggie realized as she stared dumbly at the pile of clothes. But nice in a Philippa-sort-of-way. She'd taken Maggie into her confidence, and even smiled at her in the closet.

The closet.

Maggie shut her eyes and swallowed hard. She gulped down a mouthful of spit and felt like gagging. She slid back under her covers and tried to fall back to sleep.

Percy meowed at her door. Then he started clawing at the wood.

*Damn cat,* she thought crossly. She pulled her knees to her chest and wrapped her arms around them, hoping to quell the growing nausea that was forming in the pit of her gut.

It didn't work.

The urge to vomit came on like a gale. She tore off her covers, leapt out of bed, and flung open her bedroom door. Percy howled at her in surprise. She covered her mouth with both of her hands and jumped over him as she dashed to the bathroom.

Percy trotted after her and met her at the toilet. He rubbed his ears against her legs as she knelt in front of the porcelain bowl, then hopped over her outstretched calves and started licking the upturned soles of her feet.

Maggie grabbed the toilet handle shakily and flushed away her puke. Then she fell back against the bathroom wall and sighed. Percy jumped onto her lap and purred. She wrapped her arms around him and started stroking his fur.

"You're a real kitty," she whispered hoarsely as she tickled him under his chin. "A real, flesh-and-blood kitty. And you and I are the only ones who live in this house. There are no ghosts living in my closet. I just imagined that. I've just been imagining that strange woman's voice for weeks now. It was all some sort of hallucination. A midlife psychotic crisis."

Percy butted her chest with his head, then jumped off her lap and walked to the door. He flashed her an impatient look and meowed.

"You don't care that I'm hungover, do you, you selfish little wanker?" she asked in a fawning voice. "You just want your breakfast."

Maggie stared dumbly at the cat until she felt certain that her stomach was settled. Then she climbed off the floor, walked to the sink, splashed cold water over her face, and examined herself in the mirror. A pale, puffy, bleary-eyed face stared back at her.

Percy meowed again.

"Alright, alright," she chided the cat. "Just let me wash this horrid taste out of my mouth."

She scrubbed her teeth and the inside of her cheeks with her toothbrush. Then she swallowed two aspirin, grabbed her dressing gown off its hook on the bathroom door, and followed Percy down the stairs.

She cast a quick, nervous glance at her hall closet when she reached the bottom step, but fought back the impulse to look inside. She walked to her kitchen instead, steeled her nerves, and cautiously opened her pantry to fetch a tin of meat for Percy.

No voice called out to her.

She sighed in relief, then grabbed Percy's breakfast and a box of tea bags for herself. She put her kettle on to boil, opened the tin of cat food, and scraped the minced tuna onto a plate. Then she petted Percy's back affectionately as he ate.

The doorbell rang.

"No," Maggie said emphatically to Percy. "I am not in any position to receive visitors."

The doorbell rang three more times in rapid succession.

"Lord help me," Maggie moaned. She stood up, rushed past the hall closet without lifting her eyes from the floor, and looked out the peephole on her front door.

A ridiculously handsome young man was standing on her porch.

"This must be a mistake," she grumbled under her breath.

She opened her door a few inches and addressed her visitor. "I'm sorry, but I can't see anyone at the moment."

"*S'il vous plaît, mademoiselle,*" the man replied. "I em Jean-Claude. Philippa haz asked mee to call on yeu."

Maggie ran her fingers through her unbrushed hair and sighed. "Whatever for?"

"I hev cumm to fetch ze teddy."

"You have *what?*" Maggie blustered.

"Clara's leetle bear," he explained. "She haz left eet here. Eet eez small and bleu."

Maggie closed her eyes and tried to remember if she had seen such a toy in her house. A dim memory of Clara shoving a stuffed animal into a pillowcase flashed through her mind. Her temples started to throb afresh at the effort of thinking. She opened the door.

"You can look for it," she agreed. "It's probably stuck behind one of the sofa cushions."

Jean-Claude stepped into the living room and started searching for the bear.

The kettle whistled. "I'll get that!" Maggie shouted over the shrill noise. She ran to her stove and nearly tripped over Percy as she pulled the kettle off the burner.

The telephone rang.

"Oh, *please!*" she shouted, her exasperation escalating.

"Azz you weesh!" Jean-Claude called back to her. He ran into the kitchen and grabbed the phone off the hook.

"No, no, I didn't mean—" Maggie pleaded. She put the kettle back on the hot burner, setting it screaming anew, and tried to grab the phone away from Jean-Claude.

"*Bonjour!* Who mey I zay eez cahlling?" he said into the mouthpiece. He reached his free arm towards the stovetop, deftly moved the shrieking kettle to a cool burner, and offered Maggie the phone. "Eet eez Helene Nussay," he announced. He turned to walk out of the kitchen, then spied the wine-stained goblet and two empty Zinfandel bottles resting on the counter. He flashed Maggie a knowing smile, then left the room.

Maggie glared at Jean-Claude as he retreated, her nostrils flaring in irritation. Then she sat down at her table to talk to her old friend.

"Who was *that?!*" Ellen Nussey asked in a voice so loud that Maggie had to pull the phone away from her ear.

"Nobody," Maggie stated bluntly. She rubbed at her throbbing temples. "A friend of a friend. Not even. How are you?"

"I'm fine," Ellen replied. "I just rang to ask if you're coming to my party for Mary."

Maggie stared longingly at the wisps of steam escaping from the tea kettle. "Oh, right. I've been so busy lately I'd almost forgotten about that. Of course I'll be there. What can I bring?"

Jean-Claude returned to the kitchen, clutching a small blue bear in his right hand. He leaned towards the telephone and whispered, "I hev found ze missing teddy." He waved the toy in front of Maggie's face and smiled seductively. "I weel go now. *Adieu.*"

Ellen squealed in delight, forcing Maggie to once again pull the phone away from her ear.

"Oh, bring him to the party, please!" Ellen begged. "Eet weell be zoh much fun!"

"No, Ellen," Maggie insisted, clenching her teeth. "I hardly know him."

"Really?" Ellen laughed. "You hardly know him, but he knows where you keep your teddies?"

Maggie ended the conversation as politely as she could and hung up the phone. She stood up to fill her teapot, then glanced down at Percy. He was licking the last of the tuna off his plate.

"It's going to be that kind of a day, isn't it?" she asked the cat.

Percy cleaned his paws, then started walking in circles between her legs, rubbing his face against her pajama pants.

She crouched down to pet him, then brought the teapot to the table. She opened the cupboard over her sink to pull out a clean mug. No voice addressed her.

She flashed Percy an anxious look. "Shall we brave a glimpse at the hall closet?"

Percy stretched his mouth into an enormous yawn.

"Oh, come on, you!" she exclaimed. She scooped him up and walked into her hallway. She held the cat close to her chest with her left arm and put her right hand on the knob. "Here we go, sweet boy. On the count of three—one, two, *three!*"

She flung the door open.

The Victorian woman was gone.

Percy arched his back and squirmed. Maggie let him free, then leaned into the closet and whispered, "Agnes?"

A hollow, blissful silence met her remark.

Maggie stood back, crossed her arms in front of her chest, and smiled.

# Chapter Twenty-Six

## A Spirit from the Past

Harry pulled Jim's suitcase out of the trunk of the Jaguar and rested it on the curb by the Hall of Fame's back entrance. Jim shook his hand goodbye, then turned towards the silver-haired museum curator standing in front of the door marked 'Employees Only.'

"Thanks so much for rescheduling our appointment, Mrs. Anderson," he said. He shook hands with her, then shifted his cane back to his right hand and started reaching for the bag with his left.

"No problem," the woman replied. She stepped in front of him and grabbed his suitcase. "Please—don't strain yourself. I'll carry this for you. And call me Trish. Everyone does."

"Thanks. Please call me Jim. Now let me get that door for you at least," he offered.

Trish slipped past him and propped open the heavy door before he had even taken his first step. He blushed at his helplessness, but offered her a game smile and started limping towards the building.

"Just wait here for a sec while I put your bag in my office," she directed Jim as soon as they had both stepped inside. "Then I'll take you upstairs so you can see the exhibit space. I'm sorry you weren't here for our brainstorming sessions, but I hope you'll be happy with what we've done so far." She glanced at her wristwatch. "We should have a little time to see the old pianos in private before the rest of the crew gets here."

Jim nodded and leaned on his cane while he waited for Trish to return. Then he followed her down a long corridor. She slackened her pace to match his as they walked.

"I was so sorry to hear about your injury," she said as she led him to the elevator. "I hope you had a good doctor taking care of you."

"Well—" Jim began, unsure of how much information he wanted to share with this stranger. "I think he was good. It was my first experience with a homeopath."

"Oh! I use them all the time!" she exclaimed. "Personally, I don't much care for traditional doctors. They just wave you in and out of their offices and hand you bottles of pills. I like a caregiver with a more human touch."

"This bloke didn't believe in pills either," Jim said. "He only gave me teas and—" He considered mentioning the hand-rolled cigarettes, mushrooms, roots, and puffs on the hookah that Cliff had foisted upon him, then thought better of it. "Mostly, he just gave me tea."

"Good for him!" Trish replied. "I'm a great believer in the power of herbal teas and extracts. Though I've got my reasons, of course. I'm allergic to penicillin."

Jim flinched. "Oh. Funny you should mention that. I was just talking to—to someone else who was allergic to penicillin. I hadn't realized it was such a common allergy."

They reached the elevator door. Trish pushed a button to summon a car. "I don't think it is. But it runs in my family." Her expression turned wistful. "My daughter died from an allergic reaction."

"I'm so sorry to hear that," he said gently.

"Don't be," she insisted. She tilted her head to the side and shrugged one shoulder. "I mean, I appreciate your sympathy. But I really didn't know her at all."

The elevator doors opened, and Trish motioned to Jim to step in first. She followed him into the car and pushed the button to take them to the top floor.

"I never used to tell this to anyone," she admitted after the doors had closed. "But these days—well, it hardly seems like a scandal anymore. I had a baby when I was sixteen and gave her up for adoption. One of my mother's relatives raised her for me. You know how it was back in the Fifties. I got married a few years after that and never even told my husband about my first baby. But after he died, I tried to look her up. That's when I discovered she was dead."

Jim's stomach lurched. His face blanched, and he leaned on his cane to steady himself.

Trish reached out her hand and supported his elbow as the elevator came to a stop. "Sorry, these elevators are still a bit of a rough ride. An engineer is supposed to come in later this week to adjust them."

"I'm fine," Jim assured her. He pushed aside his racing thoughts and offered Trish a weak smile. "I'm sorry you had to give up your daughter, but at least she was raised by someone from your own family. I'm sure she was in good hands."

"Oh, she was," Trish agreed as the doors opened. She led Jim into another wide corridor. "The Shaws were very good people. A bit too religious for my taste, but they had kind hearts. And I know they loved my Cathy as if she were their own little girl. Now, if you'd care to step this way, Jim, I'll show you the piano that Jerry Lee Lewis played at his groundbreaking sessions at the Sun Recording Studio in Memphis. I can almost feel the spirits of Elvis Presley and Roy Orbison every time I walk by it! Would you like to sit down and tickle the ivories on this beautiful instrument for a bit?"

# Chapter Twenty-Seven

## The Recital

Maggie fidgeted self-consciously with the belt of her new silk dress and surveyed her surroundings. The reception seemed to be going well. The cake was half-eaten. Nobody had spilled any punch yet. The parents all appeared pleased with their children's performances, and each of her students seemed relieved to be done playing their pieces.

She proudly posed for a photo with her prized student David, who was moving on to the Royal Northern College of Music next year, then looked to her side and saw Jim McCudden approaching, leaning on an old wooden cane for support.

"It was a lovely recital, as always," he said, extending his free hand to shake hers.

"Thank you so much," she replied, her knees buckling only slightly at the touch of his skin. "You, um, I see you're walking—with a cane," she stuttered.

"Yes, I am," he agreed. He smiled at her warmly. "I like it much better than the crutches."

"Oh dear," she gasped. She started to ask about his injury, but was interrupted by a boisterous set of parents who wanted her to pose for a photo with their family.

Jim winked at her, then wandered off to fetch a glass of punch.

Maggie sucked in a deep breath as she watched him hobble away.

*Wishes are like tinder,* she reminded herself as she smiled for the camera. *But they vanish immediately, unless they—oh damn, what was it Agnes said again?*

She chitchatted politely with the father who had just snapped her photo. Then she turned her head to the side and stared at Jim's back.

*The flame of hope is kindled in a moment,* she remembered suddenly. *But what kindles it? Lord help me, why am I still thinking about that dreadful woman?*

She noticed Jim was limping back towards her. Her cheeks flushed. She put her hands to her face to cover them. Her skin felt warm.

Jim reached her side and asked if she'd heard Maurizio Pollini's recent recording of Chopin's Polonaises yet. But before she could respond, Philippa McCudden stormed up to her ex-husband and cut her off.

"So there you are," Philippa said through a forced smile. "Chatting up the piano teacher again, I see."

"Hello, Pippa," Jim replied coolly. "Didn't Robbie and Clara play beautifully?"

"Don't. Call. Me. Pippa!" she replied in a loud stage whisper.

Jean-Claude maneuvered his way through an unwieldy group of giggling students and took his place by Philippa's side. Kim Park, Maggie's other top student, gawked at him as he passed, then fell into an animated discussion with another teenaged girl about the Frenchman's insanely gorgeous face and perfectly shaped bum. Maggie blushed again.

Jim offered his children's French teacher a hearty handshake. *"Bonjour! Merci bien d'avoir appris mes enfants à parler Français."*

*"Je vous en prie,"* Jean-Claude replied. He pointed to Jim's wooden cane and asked with a look of concern, *"Vous êtes gravement blessé?"*

*"Non, c'est un rien,"* Jim demurred.

Before Jim could elaborate on the status of his injury, Philippa interrupted him once more. "Robbie and Clara aren't even *trying* to learn French. They've both got a very bad attitude about our upcoming vacation. I've half-a-mind to leave them with you for the entire month of August if they don't start stepping up their efforts."

"I'll have to check my schedule, Pippa, and see if I'm free," Jim remarked casually.

"You'd *better* be free," Philippa said. "Do you know how much trouble you caused me last week when you decided to fall off the face of the earth?"

Jim smiled at her in reply and continued to make small talk with Jean-Claude in French.

Philippa grunted in exasperation, then grabbed Jean-Claude by the elbow and dragged him away.

Jim turned his attention back to Maggie and sighed. "Sorry you had to witness that."

Maggie shrugged and offered him a sympathetic smile.

He looked into her eyes. "Thank you for watching my kids last weekend," he said, the joy returning to his voice. "Robbie told me he had a wonderful time. He said you let him watch movies past his bedtime both nights, and taught him how to make lasagna."

"And what did Clara tell you?" Maggie asked, bracing herself for a candid reply.

Jim frowned. "She told me you made her go to church."

Maggie smiled shyly. Jim laughed out loud. His eyes twinkled mischievously.

Maggie looked around to make certain Philippa was out of earshot, then asked Jim if he did, in fact, have any plans for the month of August.

"I usually go to the Salzburg Music Festival," he replied. "It's a habit I got into years ago when I lived in Munich, though I usually can't find anyone to go with me.

But maybe this year I can take the kids along. I enjoy concerts so much more when I'm with someone."

Maggie held Jim's gaze as Agnes' words came rushing into her head in a rapid jumble: *Wishes are like tinder. The flint and steel of circumstances are continually striking out sparks. But they vanish immediately, unless they chance to fall upon the tinder of our wishes. Then, they instantly ignite, and the flame of hope is kindled in a moment.*

She summoned her courage and proffered an invitation. "I saw in the paper that Maurizio Pollini will be performing with the Hallé Orchestra this coming Friday. Would you like to go see him with me?"

"I'd love to!" Jim replied, breaking into an enormous smile. He squeezed her hand briefly, then let it go.

Maggie's heart started racing at the touch of his hand. "That's wonderful!" she exclaimed. But then her face fell. "Oh, crap, no. I forgot. I'll be busy that evening. I'm going to a surprise party for a friend."

Jim took her hand back in his. "I read in the paper that Pollini will be giving a matinee performance with the Liverpool Philharmonic on the following Sunday. I think he's on tour, plugging his new record. Perhaps we could see him there instead."

Maggie gazed into his eyes, her teenage crush resurging with a vengeance. *I've got a date with a pop star!* she screamed in her head. "That would be lovely," she said breathlessly, struggling to appear calm.

"You'd have to drive, though," he said. He let go of her hand and gestured towards his injured foot. "Unless you'd rather take the train."

"I'd be happy to," she offered, her knees growing weak.

"Then it's a date," Jim replied. He gave her hand one more quick squeeze, then released it as another student's parent approached Maggie and asked for a photograph.

# Chapter Twenty-Eight

## The Package

Jim threw open his car door, lifted his jacket over his head, and made a mad dash to the front door of his house through the pouring rain. A crack of thunder rumbled in the distance. He grabbed his post from the mailbox, unlocked his front door, and ran inside.

After kicking off his shoes in the front hallway, he ran to the bathroom to throw his dripping jacket into the tub. Then he walked to his kitchen, his wet socks leaving damp footprints on the tiles as they squished across the floor, and threw his mail on the table. He switched on his electric kettle, pulled his red and yellow Manchester United mug from the cupboard, and sat down to sort through his post while the water came to a boil.

A bill for the gas, the new issue of *NME*, a letter from Oxfam, no doubt requesting money, and—

"Christ!" Jim muttered under his breath. His lips bent into a grimace as he reread the return address on the small brown package:

*Shaw's Botanicals, P.O. Box 1847, Cautley, Ohio 44139*

The teakettle started whistling. Jim tossed the package on his table and filled his mug with boiling water. Then he grabbed a bag of Typhoo tea from the box he kept on his counter and dunked it in his cup while memories of the strange brews Cliff had served him flooded his head. He brought his mug to the table, opened the envelope, and pulled out a long letter and a small packet of dried leaves. He flipped through the letter, saw Nessie's signature on the last page, and sighed in relief.

*Here I go again,* he thought, bringing the mug to his lips. *Sipping a cup of tea while Nessie spins me a long story.* He leaned back in his chair and started to read:

*Dear Jim,*

*Thank you for returning Mr. Shaw's cane. He would have been happy to know you put it to such good use. I sure am glad to hear your feeling fine and walking on your own again. I told you you were in good hands with Cliff now, didn't I?*

*That brings me to the reason I'm sending you this note. Cliff died last month. Not quite sure what it was that took him, because you know he never would go to any doctor. I suspect jaundice, because his eyes started looking kind of yellow toward the end, but I don't know.*

*He started growing weaker right after you left us. Not sure why. I took over all the greenhouse work, and he spent most of his time at the Grange. Slept there most nights too. But I think he seemed a whole lot happier those last few months then he had in a long time. So I suspect whatever it was that took him, it didn't cause him much pain.*

*He left me the Grange in his will, and the greenhouse too, so I been pretty busy keeping up with the orders. No one's complained yet about the blends I send out, so I think I must be doing something right. He left the Heights and all of the land to Harry, as you probably could have guessed. Harry just hired a man from Tuscarawas County to look after the farm, so he can keep dinking with his cars and trucks. He thinks he might open up a specialty garage with some of the money Cliff left him, so he can work on more sports cars like that one you drove here.*

*And Lordy, Cliff sure left a lot of money! We all knew he was loaded, but no one had any idea just how much cash he kept in the bank. Keeps pouring in too. Just got a big old check in the mail from Japan the other day. Harry put it aside, in case he needs it to pay taxes on everything else.*

*Cliff left a nice bit of cash to me and Katie Lyndon too. She didn't want to touch her share at first, but her Grandma told her don't be a fool. Ever since you sent Trish down our way, she's been a regular guest at the Black Bull. She even managed to kick out Ernie! She talked some woman she knew from Chagrin Falls into taking Ernie's rent money, and once he left town, his cronies all skedaddled too. And now Trish is helping Katie fix up her place to look like that fancy Bed and Breakfast her daddy always wanted to run. Trish says she wants to advertise the place too, maybe to folks coming into Cleveland to see that new museum you were heading to.*

*Harry's been helping Katie with tearing down walls and putting up lights and that sort of thing. Like I told you when you were here, I think he's kind of sweet on her. I wouldn't be surprised if they ended up together. Trish wrote out a family tree, showing how she was related to Mrs. Shaw, and it seems like Katie and Harry don't really share much blood, so they could probably get married if that's what they want to do. But I'm getting ahead of myself.*

*Anyways, I sure am glad to hear your foot's all better and your walking around fine again. I do hope you might come visit me sometime, if your ever back in Ohio. Harry got the electric and heat going again in the Grange, and I sewed up some new curtains. Bet you wouldn't recognize the place if you saw it now!*

*I'm sending you some of that cherry tea you liked so much when you came to visit. It's supposed to lift your spirits when your feeling down. Don't know if that's always true, but it sure tastes good. Hope you like it.*

*Love,*
*Nessie*

Jim picked up the packet of tea and brought it to his nose. He closed his eyes and breathed in its powerful scent, and for a fleeting moment, he was transported back to his small bed in the small room in the dark cottage in Northern Ohio. Cathy was by his side once more, teasing and taunting him by the dim light of the camping lantern. Then Cliff barged into his room, hurling insults and raising his fist in fury.

Jim brought his hand to his cheek and rubbed it. The bruises that bore Cliff's mark had long since faded, but the memory of their pain still lingered.

"Jaundice," he said aloud in an exasperated voice. Then he thought about Nessie's perfectly reasonable diagnosis, and brought his red and yellow mug to his lips.

The Typhoo tea was warm and soothing, and tasted like his childhood. He closed his eyes and pictured himself sitting at his mother's kitchen table on a cold and rainy day, eating choco biscuits and Jaffa cakes with his brother and sister after school let out.

Then he opened his eyes and looked back at the letter he had just read. Nessie's handwriting seemed to suit her. He could almost hear her voice jumping off the pages.

She had been so kind to him that long, weird week he'd been trapped in the cottage. She'd passed the time of day with him, sitting by his side and telling him stories, when she no doubt had better things to do elsewhere. She'd lent him her father's pajamas, and taught him how to walk on crutches. She'd washed and ironed his clothes, prepared his meals, and even applauded when he'd played the piano for her. And he never had the chance to thank her, or even say goodbye.

He reread the last page of her letter. His eyes lingered on her wholly unanticipated invitation—*"I do hope you might come visit me sometime."* Then he picked up the package of tea she had sent him and sniffed it once more. Its pungent aroma of wild cherry bark and honeysuckle blossoms carried him back to that strange world where time and space and life—and even death itself—seemed to have no boundaries.

*I'll need to use a chipped blue ceramic mug covered in smiley faces if I truly want to enjoy this tea,* he decided on the spot. *And there's only one place on this earth where I can find such a singular cup.*

# Chapter Twenty-Nine

## Ye Who Are Weary Come Home

Nessie clasped her hands together and pressed them to her heart. "That was lovely, Maggie, just lovely. My daddy used to play that ol' hymn for Mama and Mr. Shaw sometimes. We'd all gather 'round this very piano and sing along."

"I've always had a weak spot for 'Softly and Tenderly'," Maggie admitted as she closed the cover over the keys. "It has such a haunting melody."

Jim laughed. "That's because it's a song about death!"

"Now, now," Nessie said, leaning back in her father's old rocking chair. She threw Jim a stern look. "We all have to go to Jesus someday. Might as well face that fact with a sense of hope, and not a feelin' of regret. Which reminds me. You said you wanted to pay your respects to Cliff 'fore you left."

"Yes, that's right," Jim agreed. "I saw the small graveyard beside the old barn when we were driving here from the Black Bull. I'm guessing that's the Shaw family plot?"

"You guessed right, but Cliff ain't buried there. He was laid to rest at that Episcopalian cemetery, 'longside Cathy."

Jim cocked an eyebrow in surprise. "I would have thought she'd be buried beside Joe."

"She is," Nessie agreed. "Joe's on her left side, and Cliff is on her right. Cliff made the arrangements with the pastor 'fore he died. Not sure how he convinced ol' Father Newby to let him rest there, 'cause Lord knows, Cliff ain't never set foot in that church. He didn't even go to Cathy's funeral. But I heard tell that church just put up a new roof, so I'm guessin' Cliff must have made a nice donation to the parish buildin' fund."

Jim offered Nessie a weak smile. "I suppose that's somehow appropriate. I'm sure Cliff would have wanted to be by Cathy's side in death, even if he couldn't be in life."

Nessie stood up from her rocking chair and started collecting the dirty mugs and dishes from the coffee table. "Well, you two better get a move on if you want to get there 'fore nightfall. It's gettin' on towards dark. I wouldn't want to go visit any graveyard after the sun's gone down. Might be haints hangin' 'round, up to no good."

Jim and Maggie exchanged nervous glances. Then Jim looked back at Nessie. "Do you believe in ghosts, Nessie?" he asked warily.

Nessie stacked a china cup on top of her pile of dirty plates and laughed. "Oh, don't be silly! I'm just havin' you on. There ain't no such thing as ghosts. But I don't think a graveyard's a good place to go visit in the dark. You'd be better off stoppin' by tomorrow mornin' on your way back to Cleveland. That way, you could see Cliff's gravestone proper. Got some line from a poem carved into it, 'bout fire and ice. Maybe you could tell me what it means after you read it. Makes no sense to me."

"I'll do my best to interpret it," Jim replied, biting back a smile. He stood up from his chair, grabbed the Spode teapot he had just given Nessie as a gift, and carried it into the cottage's freshly painted kitchen.

Maggie slid off the piano bench and followed Jim and Nessie into the next room. "I can help you wash up," she offered.

"No, you can't. You're my guest," Nessie chided her gently. "You two just enjoy yourselves."

Jim admired the bright, daisy-patterned curtains hanging over the sink. "You were right when you told me I wouldn't recognize this house anymore. It looks so different now."

"Electricity'll do that to a place," Nessie replied with a chuckle. "That campin' lantern Cliff lent you didn't shed much light."

Jim rested the teapot on the counter and draped his left arm around Maggie's shoulder. "I hate to leave so soon, but I want to get back on the road while there's still some sun in the sky. It's so easy to get lost on these country roads in the dark."

"Don't be silly," Nessie laughed. She turned on the tap and started filling her sink with warm water. "Just turn right at the big fork to get to the Black Bull. You can't miss it."

Jim looked down at his shoes to hide his blush.

Maggie slipped away from Jim, clasped Nessie's hands, and kissed her cheek. "Thank you for the tea and sandwiches. You've been so very kind."

"It was my pleasure," Nessie said. "And thank *you* for the teapot and the lovely flowers. *And* for playin' all them hymns. It meant a lot to me, hearin' those songs again."

"I learned them from the organist at my father's church when I was a girl," Maggie replied. "I know those songs like the back of my hand." She stepped to the side so that Jim could say goodbye to Nessie.

Jim stepped forward and extended his right hand.

Nessie pushed it aside, wrapped her arms around his waist, and drew him into a tight embrace. "Now, you take care of yourself," she directed him. "Don't go twistin' your ankle no more. And take care of this nice lady you brung along to meet me too. She's a rare one."

"She is indeed," Jim agreed. He gave Nessie a big squeeze, then stepped out of her arms. "Thank you for the mug too. It will always remind me of you."

She rolled her eyes. "I couldah given you a nicer one. That one's chipped."

"It's the one that I want," Jim insisted.

Nessie left the dirty dishes in the sink to soak, then walked Jim and Maggie to her front door. "Drive careful now. And mind that dip in the road past the mailbox. I think that pothole's got bigger since you were here last."

Maggie collected her purse while Jim grabbed the handle of the chipped blue mug Nessie had given him. They walked to their rental car, then called goodbye to Nessie one last time.

"That's such a darling little cottage," Maggie said as Jim backed onto the main road. "I can think of worse places to be stranded for a week."

"It looked a lot different when I was there," Jim said without meeting her gaze.

He turned onto a tall, steep driveway, then stopped the car at the top of the hill so he could take one last look at 'The Heights.' In his mind, he had always pictured Cliff's home as a haunted mansion—a cross between Norman Bates' 'Psycho House' and one of the crumbling gothic manors from the Hammer horror films he had watched as a teen. But the Shaw family homestead was a simple, red-brick, two-story farmhouse, with freshly painted shutters and a screened-in back porch. Its lawn was dotted with bright yellow and red tulips. Pink and purple hyacinths surrounded the front doorstep.

The sun sank behind the dense copse of maple trees that lay to the house's west, and the sky took on a purplish-indigo hue. Jim turned the car around and drove back down the steep hill. Then he eased his vehicle onto the main road and headed towards the Black Bull.

Night fell quickly, and with only a thin crescent moon shining in the east, the sky was soon an inky blue shade of black.

Jim turned a tight corner, then slammed his foot on the brake and jerked the car to a sudden stop. He cursed under his breath. His heart started racing.

Maggie threw Jim a terrified look. "What's wrong? Why did you do that?"

"Didn't you see?" Jim answered, his breath coming out in fast, shallow bursts. "Something just ran across the road! I saw a dark shape!"

Maggie looked to the right and left, then rested her hand on Jim's knee. "It must have been a deer," she replied. "It was probably running to those woods over there to find shelter for the night. Drive slowly. I don't want you to hit anything."

Jim swallowed hard and continued on his way. He crested a small hill and searched for the unmarked fork in the road that would lead him back to Katie's B&B. When the road finally divided, he turned sharply to the right. His headlights swept across a small outcropping of oaks. And there, in the middle of the trees, for the briefest of moments, he saw two sets of ghostly, yellow eyes reflecting his car lights back at him.

*fin*

# A Note to the Reader

After I finished writing the first draft of my novel *Mr. R*, a rock-and-roll reimagining of *Jane Eyre*, I started toying with plot ideas for a sequel. The story of *Wuthering Heights* immediately sprang to mind. But then I researched Emily Brontë's masterpiece, and discovered it was originally published in tandem with *Agnes Grey*, the first novel by Emily and Charlotte Brontë's sister Anne. I'd never read *Agnes Grey*, so I picked up a copy. The further I got into the story, the more surprised I was that this gently-plotted, highly moral novel was published alongside Emily's wild Gothic tale. I could hardly imagine two more disparate books!

But then I noticed a striking similarity between the two novels. *Agnes Grey* is a first-person narrative told by a virtuous but not very exciting governess, describing her encounters with two families of badly-behaved rich people. The frame story of *Wuthering Heights* is also narrated by a virtuous but not very exciting character (a soft-spoken gentleman named Lockwood), who falls ill while visiting an estate in Yorkshire and is nursed back to health by the virtuous but not very exciting maid Ellen "Nelly" Dean, who tells him the incredible story of the badly-behaved folks who live across the moor.

The selfish, rude and larger-than-life characters in both novels—the animal torturer Tom Bloomfield, the shameless flirt Rosalie Murray, and, most famously, the passionate lovers Heathcliff and Cathy—dominate these books. The unfortunate narrators, meanwhile, seem doomed to be the bystanders in their own first-person stories.

And yet the high-minded Agnes, Lockwood and Nelly survive their mishaps, while the headstrong and immoral characters appear destined to wallow forever in self-damning decadence (or, in the case of Heathcliff and Cathy, are banned from Heaven, and cursed to walk the moors eternally as ghosts).

After toying with several plot ideas, I decided it would be fun to write a novel that shed a little more light on the Lockwood, Nelly and Agnes characters. I plucked the piano player Jim McCudden out of *Mr. R* and made him the Lockwood-esque central figure in *Restless Spirits*. I replaced the opinionated Nelly with the warm-hearted Nessie, and tried to make my storyteller a bit more likable than Emily Brontë's original character in *Wuthering Heights*. And I added a subplot to my novel about an *Agnes Grey*-like teacher named Maggie Grayson.

But just to keep things fun, I handed some of the narration duties over to two ghosts. I tried to present some plausible explanations for the ghosts' appearances—Cathy visits Jim when he is feverish, in pain, frightened, under the influence of drugs, or plagued by poor sleeping patterns; Agnes haunts Maggie when she is feeling guilty, lonely, or somehow overwhelmed. I'm not suggesting that Cathy and Agnes aren't 'real.' They are as real as any fictional characters can be! But I think it's important to note that these two ghosts appear in moments when Jim and Maggie's minds are more likely to play tricks on them.

I tried to keep my story light-hearted. I toned down the moralistic messages that imbued both Emily and Anne's original novels, while still giving narrative prominence to a few church-going, God-fearing characters. And I threw in a lot of musical references as well, to continue the "Rock-and-Roll-Brontë" theme that I started in *Mr. R*.

I wrote my first draft of *Restless Spirits* in 2008, but I worked on my last major revision in the spring of 2020, when I was quarantined during the coronavirus pandemic. Being more-or-less trapped in my home gave me a much deeper sympathy for both the housebound Jim and the put-upon Maggie, who couldn't escape the needy houseguests she'd been saddled with.

I hope you enjoyed reading my story. If you did, please tell your friends about it or leave a review on Amazon. If you discovered this book before learning about *Mr. R*, please consider reading my first novel, which provides a little more background on Jim and the Pilots. And keep an eye out for the next book in my series—*Wildfell Summer*, a magical, mystery trip through Anne Brontë's classic novel, *The Tenant of Wildfell Hall*. Sex, drugs and rock-and-roll never looked so Victorian!

*Tracy Neis*

# Endnotes

This story is based on *Wuthering Heights*, by Emily Brontë, and *Agnes Grey*, by Anne Brontë. These two novels were published together in 1847 as a three-volume book by Thomas Cautley Newby. The Eddie Rochester character mentioned in this novel is based on the tortured romantic hero of *Jane Eyre* by Charlotte Brontë (also originally published in 1847). Eddie was first introduced in Tracy Neis' first novel, *Mr. R – A Rock and Roll Romance* (Mischievous Muse Publishing Alliance: 2018).

Some aspects of this story are also based on the lives of the Brontë family, including Emily, Anne and Charlotte's brother Branwell (1817-1848), and their father, the Reverend Patrick Brontë (1777-1861). Some scholars believe Reverend Brontë was the grandson of (or was at least related to) the eighteenth-century Gaelic poet Padraig O'Pronntaigh. The characters Mary Taylor and Ellen Nussey borrow their names from two childhood friends of Charlotte Brontë. Jim McCudden's band, "The Pilots," borrows its name from the original Mr. Rochester's pet dog in *Jane Eyre*.

The author wishes to thank her original readers—Megan Roxberry, Patricia Courtney, M.J. Buist, Denise Longrie, Warren Brown, Father Jack Wessling, Mercy Hume, and Mike, Emily, Karen, Laura and Maria Neis—for reviewing early drafts of this novel and offering input and insight.

Additional thanks are in order to Laura Neis for helping the author self-publish this book.

The following works of literature are quoted or paraphrased in this book:

*Agnes Grey,* by Anne Brontë (1847)
*Alice's Adventures in Wonderland,* by Lewis Carroll (1865)
*Brideshead Revisited,* by Evelyn Waugh (1945)
*Fire and Ice,* by Robert Frost (1923)
*No Coward Soul is Mine,* by Emily Brontë (1946)
*The Psychedelic Experience: A Manual Based on the Tibetan Book of the Dead,* by Timothy Leary, Richard Alpert and Ralph Metzner (1964)
*The Rubaiyat,* by Omar Khayyam (1048–1123), translated into English by Edward Fitzgerald in five editions (from 1859 through 1889)
*The Weary Blues,* by Langston Hughes (1923)
*Wuthering Heights,* by Emily Brontë (1847)


The following song lyrics are quoted in this book:

*Could it be Magic?* by Barry Manilow and Adrienne Anderson (1973)
*Get Ready,* by Smokey Robinson (1966)
*Moon Dance,* by Van Morrison (1969)
*On a Slow Boat to China,* by Frank Loesser (1948)
*She Said, She Said* (1967), *Tomorrow Never Knows* (1966), and *I am the Walrus* (1967), by John Lennon and Paul McCartney
*Wuthering Heights,* by Kate Bush (1970)

An historical note about the Walkman:

The Walkman portable cassette player was introduced to the world market by the Sony Corporation in 1979. Many members of the Sony Corporation are credited with playing a part in its development, but there is no single person responsible for its inception. According to Sony, "In 1979, an empire in personal portable entertainment was created with the ingenious foresight of Sony Founder and Chief Advisor, the late Masaru Ibuka, and Sony Founder and Honorary Chairman Akio Morita. It began with the invention of the first cassette Walkman TPS-L2 that forever changed the way consumers listen to music." The developers of the first Sony Walkman were Kozo Ohsone, General Manager of the Sony Tape Recorder Business Division, and his staff, under the auspices and suggestions of Ibuka and Morita. To date, more than 300 million Walkman units have been sold.

# Praise for Mr. R

Looking for a great summer read? I loved *Mr. R – A Rock & Roll Romance* by Tracy Neis. This modern retelling of *Jane Eyre* surprised and delighted me. For me, I know a book is great when I don't want it to end, and can't stop thinking about it after I've finished. That's what happened when I read *Mr. R.*

—**Syrie James, bestselling author of**
*The Secret Diaries of Charlotte Brontë*

*Mr. R* kept me entertained; I'd certainly recommend this one to Brontëites.

—**Nicola Friar, author of**
*The Brontë Babe Blog*

*Coming Soon...*

# Wildfell Summer

It's 1967—the Summer of Love—and the Pilots are touring America. But much to his bandmates' surprise, drummer Gerry Enis is skipping the after-show parties every night and curling up with a novel in his hotel room instead.

The hard-drinking percussionist, however, is not just *reading* his book. He's found a way to go tripping into the pages of Anne Brontë's tour de force *The Tenant of Wildfell Hall,* so he can party alongside the notorious Arthur Huntington, one of the most dissolute characters in all of English literature.

Can Gerry's bandmates and manager find a way to tear their friend away from his fictional foil? Or is Gerry destined to become the first rock star in history to succumb to the dangers of laudanum addiction and Victorian-style debauchery?

Roll up, roll up to *Wildfell Summer.* It's dying to take you away...

# About the Author

Since earning her degree in English from the University of Notre Dame, Tracy Neis has written for numerous publications, including *Cincinnati Magazine*, *Goldmine*, and *Beatlefan*. She is the author of *Mr. R – A Rock and Roll Romance* (Mischievous Muse), and the young adult collective biography *Extraordinary African-American Poets* (Enslow). She also publishes Beatles-themed fan fiction on her blog, cremetangerine.video.blog, and under the name CremeTangerine on fanfiction.net and archiveofourown.org. A proud Ohio native, Tracy currently lives in Southern California with her husband and four daughters.

Made in the USA
Monee, IL
13 January 2026